"Why shouldn't I kiss you again?" she demanded. *"Give me one good reason why we shouldn't do something we both want. And don't you dare deny it."*

He whirled on her. The look on his face was dark, pained. "You need a reason?"

She raised her chin a notch. "Yes."

Three steps and he was before her, his hands on her shoulders. His eyes squeezed closed, and he lowered his forehead to hers. She wasn't sure if touching him would help or hinder his ability to get the words out, so she held herself still.

He brushed his thumb across her cheek. "Because one kiss with you wouldn't be enough for me."

"And that's a problem?"

"Hell, yes, it's a problem. Because…" He went silent.

"Tell me."

"Because all the things you deserve, I can't give you any of them. I can't even tell you my real name."

Dear Reader,

I love setting my books in locations so vibrant and fascinating that the stories couldn't happen anywhere else in the world. Panama, the setting for *Tempted into Danger*, is just such a place.

This small strip of land—an isthmus, if you recall from your grade school geography lessons—is an epicenter of history, business, cultures and wild jungle. It is a true cross section of diversity, where the American dollar is the official currency, yet the roads are measured in kilometers. Where international banking and tourism flourish, but so does international crime.

When Diego Santero, the hero of my story, flies a helicopter over the Panama Canal into the rainforest, I want you to feel like you're right there with him. Okay, maybe not the dodging bullets part of the helicopter chase scene, but the part where you're soaring over untamed wilderness, with the Panama City skyline and Pacific Ocean behind you and the Atlantic Ocean in front of you as you race across the sky in an adventure for the ages. And when the pilot is as lethally sexy as Diego Santero? Well, that's the stuff great romance novels are made of. Open up the pages of this book and you'll never be so tempted to fall straight into the arms of danger.

Happy Reading!

Melissa Cutler

MELISSA CUTLER

Tempted into Danger

HARLEQUIN® ROMANTIC SUSPENSE

Recycling programs
for this product may
not exist in your area.

ISBN-13: 978-0-373-27828-2

TEMPTED INTO DANGER

Copyright © 2013 by Melissa Cutler

HARLEQUIN®
™ www.Harlequin.com

Printed in U.S.A.

Books by Melissa Cutler

Harlequin Romantic Suspense
Seduction Under Fire #1730
★Tempted into Danger #1758

★ICE: Black Ops Defenders

Other titles by this author
available in ebook format.

MELISSA CUTLER

is a flip-flop-wearing Southern California native living with her husband, two rambunctious kids and two suspicious cats in beautiful San Diego. She divides her time between her dual passions for writing sexy, small-town contemporary romances and edge-of-your-seat romantic suspense. Find out more about Melissa and her books at www.melissacutler.net or drop her a line at cutlermail@yahoo.com.

Every day around the world, women and men put their lives on the line in defense of freedom and the innocent. The story is dedicated to them.

Chapter 1

Panama

Gotta love Uncle Sam. He carried a big stick and an even bigger ego, which was the only explanation Diego Santero could think of for the presence of an actual freakin' sign on the door of the Department of Homeland Security's ICE attaché office advertising its presence in Panama City.

Not that Diego's ego was any less bloated than the federal stiffs who issued him a salary, but at least he had the common sense to practice discretion. Too often his life and the lives of his crew depended on it.

Diego breezed past the office's main doors without slowing, striding around the rear of the building to an unmarked entrance. Flipping the bird to the goons watching him through the security camera, he slipped his key card through the slot, verified his fingerprints on the scanner, then shouldered the heavy door open.

The first floor corridor reeked of bureaucracy—the stale odor of air conditioning and burnt coffee and the dust of constantly shuffled reams of paperwork. He peeled his sunglasses from his sweat-sticky face and tucked them in his shirt pocket, squinting up at the fluorescent lights lining the corridor's ceiling.

Most people preferred a climate-controlled office to the humid heat outside, but if ever there was a man not cut out for white-collar work, it was Diego. Thank God the U.S. Navy had offered him an alternative when he was an eighteen-year-old punk. A childhood spent under the fluorescent lights of the New Jersey public school system had been enough desk work in government buildings to last him a lifetime.

Two members of his crew met him at the base of the stairwell leading to the second-floor briefing rooms.

He nodded his greeting to Alicia and bumped forearms with Ryan. "You been upstairs yet to get a sense of what the stiffs want from us?"

Alicia shook her head. "Waiting for you."

"Chiara brothers. Gotta be," Ryan added in his deep, pensive voice.

Ryan had been Diego's right-hand man since the beginning. Before they'd signed on with ICE, they were SEALs together and had clicked instantly. Mostly because Ryan was a man of few words who let Diego run the show.

"You think everything's about the Chiara brothers, Ryan. Your brain's in a rut." Diego tapped his temple for emphasis. "You're like that dude, Moby Dick, with the white whale."

Ryan shrugged noncommittally.

Alicia, Diego's intelligence specialist and honorary sister, arched a perfect eyebrow. Stubborn as she was, she caked on the makeup and left her hair long as though to remind the rest of the crew that not only did she match them in strength, smarts and experience, but she did so without sacrificing an ounce of estrogen.

"You've read *Moby Dick?*" she asked.

Ryan snickered. "Naw, he's never read it."

"How the hell do you know that?" Diego asked, squaring his shoulders with mock indignation.

Ryan's lips twitched into a grin. "Because Moby Dick's the name of the whale, not the dude."

"Who names a whale? That's the stupidest thing I've ever heard."

As Alicia and Ryan chuckled good-naturedly, Diego allowed himself a small smile. He never got on his crew about razzing him. With the way he was constantly asking them to risk their lives for Uncle Sam, seizing on humor whenever possible was as necessary to their sanity as their firearms.

He tipped his head toward the stairs. "Enough with the book-club chat. Let's get this briefing over with. These artificial lights are hell on my complexion."

He swiped his key card to unlock the stairwell door and preceded Alicia and Ryan to the second floor.

"SeaWorld," Ryan said behind him.

Diego pushed through the door at the top of the stairs and into another unremarkable, climate-controlled hallway. "What about SeaWorld?"

"They named a whale. They've got Shamu."

Diego stopped in front of the closed briefing room door and pivoted, gesturing his hands in a circle. "Are we actually having this conversation still, or is this some sort of freaky dream I'm having 'cause I ate too much garlic sauce last night?"

Alicia gave him a playful shove out of the way and pushed through the doorway. "Don't forget *Free Willy*," she said in a singsong voice as she walked into the room.

Diego and Ryan filed in after her, nodding hello to the other two members of their team, John and Rory.

Though the stench of bureaucracy was bad in the hallway, it had nothing on the briefing room. Beige tile, white soundproofed walls and row after freakin' row of fluorescent lights on the ceiling.

The circular table that dominated the room was loaded with laptops, stacks of files and maps. A tray with a water pitcher and glasses anchored the middle. A blank projector screen occupied the far wall of the windowless space, ready and waiting for an industrious government official to start a PowerPoint presentation, no doubt. Everything a federal stiff needed to feel right at home.

The way Diego's crew stood around, shifting their weight or fidgeting with their firearm holsters, the ambiance left them as twitchy as it did him.

Thomas Dreyer, a pale-faced, pencil-pushing ICE director Diego had done business with in the past, looked up from his laptop and stood, extending his hand. "Agent Santero, good to see you again."

Diego disagreed, but until he knew what ICE wanted with his crew, he'd hold his tongue. "Sir," he said instead as they shook.

"I appreciate your team being here. Grab some refreshments and let's get started." He gestured across the room to a long table covered with pastries and coffee.

Ignoring the refreshment offer, Diego exchanged brief handshakes with the other man in the room, Special Agent Aaron Montgomery. Diego tried to keep his nose out of ICE gossip, but the last he'd heard, Dreyer and Montgomery had been tapped by Washington to head up Operation ICEWALL, the bureau's shiny new media-friendly mission to block the flow of drugs and money through Central America.

Yeah, right. Good luck with that, guys.

Despite Diego's cynicism over Operation ICE-WALL's potential for success, he understood Dreyer's and Montgomery's presence in Panama, given that the country—along with Costa Rica—was wedged between Colombia and Mexico. What piqued Diego's curiosity was why, with the entire weight of the American, Panamanian and Mexican governments backing them, and with squads of ICE agents prepared to undertake the mission's execution, they still saw fit to bring in Diego's black ops crew.

Black ops only handled the sensitive, hush-hush problems that would do more harm than good if word got out. Diego and his crew were ICE's ace-in-the-hole problem-solving and crisis-management team, executing everything from covert extractions to well-timed diversions—not overhyped, billion-dollar, multinational government projects. That is, not unless those projects had gotten out of control in a way that would be detrimental to either the government or the public's support of the operation.

Dreyer clapped his hands together. "Okay, let's get you briefed."

Thoroughly intrigued by the reason for the briefing, Diego crowded near his crew, arms folded. Dreyer consulted his notes, then flipped on the projector. His crew groaned under their breaths.

"Jesus, Dreyer. Hand me one of those dossiers."

Diego waved a hand at the table. "I can't stand another freakin' PowerPoint presentation. Where do you think we are, the Pentagon?"

Undisturbed by Diego's protest, Dreyer handed each operative a navy blue binder, then started his Power-Point presentation anyway. A photograph of a woman's face glowed from the projector screen. Diego found the coordinating page in his dossier and stared into the woman's striking, midnight-blue eyes.

"Vanessa Crosby, age thirty. A U.S. expatriate who has resided in Panama for seven years as a senior analyst in the criminal detection department at RioBank," Dreyer said. "Yesterday, ICE intelligence analysts intercepted an email from Crosby to her boss expressing concern over a possible pattern of criminal activity she discovered within the bank's system."

"Well, that's terrific news," Diego couldn't help but interject. "Bet she makes Employee of the Month. You want me to bake her a cupcake?"

Dreyer gaped at him. Like he was caught unaware of Diego's tendency to be a smart aleck, despite that they'd worked together on and off for twelve years. Diego flashed his best "you got a problem with me?" face.

Dreyer cleared his throat and adjusted his tie.

Montgomery, sprawling in a chair, took over the briefing. "It seems that Miss Crosby has created an algorithm to track the movement of bulk cash using small deposits and wire transfers. If her program works—and we think it does—it would revolutionize ICE's counterterrorism efforts."

Now they were getting somewhere.

ICE had an entire department with a massive budget devoted to combating bulk cash, aka the millions of American dollars in drug and weapon revenue that crime organizations busted their tails to launder and repurpose without tipping off authorities.

Diego knew nada about algorithms or number analysis or whatever the heck this Crosby broad did for the bank, but he was personally and painfully aware of the many ways bulk cash funded terrorist activities all over the world.

"What exactly did her email say?" Diego asked. "Is it in the dossier?"

"We didn't include it because it doesn't have any impact on the mission we're asking you to perform. To sum it up, she asked her boss for permission to initiate a more expansive test of the algorithm using customer account data. She thinks she can pinpoint the exact account that the bulk cash she detected is being funneled into."

"What was her boss's reaction?" Diego asked. "Seems like the bank's bigwigs would be falling all over themselves to get their hands on a program like that."

"You'd think, but instead he reprimanded her," Montgomery said. "Told her to hand the program over to him because it was outside her job description."

What a prick. "Did she give him the program?"

"No. She put him off. She told him it wasn't user-friendly yet and she'd need to clean it up before anyone else would be able to make use of it. He gave her a deadline of Monday morning."

Alicia slapped her copy of the dossier on the table. "How can you be sure there's a bulk cash scam at all? I find it hard to believe Crosby created an algorithm that no ICE bulk cash investigators or international banks have come up with. And then to find criminal activity that everyone else along the line of checks and balances in RioBank's infrastructure missed? You know what they say about things that are too good to be true."

Diego nodded. Great point. Who was to say Crosby knew what she was talking about? "What's the likelihood this lady's math is wrong?"

"Turn to page two in your dossier," Dreyer said. "Look at her stats and then tell me if you think Vanessa Crosby's theory is wrong."

Diego and his crew flipped the page. In his periphery, he saw Dreyer click to the next slide in his little projector show. He nearly sniggered until a glance at Vanessa Crosby's personal history stopped him cold.

PhD from Princeton after double-majoring in applied mathematics and economics, paid for in part by a load of academic scholarships, probably because she'd finished high school with a 4.4 GPA. Diego didn't even know a 4.4 GPA existed.

He toggled to her photograph. Long, straight brown hair, a smattering of freckles, those almost-black eyes. She looked sharp, smart even, but not like her life story read. He skimmed her credentials again—her transcripts and accolades from college, followed by her meteoric rise through the ranks of RioBank. No doubt about it, Vanessa Crosby had a brilliant mathematical mind.

Diego liked that. A lot.

Not that a man such as he, who'd chosen the life of a soldier and who'd barely squeaked out of high school with a diploma, had any business getting turned on by the size of a woman's brain.

Irritation washed through him. Clearly, the feds behind Operation ICEWALL wanted something big from Crosby—bigger than that algorithm she'd created. Why else would Diego and his crew be brought in?

Scowling, he snapped the dossier closed. Here was a lady who'd probably worked her tail off to get where she was and seemed to have a pretty good life going. The last thing she or any civilian needed was the U.S. government sweeping in and mucking everything up in their never-ending war against the scourges of the world. "Okay, so we can assume Crosby's not wrong about her findings. What's your plan for her?"

Dreyer's expression took on a shimmery, Christmas morning type of glow. Like Vanessa Crosby was some sort of gift-wrapped present for the Department of Homeland Security to do with as they pleased. "We believe Vanessa Crosby is the key to breaking Operation ICEWALL wide open. The weak link in the banking industry we've been waiting for."

Diego seriously doubted *weak* was an apt description of Crosby, but he decided to keep his trap shut and hear them out.

Montgomery shot to his feet alongside Dreyer. "Our plan is to convince Crosby to work as an ICE insider in the bank. Get her to run the algorithm test without her boss's knowledge and lay out her findings for us. You remember the Chiara brothers crime ring your crew chased in Honduras ten years ago?"

How could he forget, when Ryan never let him? Leo, Nico and Enzo Chiara were scumbag Italian mercenaries who'd created a hell of a business as pawn brokers for the criminal elite, coordinating million-dollar sales of everything from small arms and tanks to nuclear devices. "Yeah, I remember."

"We believe there's a connection between the bulk cash scam Crosby discovered and intel we received from an informant about a submarine sale the Chiara brothers are brokering next week. ICE has been tracking these bastards for years. This is our best chance at shutting them down. Thanks to Vanessa Crosby."

Diego glanced at Ryan, his brows raised in question. If anyone would have a hunch about the Chiaras using RioBank as a bulk cash laundering vehicle, it would be him. He'd been hunting them longer than anyone— for reasons he was irritatingly tight-lipped about—and had made it his number-one goal in life to dig for new intel on them every chance he got between missions.

Ryan's jaw grew tight. "It's a viable lead, for sure. The Chiaras are here in Panama City. I can feel it."

Diego squelched an eye roll at his hoodoo logic. The man took the Chiara brothers chase way too personally. Diego was the opposite—he never took a mission to heart. Bring down one criminal and another took his place on the Wanted poster. Each was just another target for the business end of his Sig Sauer.

"So you want me to convince Vanessa Crosby to work with ICE?" he asked.

"God, no," Dreyer said with a derisive chuckle. "You'd have her running in the opposite direction, screaming in terror."

The assessment was a stab to the gut. Here he was an elite black ops agent—the best of the best, with a service record that spoke for itself—and yet his bosses didn't trust him to open his mouth around a potential informant. True, he wasn't exactly qualified to match wits with a brainiac like Crosby, but it stuck in his craw that the stiffs thought so little of him in the smarts department.

To hide his frustration, he slipped into easy sarcasm. "Aw, that hurts. And here I thought I had a way with the ladies." He looked at Alicia to back him up on that.

She'd been around him enough to know he could talk a good game when the situation demanded.

She scrunched her face and gave a little head shake. "Sorry, you're not exactly a smooth operator around women."

"Well, hell." Life as a nomadic agent didn't exactly allow him a whole lot of opportunity to hone his seduction skills. Wasn't like he spent weekends trolling bars between missions—that was prime training time.

He studied Crosby's image on the projector screen. The dossier listed her marital status as single, but he didn't doubt for a second that a pretty, successful woman like her had some rich bigwig banker wrapped around her little finger. "All right, so I keep my trap shut. What do you need me and my crew for?"

"Your objective is to transport Vanessa Crosby to the ICE safe house without anyone finding out. Montgomery and I will be waiting there to talk to her. After we've brought her around to our way of thinking, you'll return her to her apartment as discreetly."

Diego raised his eyebrows in disbelief. They wanted to use him as a taxi driver? "Let me get this straight. You want me and my team of world-class operatives to drive a woman across town. And then take her home again. You don't want us to talk to her, gather intel off her home computer, rough up her boyfriend or shake down her boss? Just chauffeur her to and from the safe house?"

"That's affirmative."

Diego scrunched his eyes, wincing as a dozen curse words pinged around in his head. If he wasn't careful, the feds would have him working as a letter courier before too long. Just fantastic. Seemed like more and more in his line of work, success came down to the little moves: poring over satellite imagery, sifting through secrets heard on the wind, coaxing witnesses. Keeping the terrorists of the world at bay felt less and less like combat and more like building a defensive wall one grain of sand at a time.

Diego preferred the grand gestures. He wanted to blow something up or kick someone's ass. His favorite assignments had him sneaking undetected into hostile deserts, or lying in wait for days in snake-infested trees, breaking kids out of human trafficking rings or stopping thousands of pounds of cocaine from crossing the U.S. border.

He loved what ICE and the Department of Homeland Security stood for, but it was time for him to find a new employer. Maybe the CIA would take mercy on him. "I don't mean to be a douche-wad, but are you freakin' kidding me?"

Montgomery beamed at him like an idiot. "Of course you mean to be a douche-wad, Santero. It's who you are."

Dreyer strolled his way, folding his arms across his chest, drilling him with a look of challenge. "You think you're too good for this assignment?"

"Hell, yeah, I'm too good for this assignment." He gestured to his crew. "We all are. This is insulting."

"Get over yourself. This woman's important to ICE. And there are decent odds she's already on the Chiaras' radar. I won't take a chance of jeopardizing a possible RioBank insider because she's spotted in a car with known U.S. officials. This might not be running down terrorists in the Afghanistan desert, but the mission is as black ops as it gets."

Oh, please.

Diego marched to the projector screen and poked

Crosby's image in the chin. "What makes you so sure she'll agree to this? No woman in her right mind would volunteer for such a dangerous job when it means she'll have to live out the rest of her days in WitSec once ICE is through with her. Not to mention that she's an expatriate. What does Crosby care about the U.S.? Nothing, or else she'd still be living there."

"Leave that part to me," Montgomery said, grinning smugly.

According to Alicia, Montgomery was easy on the eyes, so he probably had a better chance than anyone of persuading Vanessa Crosby to work with the feds. But all Diego saw when he looked at the agent's million-watt smile and perfectly coifed blond hair was a man whose keister Diego had saved in Mexico earlier that year when he and his girlfriend had gotten in a jam against a cartel. Not that he didn't respect Montgomery, but it was tough to think of him as an equal.

Whatever. This operation was Dreyer's baby, so if he trusted Montgomery, then Diego's opinion meant diddly-squat. And he knew Ryan would be up for the job if it might break the case on the Chiara brothers. One of these days, he'd have to pin Ryan down on the reason the Chiaras dug under his skin so deep. Maybe while they sat around outside the safe house waiting to chauffeur Crosby home.

"All right. So my crew and I grab the broad, keep our mouths shut and leave the sweet-talkin' to Pretty Boy Montgomery. That's all?"

"Affirmative. Have her to the safe house tonight at dusk."

Diego checked his watch. Dusk was nine hours away. Time to get to work.

With a salute, he clutched Vanessa Crosby's dossier

and stalked from the room. His crew trailed behind on the stairwell, giving him the silence and space he needed to fume properly.

They gathered in a circle in the first-floor hallway. The expressions on his crew's faces mirrored Diego's black mood. Nobody liked to get dumped on by their bosses.

"All right, so we can start searching the classified ads for black ops job openings when we're done with this mission," Diego said. "Until then, let's suck it up and do it right. Ryan, secure clean cars. Three'll do it. Alicia, map the area around Crosby's apartment and get a bug in there. ICE intelligence claims Crosby lives alone, but I find that hard to believe."

"She's a looker," John said, admiring her photographs in his copy of the dossier.

That was a gross understatement, but Diego was all business now and so ignored the remark. "John and Rory, you're sniper lookout. Stationary. And Rory, see if there's anything along the route we can blow up. It's been too damn long since I've gotten to blow anything up."

"Whatever you say, boss."

Diego tucked his dossier under his arm and cracked his knuckles. "If the feds want to foot the bill for a five-man black ops chauffeur squad, then we're going to give 'em their money's worth. This Vanessa Crosby broad ain't gonna know what hit her."

Once, when she was six, Vanessa stole a piece of candy from her dad's private stash, simply for the thrill of trying to put one past him. But the pressure of keeping the secret was too much and within minutes of her dad's return from work that night, she'd broken down in an unprovoked, sobbing confession.

What she'd done today was far more significant than stealing candy.

She navigated the crowds of business people returning home after work, striding toward the bus stop a block south of RioBank. She couldn't wait to get inside her apartment. And not only because, after a day spent in her pleasantly air-conditioned office, she could barely tolerate the humidity and smog of the business district.

Out of the corner of her eye, she caught the shadow of a man moving between two towering office buildings. With a gasp, she picked up her pace to the bus stop. Silly, to see danger where none existed. No one was out to get her in broad daylight on a busy street. No one knew the illegal and unethical act she was committing.

She hitched her purse higher on her shoulder as she walked, the tiny zip drive inside feeling like it weighed ten pounds. That's the way deceit always felt to her— heavy and unyielding in its pressure on her conscience. The zip drive contained a massive number of customers' personal account files she wasn't permitted to copy, much less remove from the bank. In doing so, she'd violated so many rules that if she were discovered, losing her job would be the least of her worries.

But she had to get the data results from the algorithm straight in her head. Something in the numbers had put her instincts on high alert, and the way her mind worked, she wouldn't be able to think of anything else until she solved the mystery.

Mr. Tavares assured her in his most asinine, sexist tone that she wasn't to worry her pretty little head over it because that wasn't what he was paying her to do. He'd demanded she hand over the algorithm program so he could look into it, but her gut told her that he wouldn't. And then she'd never know the answer, and that would eat her up inside. Not to mention that if RioBank was being unwittingly used as a money laundering vehicle, then her bosses deserved to know, too.

The commuter bus rumbled onto the street, snorting black smoke through its muffler. Vanessa waited her turn to board, her skin pricking as though someone was staring at her. She scanned the street, searching for the man she'd glimpsed in the shadows, but saw no one suspicious.

It shouldn't have been a surprise that her imagination was getting the best of her. Horror movies had always been her thing. She loved the heart-pounding thrill of being scared—in the controlled environment of a movie theater or her living room.

Growing up, she and her friends delighted in freaking themselves out by watching scary movies at night, then imagining that every creak or shadow was actually a ghost or boogeyman. More often than not, they'd keep up the game until, on some level, they believed in the possibility.

Boarding the bus, she couldn't shake the feeling that someone was following her, even after the doors closed and the bus continued on its route. Craning her neck, she took stock of the passengers. Only ordinary people. Mothers with cranky kids, businessmen and women in rumpled suits, a group of young teenage boys going who knew where, snickering while they watched something on a cell phone. No one was paying her the least bit of attention, much less following her.

Nice going, Vanessa. Way to conjure up a healthy serving of paranoia with your guilt.

Huffing with amusement at her anxiety, she dialed

Jordan's number. Her best friend since seventh-grade math class, Jordan was the reason Vanessa had ended up in Panama. Jordan had followed her college sweetheart here, and Vanessa had followed Jordan. Seven years later, Jordan and Carlos were married with two kids.

In the years since Vanessa made the choice to leave the U.S., Jordan and Carlos and their kids had become her anchor—closer than her own family had ever been. She still talked to her dad occasionally and would always love him, but they were more like acquaintances.

"Hey, Jordie. Are we still on for dinner tomorrow night?"

"You bet. Hope it's okay that Carlos invited some friends from work to join us."

She pictured a room full of cute, successful building engineers. "Single?" She cringed at the note of desperation in her voice, hoping that Jordan hadn't noticed. Then again, Jordan was well aware that it'd been too long since Vanessa had met a man worth risking her heart on and that desperation was definitely becoming an issue.

"No, sorry. But I made him swear he'll keep his eyes open for hot boyfriend material."

"I don't even need a hot boyfriend anymore. I've been so long without the company of a man who's capable of sustaining a conversation, other than Carlos, of course, that I'd settle for someone old and unattractive, or maybe a gay bestie."

"Vanessa Marie Crosby, you will not settle for a gay bestie on my watch. You need a man you can talk to *and* fondle."

"You're right. I do need that." She groaned. "It's hopeless anyway, because Panama has a serious lack of potential gay besties."

Jordan laughed. "Oh, sweetie, someday you're going to find a smart, cute guy who's great at conversations and who'll love you like you deserve."

Vanessa dropped her voice to a whisper. "Okay, since we're dreaming up a totally implausible fantasy boyfriend, we might as well make him good in bed, too."

"That goes without saying. A girl's got to have standards."

The bus reached Vanessa's stop, three blocks from her apartment building. Though less paranoid now that she'd connected with Jordan, she still took one last look over her shoulder before getting off. "You know how in horror movies, when a woman walks alone, it's practically a given that something terrible is going to happen to her?"

"Okay, random."

"Humor me," Vanessa pressed, glancing side to side like she might see that man again. She rolled her eyes. Stupid. "Like in *Halloween,* every time Laurie walks down the street, there are flashes of Michael Myers looking out of a window and the shadow of someone lurking. And you know at any minute he's going to jump out and grab her."

"Classic movie," Jordan said. "Definitely one of my top fifty horror flicks of all time."

"Mine, too. Remember after we watched it the first time, we went on a walk around your neighborhood to freak ourselves out? We actually convinced ourselves we were being followed."

Jordan let loose with a belly laugh. "That was so much fun! We sprinted the whole way home. I didn't feel safe until we'd snuck back into my room and closed the curtains."

Vanessa was smiling now, too. "Then I dared you to

open the curtains again to check if anyone was out there watching us, but you wouldn't take the dare."

"What goofballs we were. Why did you bring it up?"

Vanessa opened her mouth to explain, but words caught in her throat as she thought better about it. There was no use worrying Jordan when the only ghoul haunting her was her guilty conscience. She eyed a white sedan with dark tinted windows cruising past her and the tingle on the back of her neck kicked up again. With a look over her shoulder, she quickened her step. Only two more blocks to her apartment.

"Hello, Vanessa? You still there?"

"I'm here. Just thinking about how easy it is to make myself spooked when I want to."

"You like getting spooked."

"Normally, yeah." Just not while she was engaging in illegal behavior at work and feeling pretty conflicted about it.

The white sedan flipped a U-turn and headed toward her.

"What's up, Vee? You want to rent that movie tomorrow night? Might be fun. We could go on a midnight stroll through the neighborhood afterward, get ourselves scared all over again."

"Sounds great. Look, I've got to go. There's some creep in a car cruising the street, and I don't like the look of him. I'm going to hurry home." With a promise to text Jordan the minute she got to her apartment, she stuffed the phone into her purse and kept her eyes on the car's approach. She could dart into an alley or store, but then what? Eventually, she'd have to walk back onto the street to get home.

And she was only one block away. That was two hundred and two meters. With her average stride of 0.67

meters, that only left her with two hundred and ninety-nine steps to the building. Better to stay the course and not give in to irrational fear.

She felt stronger and calmer now that she had numbers to focus on. That's what she loved about math. Its constancy soothed her like nothing else could.

"Two ninety-eight, two ninety-seven," she said aloud, counting her steps.

The sedan grew close enough for her to study the driver through the glare of the afternoon sun. He wore dark sunglasses, and maybe it was because she'd seen one too many scary movies, but she would've sworn he was staring at her, the hint of an evil smile on his lips.

Nice, Vanessa. Real special imagination you've got there, to turn your mundane life into your own personal slasher movie.

As soon as she was home with the dead bolt locked on her front door, she'd have a good laugh about getting herself worked up over nothing. She'd traversed the same exact route to and from work for the past seven years without a single bad thing happening to her. Today was no different.

"Two eighty-two." Which meant a hundred and eighty-eight meters to go. Not a problem. She could do this.

Movement in a window of an abandoned warehouse across the street diverted her attention. She glanced past the car in time to see the stained, beige sheet covering the window swish closed. Now she was being watched from buildings, cars and men in dark jackets lurking in alleyways. All she needed was a man with a white mask to appear or some angelic-looking kid with huge saucer eyes to say something creepy about seeing dead people and her scary movie fantasy would be complete.

With her apartment building in view, she fished her keys from her purse. The zip drive came up with the keys and skidded across the sidewalk. Her heart thudding wildly, she scooped it up and stuffed it in her skirt pocket, then stumbled sideways as a mom with a double stroller bullied past her. She searched the street for the white sedan in time to see its rear bumper disappear into the alley around the corner.

From here, it was a clean shot to her apartment lobby, then one flight of stairs up to her unit. She set off at a trot, her one-inch heels clicking noisily but not slowing her down. As soon as she tested the algorithm and figured out why the numbers were bugging her, she'd destroy the zip drive and no one would be the wiser about what she'd done. Then her paranoia would evaporate and her biggest problem could go back to being about her pathetic love life.

The feeling of being watched stayed with her in the lobby and stairwell despite that the only sound was the echo of her heels on the tile. A rent increase a few months ago had induced a mass exodus of tenants, resulting in the building being only partially occupied. Of the ten units on the second floor, only Vanessa and two elderly couples at the end of the hall remained.

A dizzying sense of vulnerability crawled up her spine as she shoved her key into the dead bolt. The vacant hallway suddenly seemed as ominous as a dark alley in one of Panama City's slums. If someone had it in mind to attack her here, no one would witness it. No one would know she was in trouble.

As clammy sweat erupted on her skin, she shouldered the door open, slammed it behind her and reengaged the dead bolt. Standing against the closed door, a giggle burst up from her throat as she realized how completely she'd whipped herself into a frenzy over nothing. Maybe she should lay off the horror movies because her imagination was out of control.

Still chuckling, she texted Jordan, then tossed her key ring on the kitchen counter en route to the bathroom. A cold washcloth would work miracles on her perspiring skin and settle her still-pounding pulse. She flicked the bathroom light on and barely had time to scream before a hand closed over her open mouth.

Chapter 2

Diego stared down the slide of his Sig at the driver of the white sedan that had been circling Vanessa Crosby's block for a half hour, marveling at how the seemingly simplest mission his team had ever undertaken had just gotten a hell of a lot more interesting.

He shoved the muzzle of the gun into the man's Adam's apple and asked him in Spanish, for the tenth time, who he worked for. The driver begged for his life but wouldn't give up any information on his boss.

Through his earpiece, he monitored the bug Alicia had planted in Crosby's apartment that afternoon. A rattle, then the door opened. It slammed and she released a peal of nervous laughter. She'd seemed agitated as she'd left her office, like she felt the charge in the air from his team watching her.

He'd felt the charge, too. And not only from the shock of how much prettier she was in person than in the surveillance photos. No, he felt the buzz of trouble humming in the atmosphere. Something bad was going down tonight.

The sedan, with its heavily armed driver, confirmed his suspicions.

He listened to Crosby's shoes clip-clop along the tile, past the bug in the kitchen. The sound dulled as she moved onto the carpet. Diego raised his radio to his lips, ready to pass the driver to Alicia for questioning. Before he could speak, Crosby screamed.

Not the yelp of a chick being surprised by a spider crawling on her leg, but a piercing scream of terror. No sooner had the scream started than it cut off, like someone had shut her up against her will.

Cursing, Diego backhanded the driver's skull with the side of his gun, knocking him unconscious. He sprinted around the back of the apartment building.

"Eight Ball," he shouted into his radio, using Ryan's call name, "did you hear that?"

"I'm on my way."

Diego rounded the corner. Crosby's second-floor window came into view. Over the wire, he heard muffled movement and a thump, maybe a door closing. Hard to tell with the bug in the kitchen. "Cover her front door. I'm going in the window. Ghost Rider, Thriller, do you copy?"

"Copy," John and Rory said at the same time.

No time for subtlety now that the asset was in danger, he shed the jacket concealing his utility belt and firearms as he ran. "Hold your positions. You see anyone suspicious leaving that building besides me, Eight Ball and Crosby, take them down. Phoenix, handle the man in the alley, then be ready in the follow car."

"Roger that," Alicia answered.

The wire tap had gone dead-silent. He stared up from the alley at Crosby's windows but registered no movement inside. Whatever the identities of the hostiles, they were highly trained professionals. Diego probably had a matter of seconds to recover her before her odds of survival plummeted. "We're going balls to the wall, guys. Our sneak-and-peek just turned into a hostage rescue."

He stuffed the radio onto his utility belt and swung the rifle with the mounted grappling-hook launcher around from his back. Aiming for the roof between Crosby's living room and bedroom windows, he fired. Pressured air from the pneumatic gun cracked the silence in the alley, but the sound wasn't sharp enough to draw attention.

A tug and the hook caught on the lip of the roof. From there, training and brute strength took over as Diego hauled himself hand-over-hand until he was eye-level with the base of the second-floor windows. He wrapped a hand and a boot on the rope to lock himself in place, then grabbed his Sig and sidestepped against the stucco wall to look into Crosby's living room.

Nothing and no one inside.

He swung right and peered through the bedroom window, which had an unobstructed view into the bathroom.

Again, nothing.

They weren't in the kitchen or he'd have heard it through the bug. He shoved the Sig into his thigh holster and took his radio in hand. "Eight Ball, you at her door?"

"Affirmative."

"Any movement or sound? I have visual through the windows. The place is empty."

"Nothing here. If they left her apartment, it wasn't through the door."

He looked up. They could be on the roof, but if that were the case, they'd have seen Diego's grappling hook and he'd be dodging bullets right about now.

The bed was made, the flowery quilt without a wrinkle on it. He replaced the radio and took up his Sig again. *Where are you, Vanessa?*

The bathroom door had been moved, closed about a foot from where he'd seen it during her apartment sweep. The hand soap at the sink had fallen over and a pair of women's heels sat on the linoleum. No blood on the floor or walls, as far as he could tell.

Then he saw it and cursed. The closet door was ajar. It was time to choose—stealth or speed.

Speed. Definitely.

Using the barrel of the gun, he punched a hole in the window, then cleared the pane with his boot. Glass shattered to the apartment floor and rained into the alley. He swung into the room and hit the ground running.

"Eight Ball, get in here," he shouted into the room.

Sig aimed and ready, he sprinted to the closet and threw the door open. Empty.

A crash sounded, then Ryan was behind him. On a hunch, Diego cleared the hanger rods, dumping clothes to the floor. Bingo.

A three-foot square hole had been opened through the drywall into the closet of the adjoining apartment. The vacant room beyond it was bare. He signaled Ryan to cover him, then climbed through the opening in time to see a man lowering himself into a hole cut in the bedroom floor.

Diego threw himself across the room. He crushed the man's hand against the lip of the hole with his knee.

Seizing a fistful of the man's shirt, he hauled him up through the hole. Before the guy had a chance to aim the gun wildly waving in his right hand, Diego caught him with a left hook in his jugular that sent him to the floor in a heap.

Ryan appeared behind Diego and hoisted the man away from the hole.

Diego flattened to his stomach and looked over the edge. The only thing visible in the first-floor apartment was a stained mattress. He had a hand on the telescopic mirror he carried on his belt when the radio sounded with Rory's voice. "A van pulled into the alley and stopped five meters west of Crosby's apartment, next to a window. The sliding side door is opening."

That put the van right outside the apartment below. These guys weren't messing around with getting their hostage out of the building. He beat a hasty path to the window past Ryan and the hostile he was smacking around in an attempt to get information out of him. A blue van idled directly below them, only a scant foot away from the outer wall of the apartment building.

"I count three men in the van," John said. "I have a clear shot at the driver."

Diego threw the window open. "Take it. Then disable the tires."

"Roger that."

He pulled the screen out of the way as the roar of shots reverberated through the alley. A bullet hole pierced the van's front windshield. Given the steep angle of his line of sight to the van, Diego couldn't confirm that the driver was dead, but John never missed a clear shot.

It took the men in the van only a second to respond. On the far side of the van, one hung out the passenger window and opened fire in John's direction on top of the building directly in front of them. The second man leaned out the open sliding side door and reached in through the apartment window, dragging a woman's limp form into the recesses of the van.

Vanessa.

"Ghost Rider, Thriller, hold your fire. The asset's in the van."

Once she was out of sight, the man in the van helped a second figure out the window. Diego chose the perfect moment when both men's hands were busy, then fired at the man coming through the window, shooting to kill. With an asset's life in the balance, he didn't have the luxury to chance a nonfatal shot.

The man in the van turned his gunfire on Diego.

Diego ducked back into the room. He glanced behind him to see Ryan trussing up the hostile with zip ties around his wrists and ankles.

"Thriller, what's the situation?" he asked into his radio. As he spoke, the shooting from the van ceased.

"The man who was firing at you moved to the driver's seat and pushed the driver's body out. Looks like they're going to leave their fallen comrades and take the girl."

Like hell they were.

Diego climbed onto the window sill. "Phoenix, I need a roadblock on the east side of the alley. Eight Ball, cover me. I'm going down."

Ryan appeared next to him, his rifle at the ready. "On it."

Diego jumped, landing on his feet on the roof of the van as it lurched forward on flat tires. As the van picked up speed, he dropped to his stomach and shimmied toward the closing sliding door, smoke grenade in hand.

At that moment, the white sedan from earlier rolled forward to block the exit, Alicia at the wheel. The men in the van fired on it as Alicia executed a perfect rolling fall from the car and disappeared out of view around the corner.

Diego pulled the pin from the smoke grenade with his teeth and chucked it through the open passenger window. The men inside fired on him through the roof until the grenade detonated, filling the cab with thick gray smoke, harmless except that it obscured their view.

Boots first, he pushed through the passenger window into the lap of the man sitting there. The van plowed into the car barricade at full speed. Diego vaulted forward amid shattered glass and landed hard on the hood of the barricade car, then tumbled behind it to the ground.

No time to recover from the impact, he leapt to his feet and ran around the crushed metal. The two remaining hostiles took off through the alley in the opposite direction, one of them with Vanessa slung over his shoulder.

Diego gave chase.

Pushing against the hostile's back with her bound arms, Vanessa raised her head and they locked gazes. Man, it was hard to concentrate with her dark eyes on him. The fear and hope for rescue in her expression hit him straight in the gut. He refocused on her captor's head, anywhere but at those eyes, as he swiftly bridged the distance separating them.

Though his earpiece had dislodged and he had no idea where his radio ended up, he could feel the presence of his crew around him, closing in on the hostiles from all angles, a pack of wolves moving in for the kill.

Ryan fell in step next to him and they ate up the ground between themselves and the hostiles.

"The one with the asset is mine," Diego said, lengthening the stride of his sprint.

Vanessa squirmed against the hostile's hold, pummeling his back with her joined fists hard enough that he slowed and stumbled to the right, opening a gap between himself and his cohort.

Ryan ground to a halt, raising his gun. A boom sounded and the hostile on the left fell face-first onto the asphalt, a single bullet wound in his back.

Weighed down with a still-struggling Vanessa, the remaining hostile darted toward the apartment building. At the wall, he whirled, dragging Vanessa around to stand in front of him. He jammed his gun against her neck. In his other hand, he held what was clearly a detonator.

Diego froze ten meters away, with the hostile in the sights of his Sig. Ryan stood flush with him, his gun at the ready, too. He couldn't see a bomb on Vanessa. Her work outfit was made of thin material and hugged her every curve in a way that no bomb could go unnoticed between her clothes and her skin. Could be that the bomb was on the hostile, but what would be the point of that?

His best guess was that the explosive was either in the van or the apartment building. Not that he was about to take the chance of shooting the hostile in the chest or back and hitting a bomb should the opportunity to strike arise.

Vanessa slouched against the hostile's bracing arm, her wrists still bound in front of her. She fixed her eyes on Diego again, this time radiating a little less hope and a lot more fear than they had before.

He looked past her to the hostile's trigger finger, then his face. The hostile's eyes mirrored hers—wide with anxious fear. He shouted in Spanish for Diego and Ryan to drop their weapons, but both men held steady.

Patience was the name of the game now. Any second, something was going to change the balance of the situation. Either Alicia would drive up, civilians would walk by or the hostile would lose focus. All Diego needed was the slightest hairline fracture in the tension to give him the perfect opportunity to strike.

Vanessa's shoulders shifted, recapturing his attention. He watched her bare feet plant more firmly on the ground. The muscles of her calves and quads stiffened, like she was bracing for something. Then, so gradually that the hostile didn't notice, she brought her hands up below her collarbone. He wished he could tell her to give it a rest and let him handle the heroics, but his only viable option was to be ready to respond to whatever plan she had cooking.

With a shriek that nearly made Diego flinch, she shoved her elbow back, straight into the man's gut. Ballsy move for a civilian. Stupid as hell, but impressive nonetheless.

The hostile folded over, grunting.

"Get down!" Diego shouted.

She didn't hesitate, but dove sideways onto the ground. Doubly impressive.

The instant she was clear, Diego shot the hostile through the neck. He would've rather not, but an armed, wounded kidnapper was as lethally dangerous to Vanessa as an unwounded one. Perhaps more so.

The man crumpled to the ground, raising the detonator above his head. Ryan fired, hitting the hostile's hand dead-on, but not before he depressed the button.

Diego lunged forward and threw his body over Vanessa's, collecting her limbs beneath him as a roar sounded all around them. The shock wave smacked him hard but didn't scramble his brains the way it sometimes did, telling him the blast wasn't all that close. He raised his head and looked the length of the alley. Smoke and flame poured from the broken windows of Vanessa's apartment.

Sirens sounded in the distance. Besides the possibility of getting sidetracked by local police and fire response teams, they were way too exposed for Diego's liking. He didn't particularly care to find out if there were any more hostiles waiting to pounce.

"I'm getting her out of here," he told Ryan, who was busy with the fallen hostile.

He stood and waited for Vanessa to follow suit, but she remained huddled in a ball.

With no time to explain or wait for her to recover her wits, he swept her into his arms and bolted toward his getaway car around the corner from the alley. Until they turned onto the street, out of view of the alley, her gaze stayed firmly fixed over Diego's shoulder at her burning apartment.

He set her onto the backseat and tore the tape from her mouth. She drew a labored gasp and stared up at him, her eyes wide with confusion and terror. Even if he wasn't in a race against the clock to get her to safety, soothing frightened broads wasn't his gig. Pretty tough to pull off a comforting smile while covered in blood spatter and shrapnel.

Still, irrational though it was, the urge to reassure her burned bright inside him, so he said the first thing that came to mind. "Nice jab to the gut back there."

"What?" she breathed.

Good job, Slick. Real soothing. Maybe he ought to

heed Dreyer's advice and keep his mouth shut. Scowling, he pulled out his knife to free her wrists.

She gasped and pedaled her feet backward, scared, like maybe Diego was going to carve her up with the knife. Like he hadn't just saved her life. "Calm down. If I wanted to hurt you, I wouldn't need this knife to do it."

She gasped and scooted farther away.

Not sure if he was more irritated with her for her lack of trust or himself for saying the wrong thing again, he swore under his breath and grabbed her hands. "Stop squirming. We need to get out of here."

She complied. Thank God for small favors.

One slice and her wrists were free. He replaced the knife and grabbed the flak vest from the seat. Jerking the straps open, he held it out to her.

She stuck her arms through the holes. "Who are you?"

"Doesn't matter. I'm only the chauffeur." He pulled the straps tight and secured the vest around her. She started to ask something else, but he missed it as he slammed the door closed and dropped into the driver's seat. From the center console, he found the spare radio he'd stowed. "Phoenix, you copy?"

"Copy, Devil."

He turned the engine over. "Pulling away. You and Eight Ball ready to roll?"

"Right behind you, boss."

He twisted to look over his shoulder at Vanessa. She was acting scared again—breathing shallow, eyes wide, jaw tight. He hated that it had to be like this for her. He wished as badly as she probably did that her life could've stayed the way it'd been up until that afternoon. Peaceful and average. Without the taint of corruption and the evil of men.

Wouldn't do either of them any good for him to say that, though. Knowing him, it would come out all wrong anyway.

Best he could do for her was keep her unharmed until he delivered her to Dreyer and Montgomery, then hope they cared as deeply about her safety as he did.

Chapter 3

Chauffeur wasn't the word Vanessa would use to describe the man driving her God knew where—the man who'd saved her life.

He wore a black T-shirt that did little to mask the muscles that had wrapped around her like a shield when he'd thrown himself on her before the explosion. The gun he held like an extension of his arm while he drove was black and massive, and she'd seen two more like it strapped to his body.

He'd shot at least one man with that gun in order to save her. Probably more, judging by the gunfire she'd heard. Actions that weren't in the typical chauffeur playbook.

From her position on the floor, her only view was of the sky and the gray-brown edges of building roofs. Time and silence stretched on until the buildings disappeared from sight, leaving only trees and dark clouds as an afternoon rainstorm rolled through. As fast as they were moving, it wouldn't be long until they disappeared into the thicket of jungle that surrounded the city.

Her fear and lack of control made it tough to breathe. Her body was sore from being tossed around and her head hurt from the initial blow she'd endured in her bathroom. She tried to think up a number to focus on, something big with a decimal point, but she couldn't even conjure *pi* past five digits.

Worse, it was impossible to know who she could trust.

Except that her instincts told her she could depend on the chauffeur—Devil, the woman on the radio called him. She had no idea how the nickname got started, but from what she could tell, he was the least likely devil she'd ever met. More like a guardian angel, if today's events were any indication.

He'd taken down the men threatening her, guarded her from the blast that destroyed her apartment and given her a bulletproof vest. More telling was his genuine annoyance when he derided her for being afraid of him and the honest admiration in his compliment about her elbow jab. He wasn't some smooth operator with slick words and fake sincerity aimed at lulling her into compliance. She'd been around enough of that kind of man that her radar was finely tuned. Without any better options, she decided to go with her instinct and trust him.

God help her if she was wrong.

She studied the wound on his neck below the neat cut of his dark brown hair, a bloody cocktail of glass shards, asphalt and black flecks she suspected were shrapnel—not that she'd ever seen shrapnel before.

"You're hurt," she blurted.

"Huh?"

"On your neck."

He touched his fingers to the wound. "I thought it felt itchy. What is that, glass?" He picked out a piece and examined it, then dropped it out the window.

Itchy? How about excruciatingly painful? Or maybe this guy didn't feel pain like a normal person. Wouldn't surprise her given the other superhero-like stunts he'd pulled off already. "Do you have a first aid kit in the car?"

He snorted, like he found her suggestion amusing. "It's nothing. Doesn't hurt at all. I'll deal with it later."

"Did the bank send you to get me?"

His head twitched in her direction, but he kept his eyes on the road. "No. U.S. government. Uncle Sam would like a word with you."

Though his olive complexion and dark eyes spoke to Latino roots, she'd known he was American before he'd said a single word in that New Jersey accent she'd become so familiar with during college. It was evident in the way he held himself, the cocksure set of his shoulders and the way his lips moved when he scowled. Even the crooked angle of his nose, most likely the result of a bad break, looked American somehow.

"Am I in trouble?"

He chortled. "Well, a bunch of not-so-friendly thugs were waiting to ambush you and blow up your apartment. If that doesn't qualify as trouble, I don't know what does."

She ignored his words so she wouldn't freak out by thinking about what'd happened to her. "No, I meant in trouble with the law. This is about the account information I stole today, isn't it? People found out. I knew it was wrong, but I didn't mean any harm. You have to believe me."

"Hell of a poker face you've crafted there, Vanessa. How about, from now on, you play your cards a little closer to the vest, if you catch my drift."

That he would coach her like that reaffirmed her decision to trust him. "I take it you're not arresting me?"

"Like I said, I'm just the chauffeur."

She studied what she could see of him from where she crouched on the floor. Beneath the wound that had gnarled his flesh, he had muscles that started in his neck and extended through his shoulders as thick and strong as the roots of a tree. The biceps of the arm on the steering wheel, the arm that had carried her effortlessly, strained against the fabric of his shirt.

Unexpected attraction pulsed through her. She could practically smell the testosterone rolling off his body. His massive bruiser of a physique took up all the air in the car, pressing into her awareness, calling forth an ancient, wholly feminine part of her that hadn't surfaced since she used to steal glances at her father's football players after practice, sweaty and brutish as they lumbered to the locker room.

This man was no athlete. His skills, guns and tough Jersey accent told a different story. He said he worked for the government, so there was only one possible explanation.

She poked her head higher to look at the side of his face. "It's been a while since I've lived stateside, but when did they start calling American soldiers *chauffeurs?* That some kind of new code word?"

He glanced at her through the rearview mirror. Though all she could see were his eyes and the side of his cheek, she knew he was smiling. "That's just me playing it close to the vest, like I'm trying to teach you."

"You're going with stick with the chauffeur story? You must be super top secret. Wait—are you part of SEAL Team Six?"

He strummed his fingers on the steering wheel. "You know how you can tell I'm not part of SEAL Team Six? Because you've heard of SEAL Team Six. What I am, you don't need to worry about."

She opened her mouth to question him about which branch of the military he worked for, when he released an exasperated sigh. Somewhere nearby, gunshots rang out. The engine roared in protest as she felt their speed increase.

"Stay down," he said as he exchanged his handgun on the passenger seat for a radio. "Phoenix, Eight Ball, you copy?"

Vanessa ducked lower, hugging herself and trying to breathe through her fear. She didn't understand why the chauffeur sounded so calm about the new round of gunfire. If she hadn't heard the shots, she wouldn't have had any inkling there was trouble.

"Copy, Devil. We're returning fire on two cars." It was the woman's voice, as even-keeled as the chauffeur's.

He transferred the radio to his steering hand and reached across the seat, bringing a massive black, Rambo-like rifle across his lap. "Everything under control?"

"Affirmative," said a man's deep baritone over the radio. "The bridge we rigged is less than four clicks from here. A Boom and Block ought to throw them off your tail."

More gunfire sounded in the distance.

"Roger that," the chauffeur said. He fiddled with the rifle, flipping levers and checking the chamber, then tipped the muzzle out the open driver window.

Curiosity got the better of Vanessa. She popped her head up to look through the rearview mirror. They were ripping along a road, walled on both sides by curtains of thick, lush foliage. Two nondescript sedans drove side by side several car lengths behind them. Behind those were two more.

"What are you doing? Get your head back down."

She ducked. "Are those cars the ones firing at us?"

"Not the closer two. That's my crew. They've been trailing us this whole time, but there's two more cars behind them giving us some trouble. You know those wire transfer numbers you thought might be a bulk cash laundering operation? Looks like you were dead-on about that. And now the men responsible want to shut you up in a bad way."

The moment the men in her bathroom had grabbed her, she'd known it was related to the algorithm she wrote, but it finally hit home hearing it said aloud. She'd thrust herself in the middle of an international war in which no side ever won. She couldn't die now, and not because of some stupid number patterns she'd spotted at the bank. Her stomach lurched. Every gunshot she heard kicked her heart rate up another notch.

It was unendurable, feeling this vulnerable. "You're not going to let that happen, right?"

He scowled. "What kind of question is that?"

Before she could respond, he brought the radio to his lips again. "We're at the bridge. You need any help from me on the B&B?"

"You take care of the asset. We've got this covered."

Devil—or the chauffeur or whoever he was—looked

into the rearview mirror. "Roger that. See you at the safe house."

Risking his wrath again, she scooted her butt onto the seat and sat up as the car thumped onto a wooden bridge over a river. "What's going on? What's a B&B?"

"Now's not the best time for questions. Brace yourself, there's gonna be a blast."

No sooner were the words out of his mouth than a tremendous quake of force and noise pushed on the back of the car. She got up on her knees and looked behind them. The bridge they'd crossed was engulfed in flames. None of the cars that had been following them were in sight.

Vanessa's heart pounded in her throat. "That was the B&B?" she choked out, mesmerized by the flames and smoke licking up toward the clouds.

"Affirmative. We wired the bridge with explosives this morning in case we were followed. In a B&B, the crew goes off-road before the downed bridge and circles back, trapping the hostiles against the roadblock and neutralizing them with heavy artillery."

His tone remained flat and distracted, as if what he was describing didn't put people's lives in mortal danger. Soldiers she'd never met who were risking everything because of her. *Neutralizing* people because of her. She braced a hand on her chest and tried not to think of the bloodshed, wishing she could make it all stop. "I couldn't live with it if someone on your team got hurt protecting me."

He took a sharp left turn at a breakneck speed, plunging them onto a twisty, single-lane road made dark with tree cover. "Hate to sound like a jackass, but it's not about you. We're just doing the job Uncle Sam pays us to."

In other words, he only cared about her life because it was in his job description. And whoever he was delivering her to would feel the same way. The minute the bulk cash smugglers and U.S. government had gotten wind of her discovery, her life-worth had become finite, limited to the algorithm she'd created. She was expendable and she'd do well to remember that.

A sharp pang of loneliness rippled through her, as intense as her fear, leaving a sickening trail of emptiness in its wake. No one was going to care about what happened to her, other than her dad and Jordan. And wasn't that the story of her life? When they learned of the blast that destroyed her apartment, they'd each be devastated, thinking Vanessa dead or kidnapped. But, then, if Vanessa was being truly honest with herself, even her dad hadn't cared about her enough to—

No. She wasn't going to go to that dark place in her heart again. Wallowing didn't serve any purpose that could help her now. At least the chauffeur was still with her, and although he was only doing his job, he was better than not having anyone in her corner at all.

She brought her feet up to the seat and hugged her knees, willing the fear and loneliness away as she watched the trees pass in a blur.

A deep sigh from the front seat had her shifting her gaze around, nervous. The last time he sighed like that, the kidnappers were on their trail.

"I'm not… I didn't mean to… Damn it…" Wringing the steering wheel, he shook his head, clearly frustrated, though she had no idea why. "How did you come up with the idea to jab that guy in the gut? I don't know many chicks who would think to do that while they had a gun to their throat."

It took a bunch of blinks before she caught up to his

topic change, and when she did, his praise evoked a warm glow of pride inside her. "Um, thanks. My dad suggested I take a self-defense class before I moved to Panama, and I liked it so much that I take one every few years as a refresher. I was aiming for his junk, but I couldn't scoot over far enough to make it work, so I improvised."

He snorted. "Aiming for a man's junk is definitely an effective technique, and you did fine. Gave me the window I needed to strike."

All warmth vanished as the image flashed in her mind of the bullet hole in her kidnapper's neck, his gasping inhale and exhale, the spatter of blood. She touched her cheek, wondering if his dried blood remained on her skin. It was the first time she'd seen someone die, and she was having trouble wrapping her brain around any kind of coherent feelings about it.

She was relieved and sickened at the same time, having no doubt in her mind that the events of the last hour boiled down to a kill-or-be-killed situation. But though she would be forever grateful that the chauffeur hadn't hesitated to do what was necessary, she regretted that it had been. She would never forget the look of absolute focus on his face when he'd chased down the kidnapper carrying her—the agility in his steps, the singular power of his movement, the lethal grace.

Her gaze slid up the thick muscles of his arm, imagining her hand doing the same, imagining what it would feel like to explore a body of such raw, masculine energy. No doubt about it, he was a man built for battle. Yet she could see in his sharp, dark eyes, and in the glimpses of humor and caring he'd let slip, that there was so much more to him than the fight.

How many men had he killed? How did he make

peace with that part of his job? How old was he the first time? Did the dead haunt him as she imagined they would her? She wanted desperately to ask but couldn't figure out a way to phrase the questions without sounding judgmental, and the last thing she needed was to get on his bad side.

She allowed several silent minutes to pass before she asked a different question. "Once you deliver me to the safe house, is your job done?"

Her insides twisted. Why did it bother her, thinking she may never see him again after today? Fear of being left unprotected, of course, but more than that. Deeper—a frustrated hollowness, as if they had unfinished business. There was so much more about him she wanted to know.

She watched the mirror, waiting for him to look at her through the glass, but he kept his eyes straight ahead.

"Not sure." His jaw was tight, his words clipped. "I was supposed to escort you home, too, but that's obviously not going to happen."

"Whose job is it to decide my fate?"

"You'll meet them soon enough."

The vagueness of his answer incensed her. She wanted to climb into the front seat, take that iron jaw in hand and force him to look at her. To level with her about the future and steady her nerves with the promise that he'd keep on protecting her. *If I can't be in charge of my own fate, then you be the one,* she wanted to demand. *Not some unknown government official, but you.*

Wrenching her gaze from his unyielding profile, she hugged her knees tighter and fought to keep the frustration out of her voice. "Can you at least tell me how much longer it is until we get there?"

"That post up ahead marks the driveway." As he spoke, the car slowed. His gaze flickered to her through the rearview mirror. "I should've added that I wish you could be in charge of your own fate. And I'm sorry it's not that way for you anymore."

"Thank you." And for whatever reason, she felt better. Like at least he cared enough to feel sorry for her.

The car turned left onto a narrow road at a steep incline.

A radio chirped to life somewhere at the front of the car. "This is Montgomery. Devil, do you copy?" The male voice was strained, his words rushed.

He lifted a radio. "Copy. We're here, right on schedule."

"Abort the mission. We're taking fire."

He slammed on the brakes. "You're what?" For the first time since they started driving, his tone held a note of concern.

"The safe house has been compromised," the man on the radio—Montgomery—said. "We're under attack. We can't—"

The radio signal cut out.

Chapter 4

A series of gunshots sounded nearby. Cursing, Diego threw the car into Reverse. No time or space to get turned around, so he barreled backward down the hill.

"Get low," he said. "Cover your head and don't get up until I tell you."

Thank God Vanessa didn't fight him on it. She threw herself to the floor behind his seat.

He negotiated the final turn before they reached the main road at a speed that sent the tires skidding, but he muscled the car back under his control in time to see three vehicles stopped at the intersection of the driveway and the road, blocking him in. He stomped on the brakes.

They opened fire. Diego slouched in his seat. The rear window shattered, but at least Vanessa was on the floor. He reached onto his belt for a grenade and lobbed it through the broken window.

The gunfire stopped. Shouts sounded behind him as he jammed the gear into Drive and ground his foot on the accelerator, his goal the fire access road thirty meters ahead. Not a second later, a huge blast propelled the car forward. Through the mirror, he watched a cloud of smoke and flame belch into the sky. Looked like all three cars took a hit, though two men on foot had escaped the blast.

They ran toward his car, shooting, but there was no time to worry about them. Two armored SUVs appeared ahead, coming straight at him from up the driveway. He hooked his rifle out the window, threw the car back in Reverse and got busy squeezing off rounds at the same time a hooded man popped up through the sunroof of one of the armored SUVs and took aim.

Firing at the shooter and driving with his knee, he reached for another grenade, pulled the pin and stuffed it in his rifle-mounted launcher.

Aiming at the open sunroof, he fired. Rather than dropping through the sunroof, it caught on the hood up close to the windshield. Good enough.

The SUV driver must've figured out he had a live grenade hooked to his vehicle because the car screeched to a stop. The shooter from the sunroof leapt onto the roof and slid over the windshield, his arm out to knock the grenade off. He was nearly to it when it exploded, blocking the second SUV from passing but not stopping the passengers of that car from firing at them through the smoke and flame of the demolished lead car.

The bushes and trees lining the road were too thick for him to blaze a path through, so the only option he could see besides heading out on foot was to muscle his way past the burning cars at the base of the driveway.

He stretched his rifle over the backseat.

"Stay down, Vanessa," he commanded before spraying rounds through the blown-out rear window at the blast survivors. One dropped and the other ran for cover in the forest.

Diego swung the rifle forward again and emptied the rest of the rounds at the still-shooting SUV as he gave the car more gas, working up a nice, powerful helping of backward momentum.

"Impact," he barked.

The rear of their car slammed hard into a burning vehicle. The force whipped their car around, spinning it head-on into the second car. Somehow, and he wasn't sure how he accomplished it, he spun the wheels in reverse and zipped backward through the opening he'd created between the cars and the shoulder of the road.

He kept up the spinning, ramming one of the cars out of the way behind them, until he saw open road. Working the brake pedal, he pushed the gear to Drive and got them the hell out of there.

He remained silent until the battle was out of sight, coming down from the adrenaline spike. That had been close. Way closer than he liked when it came to protecting an asset. He should've known better than to accept the safe house ICE had chosen—the long, isolated driveway was way too convenient for someone to stage an ambush. Bugged the hell out of him that he hadn't seen it coming.

He shook off his building aggravation. There'd be time enough later to beat himself up over what he'd allowed to happen. "You okay?"

"I think so." Her voice was shaky.

"You're not sure?" If she were injured, he'd have to rethink his whole getaway plan.

"No. I'm sure. Not hurt. Just rattled."

Women. They could transform an easy question into something complicated. His sisters were the queens of that sort of crap. In his world, everything was black-and-white. Save who needs saving; kill who needs killing. Bam. It was that simple.

Sighing through his nose, he lifted his radio. "Crew, do you copy? How close are you to the safe house?"

"Copy, Devil. We're two clicks away," Ryan said.

"Abort mission. Safe house was ambushed."

"Are you and the asset all right?" Alicia asked.

"We're fine. On the road again. What do you think the chances are that someone in ICE leaked the operation to the Chiara brothers?"

"Either that or there's a bug on the asset. No other way for the safe house to come under attack," Ryan said. "How do you want us to play it?"

"Dreyer and Montgomery were fighting hostiles when we beat it out of there. I'm not sure it's the right call for you to blast in there like the friggin' National Guard and save them, since we don't know who we can trust anymore. If you decide to go in there, watch your backs."

"What's your plan, Devil?" Rory asked.

"I'm calling a Leroy. And I suggest you all do the same. Do you copy?"

"Copy on the Leroy," Alicia said. "Eight Ball and I are close enough to the safe house that we can see Panama army helicopters buzzing the area. Troops are moving in. There's nothing we can do to assist without getting caught by the wrong people."

It was a relief that his crew agreed with him about going Leroy, rather than jumping into the fray. "Ghost Rider, Thriller, you copy, too?"

"We're here. Copy on the Leroy."

"Okay, then. Stay safe. We check in tonight no matter what, then decide what we want to do."

"Good luck," Ryan said. "See you on the flip side."

It took Vanessa a few tries to string enough words together to ask a question. She pushed up onto the seat and smoothed an unsteady hand over her skirt. "Tell me what's going on. Please."

"You probably already guessed that your chat with Uncle Sam is a no-go. The rendezvous place is under attack, presumably by the men who are after you. The mission's been aborted." The way he said it, he could've been talking about the results of last Sunday's ball game. Like there was nothing life could throw his way that would scare him, nothing that would rattle him to the core.

And maybe that was a good thing, because Vanessa was terrified enough for the both of them.

"What are we going to do? I mean, your mission's aborted, but you're going to stay with me, right? Is that part of whatever the Leroy plan is? The man on the radio, Eight Ball, said the asset could be bugged. That's me, right? I'm the asset?"

He swerved right, onto a dirt road she hadn't noticed. The highway disappeared behind a curtain of trees. "You're the asset, yeah."

She fingered her dress shirt, royally spooked by the idea that she might have a tracking device somewhere on her body. "Okay, so how do I know if the bad guys planted a tracking device on me? I've got to get it off."

He afforded her a passing glance through the rearview mirror. "We're not going to try to find it. If they bugged you, it'll be on your clothes. Grab the bag by your feet."

Inside the brown paper bag she hadn't noticed before, she discovered a complete change of clothes in her size, including sneakers and undergarments. Without removing the bra from the bag, she fingered the cream-colored, satiny material, her cheeks flushing. The matching panties were edged in lace.

Had he chosen them for her?

As if in response to her silent question, he looked out the side window, clearing his throat. "Phoenix, uh, Alicia, on my team, bought those. I have no idea if she got the right fit. I…" His voice trailed off. He adjusted the rifle lying across his lap and shook his head again.

The car slowed to a stop on the edge of the road. He slung the rifle strap over his shoulder and opened his door. Once out of the car, he ducked to look at her. "After you change, I'll destroy your old clothes. When we're back on the road, I'll do my best to answer your questions. Be fast about it, will you? We're killing time."

He closed the door and set his back to her, facing toward the road with the rifle in his arms, his posture vigilant. Protecting her. She counted the weapons she could see. Besides the massive rifle he held, there was a handgun in a shoulder holster, another strapped to his thigh and a third on his belt. Two knives on the belt, along with an array of other cartridges and cases she couldn't name.

Studying him, knowing he wasn't going to let anything or anyone get to her for the moment, she allowed the silence and warmth of the car to wash over her like a wave of calm. She removed the bulletproof vest and released a long, slow exhale for the first time since before she'd copied the account files onto the zip drive that afternoon.

The zip drive.

She wormed her fingers into her pocket and brought out the drive. With all that had happened, she'd forgotten about it. Perhaps the best plan would've been to drop it into the paper bag to destroy it along with the clothes, but the chauffeur's advice came back to her about playing her cards close to the vest. So instead, she set it on the seat.

With one eye on her protector's back, she wiggled out of her skirt and panties. The panties from the bag were a perfect fit. Over them, she pulled up a pair of roomy khaki pants and tucked the zip drive into the front pocket.

As she unbuttoned her blouse, her eyes slid along the curve of the chauffeur's spine. There was a mesmerizing juxtaposition of physics at work in his muscled build. Though his physique seemed carved from stone, he gave the impression he could move effortlessly and instantaneously in any direction, as if he were solid and fluid at the same time. Constantly at the ready, yet relaxed.

Reaching behind her, she unclasped her bra. Heat was building in the closed car. The bra stuck to her perspiring skin as she peeled it away. She was confident he wouldn't turn around, but she still felt exposed, admiring a strange man's body while partially nude. She blotted the perspiration on her chest with her discarded blouse, then fitted the new bra and stretchy white T-shirt on.

The socks and sneakers went on last. His crew member Alicia had even chosen the right size shoe for her. Maybe she should've been creeped out that someone she'd never met knew her every measurement, but her mind was too full of real problems to care. She stuffed her old clothes in the bag and then stepped outside.

He turned and looked down her body with dark, in-scrutable eyes. A muscle in his jaw near his ear rippled.

"Everything fits," she said lamely, handing him the bag. "It's nice to have shoes again."

Walking to the middle of the road, he peeked inside and she was extra glad she'd stuffed the underwear to the bottom. He set the bag on the ground and reached for a canister on his belt, emptying the liquid over the paper. An accelerant, if she had to guess. Next from his belt came a match. The bag burst into flames.

Watching fire consume the last of her possessions, an unexpected ache started inside her, like her very being had been bruised. She drew a ragged breath, then clutched her upper arms. Besides the few trinkets she kept at her cubicle in the bank, she had nothing left.

"I've been thinking about the questions you asked."

She wrenched her gaze from the burning clothes and watched him move toward her, his eyes radiating the same unflappable grit he'd exhibited from the moment she first saw him.

"You wanted to know if I'm going to let the bad guys get you or if I'm going to help you, even though the mission was aborted."

Though her heart rate picked up in anticipation of his answer, she squared her shoulders and raised her chin. If he didn't offer his help freely, she'd fight for it. Beg if she had to. Her survival depended on him. "I don't know who else I can trust. I don't have a car or family here, and my ATM card and ID were probably lost when my apartment blew up. I don't know how I could stay safe without your help."

He stopped more than an arm's length away, his hands loose on top of his rifle, his posture that of a soldier at rest. "Do you know what my job is?"

Was that a trick question? "You're the chauffeur."

He nodded. "And do you know why my bosses signed me up to be your driver?"

"No."

"Because the people I'm assigned to help, they come out the other end of trouble without a scratch on them. That's my job—keep the asset safe or die trying. Do I look dead to you?"

She inhaled and shook her head.

"That's right." He opened his arms and let the rifle hang from its strap around his shoulder. "The fact that I am standing here with you in the middle of this god-forsaken jungle means I have a perfect record when it comes to protecting people. I don't mess up. I don't fail. And I'm sure as hell not going to screw up that reputation with you. Are we clear?"

They weren't pretty words, but they were the most comforting she'd ever heard. He didn't know her, yet he'd protect her with his life. She was going to be okay. Relief snapped the dam of her emotions. She gritted her teeth and stared at the dirt near his boots.

There was no way, in her lifetime, she could repay him or adequately express her gratitude. He could claim all he wanted about this being a job for him, but this was her life they were talking about. "I think it's time to tell me your name, because I'm not going to call you Devil."

Perhaps she'd caught him off guard because he pulled his face back. Then he stepped closer and stuck out his hand for her to shake. "ICE Special Agent Diego Santero."

She'd dealt with Immigration and Customs agents off and on over the years with her job at the bank, but none of them looked remotely like the man whose hand currently enveloped hers in a confident handshake. A ripple of awareness coursed through her. "Nice to meet you, Agent Santero."

He released her hand and reestablished the space between them. "Diego's fine. But I'm not sure how nice it is. Most civilians, if they have to meet me, that means they're having the worst day of their lives."

That was certainly true for her. Her eyes slid to the clothes bag, now a smoldering pile. Bits of gray ash swirled in the breeze. Her life would never be the same again. She swallowed and blinked, working to regain control of her emotions.

"You're not going to cry, are you?"

The ludicrous question jarred her from her trance-like melancholy. Diego's brow was furrowed and his lips had stretched into a cringe. He fidgeted with the rifle, his gaze darting anxiously to the car as though he was contemplating escape. Here was a man who'd jumped onto the roof of a moving minivan, shot and killed at least one man and shielded her from an explosion with his body…and yet he was threatened by the possibility of a few tears?

Despite everything she'd been through and her fear of the future, a spark of affection had her biting her cheeks to hide a grin. Apparently there wasn't much difference between the college football players her dad coached and macho military alphas. Nothing brought them to their knees faster than the threat of genuine emotional expression.

She drilled him with her best offended look and set her hands on her hips. "I might cry. What are you going to do about it?"

He squirmed, then scratched his head. His eyes shifted to the car again, then the jungle beyond. "Look, forget I said that."

She shouldn't mess with him, really. This man was the only thing standing between her and certain death at the hands of a whole bunch of bad guys—but she couldn't help it. She sniffed to draw his gaze back to her, then blinked hard, jarring a tear loose. It started a slow roll over her cheek.

He stared at her, his eyes dark and serious. Then he startled and took off in a fast stride to the car. "Time for us for bolt. The longer we're on the grid, the more danger you're in."

He opened the backseat door for her and jumped into the driver seat.

Yep. Her assessment had been right. The man of steel had a soft and gooey center. She settled into the seat, contemplating that revelation as she watched the play of skin and muscle on his arm as he shifted the car into gear and pulled onto the road.

Once they were moving again, she set her hand on his shoulder. She had a feeling that touching him would spook him all over again, but like unleashing that tear, she couldn't help herself. He tensed at her touch but met the look she gave him in the mirror. "Just so you know, for future reference, the best thing to do when a woman cries is to keep your mouth shut and hand her a tissue. Cringing and running away is definitely not recommended. You've got to learn how to play it closer to the vest."

The edge of his jaw grew tight, not with a scowl of irritation, but as though he was fighting a grin. "I must've skipped that day in guy school."

Though she wanted to squeeze his shoulder, to test the breadth of it against her palm, she forced herself to let go and sit back in her seat. "Then I should also mention that the only exception to the tissue rule is if the woman crying is someone you care a lot about, then you have to hold her until she's done. Think you can handle that, soldier?"

"Roger that. Mouth shut. Weepy chicks get tissues except girlfriends, then you have to offer yourself as a tissue."

It was useless to resist his dry wit. Her chest shook with a silent chuckle. "You have a way with words."

"Yeah, right. You should know you're the first person in the history of the world to pay me that particular compliment." He glanced to the passenger seat, then opened and closed the glove compartment. "There are no tissues in this car. Unbelievable."

"Not even on your Batman utility belt?"

"You think maybe I tucked one of those travel packs of tissues next to my grappling hooks and spare magazines? No dice. Sorry."

They thumped onto a paved road and sped southwest at an impossibly high speed. Given how far away from the city they were, they hadn't passed a single car or person, reminding Vanessa that she still had no idea where they were going or what the plan was.

"What's a Leroy?" she asked.

"I was trained by a man named Leroy Yarborough. Taught me everything I know to stay alive and do the job right. One thing I learned from him was that going into any situation, you have plan A, plan B, and going on down the line, but you always have one last plan no one knows about but you, completely off the grid. Plan zero, he called it. The ultimate failsafe. So when you get in a jam and don't know who you can trust or what's going on, you have a ready response."

"Makes sense."

"When I started with ICE, I made damn sure I had

a plan zero in place, and I insisted each of my crew members did, too. After a while, we got to calling it a Leroy because it sounded less dramatic, you know? I've only had to use it three times in twelve years, but that's three times Leroy's lessons saved my life and the lives of my crew."

"How many people are in your crew?"

"Four plus me."

"Do you know what their Leroys are?"

"No clue, and they don't know about mine. They could be on a boat for Mexico or hiding out in a monastery for all I know. That's why it works. Not a soul in the world will be able to find me, or in this case find us, until we want them to."

She was about to go off the grid with a man she'd just met, without anyone knowing where she'd be. She'd made up her mind to trust Diego implicitly, but that trust was being put to the test sooner than she would've liked.

She was about to ask if she'd have a chance to let Jordan know she was safe when a chain-link fence came into view. They blazed through the gate, waved on by a weathered old man, and onto a bare, grassy field in which sat a huge metal building the size of an airplane hangar.

Diego parked in front of the building. He jogged from the car, worked a padlock and pushed the heavy metal door open, revealing several helicopters and canvas-tarp-covered cars.

Vanessa scrambled out from the backseat and followed him inside. He stopped at the first helicopter, a tiny, black two-seater model.

The closer she got to the helicopter, the more trepidation made her heart pound. That piddly little sphere of metal was his plan zero—the Leroy? Flying wasn't her favorite, especially in itty-bitty planes. And she'd never flown in anything as tiny as a helicopter, or one missing its doors, such as this one was. It looked like a toy. "You know how to fly this thing?"

Busy inspecting something inside a panel toward the tail of the helicopter, near splashy red lettering declaring Panama Canal Photography Tours, he glanced sideways at her. "I might've missed a few lessons about how to deal with weepy broads, but I aced flight school. Try not to look so nervous. You're bruising my ego."

With that, he strode to the wall and punched a button. Gears whirred to life, then the ceiling of the hangar began to retract.

The doorway darkened with the form of the old man from the gate. Rattling something in Spanish, Diego flipped him the car keys. For a second, she contemplated swiping the keys away and making a break for it. Ridiculous idea, sure, but at least she'd be near the ground in case of a crash. With mounting anxiety, she calculated how many seconds it would take to hit the earth after a free fall from ten thousand feet. Not a number designed to bring her comfort.

Diego angled himself into her line of sight. "I see your mind working overtime, trying to make sense of it all, but you've got to stop thinking so hard. You know that primeval instinct we've all got for fight-or-flight? It's flight time."

"That thing is really small."

He slung an arm across her shoulders and guided her to the passenger side. "Aw, now, don't you know it's not polite to go around insulting the size of a man's helicopter?" Offering his hand, he added, "In you go."

Events were happening way too fast for her to process. How could she decide if she was making the right choice if she didn't have time to stop and think about it? Then again, taking too much time to contemplate her options might get her killed. Drawing a steadying breath, she accepted his hand and climbed inside. The copter looked bigger from this perspective, but it shook when Diego climbed in. Not exactly comforting.

He handed her a headset, checked her harness seat belt, then fiddled with various gears and switches. The engine fired up, building to a deafening roar, and she could tell the rotors were spinning by the swirl of dust on the floor and the flap of the papers tacked to the wall.

The entire helicopter vibrated as it rose from the ground, including Vanessa's teeth. She clutched the arms of her seat and squeezed her eyes closed.

"Relax. Seriously," said Diego's voice through her headset. "Of all the things in your life right now worth getting scared about, this isn't one of them."

That was sound logic, sure, but since when did logic ever work against fear? "I've never flown in a helicopter before."

"I kind of gathered that. How about you consider this one of those expensive aerial rainforest tours all the cruise ship tourists pay the big bucks for? And bonus for you, because you've got your own personal guide."

Although she wasn't ready to open her eyes, she managed to unclamp her teeth long enough to attempt some desperation humor. "From chauffeur to tour guide, huh? Would you consider that a promotion?"

He squeezed her shoulder, which was probably meant as a gesture of comfort, but it made her stomach drop. "What are you doing? Get both your hands back on the wheel, or whatever that thingy is called."

He chuckled but removed his hand. "Cyclic stick."

"Whatever."

"As your tour guide, I suggest you open your eyes and look out your door. The view of Camino de Cruces National Park is pretty freakin' cool, and in about five minutes, we'll be crossing over the canal."

"Nice try."

He chuckled again, and she was about to give him a piece of her mind for his lack of sensitivity when his laughter cut off.

"That ain't friendly," he muttered.

"What's not?"

Without warning, the helicopter swerved right and dropped altitude. She yelped, her eyes flying open and arms flailing. "What are you doing?"

"Hang on. We've got company."

Chapter 5

Vanessa dug her nails into the armrests of her seat. She gritted her teeth against a yelp as Diego banked along the tree canopy of a steep mountain ridge, a huge camo-green Panama army helicopter hot on their tail.

He leveled out and she caught her breath enough to speak. "Why would the army think anything suspicious when your helicopter says it's part of a tour company?"

"That is an excellent question that we can definitely discuss later. Right now, I'm going to concentrate on not getting the two of us stuck in military custody."

They wove through valleys between mountains of dense greenery and burst out over the open space above the canal. The skyscrapers of the Panama City skyline looked small against the western horizon. She glanced behind them, her heart sinking at the sight of the army helicopter still in pursuit.

"Do you think you can outrun it?"

He ground his lips together. "Outrun, outmaneuver, outwit—whatever it takes. I feel like a broken record, but could you please have a little faith in my abilities? This is getting old."

He swerved left, crossing the canal, then wrenched the control stick forward. They dropped low and followed the path of the water. This far east of Panama City, the canal looked more like a river, green and wide and dotted with boats that zoomed past her line of sight. In the distance ahead of them, she could barely make out a strip of gray-blue. The Atlantic Ocean.

"Are your eyes open?" Diego asked.

"Mmm-hmm," she hummed behind her cringing, closed lips.

"Go ahead and close them again. And hang on."

That was one command she wouldn't argue about. She mashed her eyes closed as they lost altitude so suddenly, her stomach felt like it hit the ceiling. In the next moment, their helicopter started to weave like an orb at the end of a pendulum.

She thought it couldn't get any worse until she heard a loud series of cracks.

"What's that?" she said.

"They're firing at us," Diego said in a calm voice.

"Oh, crap."

"Relax. They're getting desperate."

"How is that a good thing? Seriously, I want to know."

The swerving stopped, so she snuck a peek, seeing only a wall of mossy green rock face on either side. Ahead of them, more green as the narrow canyon they were flying through curved right.

"It's a good thing because it means I've just about lost them," Diego said. "They were too far away to hit us anyway. Probably a couple of rookie soldiers piloting it. You can open your eyes now. There's a great view here out my side."

She unstuck her neck from its forward position and looked across Diego. They were hovering near the face of a waterfall. "Nice," she said, and meant it.

He offered her a lopsided grin of pure male pride. "Since I know you're going to insult me by asking, I might as well cut right to the answers. Yes, I did lose the army chopper. No, they won't find us. We're perfectly safe with just enough fuel to get us to my Leroy. Did I miss anything?"

She shook her head.

"Okay, then. We're leaving the waterfall-in-the-canyon part of the tour. Next photo op will be the Atlantic Ocean."

For the time being, she wasn't afraid. She returned his smile and settled back as the helicopter surged forward and followed the path of the canyon's river all the way to the sea.

Their time over the Atlantic was short. Heading north, they flew over numerous islands and luxury resorts dotting the coast before turning west at the mouth of a river and heading over land, into a dense, deep green spread of mountainous wilderness.

They followed the path of the river into the mountains, climbing ever steeper and farther from civilization. Where the river became a lake, they broke away from it and headed north once more.

A beep sounded from the instrument panel. She looked at Diego, who didn't seem concerned. Then again, nothing seemed to faze him except tears and questions or comments doubting his skills and intentions.

"Low fuel warning," he said. "But that's fine because we're here and I've got more fuel in my cabin to get us wherever we go next."

He crested a mountain peak and hovered over another section of river.

"The fun just keeps on coming today," he grouched, looking out his door at the water.

"What do you mean?"

He scratched his chin. "This is my landing pad."

"Where?"

He pointed downward, indicating the water directly below them. "I was only here a month ago. The river's changed course."

The fuel gauge beeped again. "You have to find another clearing."

"Thanks for the tip, but there are no other clearings, okay? It's a rainforest. And even if we did want to search for one, we're out of fuel."

He was right about the fun keeping on coming, as long as if by *fun,* he meant moments of excruciating terror. Knowing that any questions she asked or doubts she showed about his ability would only make him surlier, she clamped her mouth shut and sat as still as possible.

On the third low-fuel warning beep, he nodded. "I've got an idea." He lifted the helicopter and skimmed the canopy of trees, retracing the way they'd come.

He hovered the helicopter over the trees near the lake where they'd made the turn and dropped altitude. After unbuckling his harness and utility belt, he tossed the belt out the window. Ignoring her questioning look, he sped the helicopter backward for the count of a few seconds until they were over the center of the lake below the level of the canopy.

He reached over and unbuckled her harness. She clutched the armrests. "What are you doing?"

"There's a cabin two kilometers due north of here. If I don't make it, you'll find what you need there—food, water, the works. Get the phone out of the belt I dropped on a boulder and call my crew. They'll take care of you." With that, he pulled her headpiece off.

"What are you talking about?"

He pointed across her, out the door. "You have to jump, Vanessa."

Oh, no. Absolutely not.

Clutching the doorframe so hard her fingers ached, she shuffled her feet toward the edge and poked her head out the side to stare at the green water below. They were close enough that a jump would be safe as long as the water was deep. She was a decent swimmer, but the relative height and the idea of actually making that leap left her feeling inextricably lightheaded.

Over the roar of the rotor blades, she shouted, "Are you crazy? How high up are we?"

"Fifteen meters. It's as low as I can get with these trees."

Fifteen meters was fifty feet. A five-story building. Her stomach heaved. To help her cope, she needed an equation to solve. "Fifteen meters means I'll hit the water at a velocity of..."

Determining velocity required her to first calculate the speed of the fall. She saw the two equations in her head and had the answer on the tip of her tongue when Diego beat her to it.

"Seventeen meters per second, I know. Nothing I can do about that."

An ICE agent who could solve physics equations in his head faster than she could? Impressive. Not that it made her any more eager to hit the water at that speed. "Never mind the velocity, there could be barracuda in there, or crocodiles. Leeches, even."

"That's a chance you have to take. There's nowhere else to land. The rainforest is too thick and we're out of fuel. You have to suck it up and jump."

"What about you? What did you mean by 'if you don't make it'?"

"I'm going to jump, too, but I have to wait until you're clear of the chopper. And there's a chance my jump won't go off as planned. We're running out of time."

She knew she needed to trust him not to leave her, but it was hard. She'd never been this far out of control of her life and she couldn't stop the questions, couldn't let go of the fear that he'd abandon her to fend for herself. "How do I know you're not going to dump me here and fly away?"

"I thought we went over this. Did you forget my speech already?"

"No." But promises were as fluid as water, she wanted to add. People made promises all the time that they didn't keep. They left without warning, just slipped through your fingers while you tried to hold on to them.

"Okay, ready? On the count of three. One…two…"

"Wait!" She stuffed her hand in her pocket and pulled out the zip drive. So much for having an ace up her sleeve. "This can't get wet."

"What is that?"

"Data I copied from the bank about suspicious transactions."

"Aka, the reason you're in this mess?"

"Yep."

He took it from her and sealed it into a compartment on his thigh holster.

"You gotta hustle now. We don't have much time left in this bird."

She stood and faced the opening, then twisted to take one last look at Diego. What if he didn't make it? What if this was the last time she saw him? "Diego…"

"Jump into the damn water or I'm going to push you. Right now."

She whipped her head straight. Like everything else that had happened in the past couple hours, with this, she didn't have a choice. She sucked in a breath and flung herself over the edge.

At seventeen meters per second, she dropped through thin air in a free fall that seemed to last forever and hit the water so hard it stung. Then cool water engulfed her. She pulled to the surface, gasping for breath.

The noise of the helicopter still roared above her, loud and steady as she scrambled for shore. Every swish of something brushing her legs reminded her of the predators that could be lurking below the surface, hungry for their next meal.

Finally, she reached the bank and hauled herself onto the exposed roots of a mangrove tree, then to the solid ground beyond it. From there, she watched the helicopter rise to the height of the canopy, Diego's form growing smaller in the distance. Removing the headpiece, he stood and curved one booted foot over the open pilot door. Despite his impossible height, his gaze found hers. His face was a mark of calm concentration.

Rising from the ground, she locked eyes with him, so nervous that the pounding of her heart made her ribs hurt. He was so high up, she didn't see how he'd survive the force of impact of hitting the water. She rocked onto the balls of her feet and bent her knees, ready to spring into the water and help him if need be.

The helicopter swerved down and left, toward the tree canopy lining the bank, as his arms swung up above his head. In seemingly slow motion, he pushed off the doorway of the plummeting aircraft and arched into a perfect dive.

Coherent thought evaporated. Sound and time ceased to exist. She was vaguely aware of the helicopter chewing up trees as it crashed into the jungle on the far bank, but her focus remained wholly captivated by Diego.

He was a wonderment to behold. Stunning, beautiful. Like an arrow of pure power and control slicing through the air.

A soft sound of admiration and relief escaped her throat when he slid past the surface of the water into its depths. She'd never seen his equal in all her days. Bracing herself against the trunk of a mangrove, she drew a ragged gulp of air, counting the seconds until he emerged.

He came up swimming toward her, his arms stroking and his broad shoulders undulating with machine-like precision until he reached the bank.

An explosion sounded behind him and he twisted. Vanessa's attention shifted along with his in time to watch a belch of flame and smoke erupt from the pocket of trees the helicopter had crashed into. Once it subsided, Diego resumed his swim to shore. Wrapping those large hands around mangrove roots, he hoisted his body out of the water, a move that transformed Vanessa's breathless admiration into serious, skin-tingling lust.

Hot damn, Diego Santero looked fine soaking wet. Everything about him radiated potent masculinity, from

the slick, dark hair that drew emphasis to the angles of
his cheeks and jaw, to the water beading off his forearms and the soaked black shirt and cargo pants that
clung to every curve of muscle and flesh below.

Delicious, wicked awareness sped through her system, rendering her weak-legged and warm all over.

"What is it? Are you hurt?" he asked, stepping
nearer.

Gripping the tree for support as he touched her arm,
she dragged her gaze from his body to his face. And all
she could think to say was, "You make velocity look
good."

Chapter 6

A tight, white T-shirt—that was the best Alicia could come up with for Vanessa's change of clothes? A body-hugging shirt and bra that turned translucent when wet. Nice going, Phoenix. Way to boost his objectivity during the mission. Nothing helped him make life-or-death decisions better than the outline of a beautiful woman's nipples staring him in the face.

Next time, the asset was getting a bright orange sweatshirt and a granny bra. Then again, the next asset he protected wouldn't be Vanessa Crosby, so maybe he stood a chance of maintaining his dignity. Because he sure wasn't dignified now, what with all his blood pooling in inconvenient places.

"You're not hurt?" he asked again, bending over her. Her comment on velocity hadn't made much sense, and she sagged against the nearest tree like it was the only thing keeping her upright.

She ran her fingertips over his arm, a light touch that probably meant nothing to her but got him wondering how big of an ethical violation it was that he was picturing his asset in her birthday suit.

Then she gasped. He edged back to figure out why. She was staring at water-diluted blood running down her arm. His blood.

"You're bleeding. Oh, my God. I'm so sorry, I... Are you okay?"

"Never better." He meant to say it sarcastically but wasn't sure he achieved that effect. The wound hurt like crazy—glass usually did—but he hadn't given it a whole lot of thought. Funny how an attempted kidnapping, a firefight, an out-of-fuel helicopter and a woman in a wet T-shirt worked to take his mind off the pain.

"I've got first aid at the cabin. If you're not hurt, then let's start walking."

At least he was the one leading the way to his cabin. That gave him a little time to get over the desire to peel her wet clothes off and ask her to calculate another velocity equation, this time out loud so he could hear the numbers falling from those sweet lips while he helped himself to the softness of her body.

You're such a freak, Santero. Who ever heard of a math fetish?

"I'm sorry you had to crash your helicopter," she said.

He kept his eyes on the jungle, clearing a path through the dense underbrush with his knife as he went, searching for the boulder he'd tossed his gear belt onto. The relentless manual labor helped him resist the urge to turn and look at her every few steps. "Yeah, that kind of sucked."

The helicopter had been one of his few possessions

that didn't fit in a duffel bag. He had an ancient jeep garaged in Germany and a second chopper stashed in Kenya, but it was a piece of junk compared to the one he'd just sent into the trees. "The worst part of losing the chopper is that we're going to have to trek out of this place on foot."

"How long will that take?"

"Depends on what direction we head. At least two days, maybe three. Been a while since I've hiked it."

The gear belt was an easy find on top of the long, flat boulder he'd aimed it at from the chopper. After a quick inspection to make sure the grenades and ammo hadn't gotten damaged during the fall, he strapped it around his waist.

He looked up to find Vanessa watching him and made a halfhearted effort to keep his eyes on her face.

"I bet you feel better now that you've been reunited with your Batman belt."

"Definitely." He lifted his knife out of its sheath on his thigh and gestured north. "Let's keep walking. It looks like the clouds are about to open up and I'd like to make it to the cabin before it gets too dark."

And get you out of those clothes into something dry. But then he visualized her peeling her pants off. In his mind's eye, her panties were as see-through as the bra—and, just like that, he had to put his back to her so he wouldn't embarrass himself with the arousal that he apparently had no control over.

They plunged into the shadows of the forest as the first drops of rain fell.

He was feeling the glass and shrapnel with every step and every slash of his knife through the underbrush and decided that concentrating on the pain was a better use of his energy than lusting after an asset.

The pain cleared his head real good, and in no time flat he could think straight again.

The denseness of the canopy kept the fading daylight out, as well as the larger drops of rain. Diego had a small flashlight on his belt, but it wasn't going to be all that effective for jungle hiking. The way he figured it, they had about a half hour until the forest was as black as midnight.

"While we hike, I want to hear more about the algorithm you wrote and what it has to do with that zip drive you gave me to hold."

"The algorithm was something I wrote in my spare time at work. I didn't tell anyone I was attempting it because my boss is a jerk and I didn't want him finding out I was doing something that wasn't in my job description—especially if the algorithm failed."

He hacked at a particularly thick branch and hissed through his teeth at the sting of pain in his neck. "How is tracking bulk cash not in your job description? I thought you were a criminal activity analyst."

"Yes, but only for possible security breaches in offshore accounts. The million- and billion-dollar corporate clients of the bank. Wire transfers and small cash deposits don't qualify."

"So why'd you do it?"

"To see if I could. I overheard two of my coworkers talking about how it was impossible to track bulk cash because criminals know all the tricks to flying under the radar. And I like a good challenge."

She said it like she'd taken up oil painting, not chosen to single-handedly take on the crime world's billion-dollar bulk cash smuggling network as a hobby. And he'd thought her jab to the kidnapper's gut had been ballsy. "So you made the radar bigger in scope, so to speak?"

"No. I decided the radar the bank used wasn't working, so I built a new one."

The self-assuredness in her tone had him glancing back to see the expression that accompanied it. She grinned at him, proud, those Princeton smarts of hers radiating from her eyes and the set of her shoulders. Helicopters and high dives might be out of her comfort zone, but looking at her now, it was easy to see how she'd rocketed to the top of her field. A person couldn't fake confidence like that.

"What I can't figure out is why the men waiting at your apartment wanted to kidnap you. From what I can tell, it would've made more sense for them to kill you, but they clearly wanted you alive. Why do you think that is?"

"I hadn't considered that, but I guess you're right. They must've known that there's only one copy of the algorithm program. It's stored in an encrypted internet storage cloud and I'm the only one who can access it. Whoever those men were, they can't destroy it without my codes."

She hadn't complained about the exertion of thrashing through the underbrush at an uphill angle, but she was starting to sound winded, so he slowed his pace. "According to the file ICE gave me, you emailed your boss about the algorithm yesterday. What made you decide to tell him about it?"

"I ran a preliminary test and got a hit. I thought the bank deserved to know if someone was using it for criminal activity."

Good plan, if also a smidge naive about the way the criminal world worked. Then again, part of the reason he did what he did was so innocent people like her didn't have to live in constant awareness of the evils of the world. "And he told you to hand it over. Why didn't you?"

"Call it instinct, but something about the situation didn't feel right. I put him off, telling him I needed to clean up the program and make it user-friendly. I was going to run a small-scale test this weekend at my apartment, which is why I brought the zip drive full of account information home."

"That's a bold move. You could've been arrested for stealing customer information if you were caught." He high-stepped over a felled tree, then offered her a hand over.

"I know, but I have a thing about puzzles going unsolved. I was going to destroy the zip drive after I—"

Despite the hold he had on her hand, she still managed to snag her back foot on the log and trip, falling forward with her arm out to brace herself. No big deal because he caught her right away, but he wished he hadn't discovered that he liked the way her palm felt splayed on his stomach while she worked to right herself.

"Thanks." She gave him a sheepish smile and wiped her hands on her pants. Like they weren't as soaked through as the rest of her.

Before his overeager libido embarrassed him, he started hiking again.

"Did ICE know I was in danger today because they were spying on me?" she asked.

"Not only you, but the whole bank. The Panama office has been monitoring RioBank communications for a while. I don't have the whole scoop because my team was only brought in this morning and the feds aren't big on sharing their intel.

"What I can tell you is that the men believed to be

after your algorithm are three brothers, the Chiaras, who are black-market merchants. ICE got an insider tip that the Chiara brothers have a RioBank employee on their payroll and are using the bank to launder and store their money. When ICE intercepted your email this morning, they called my crew in. They think the suspicious number pattern you isolated is related to the Chiaras' criminal activity."

"So ICE wants my algorithm?"

"They wanted more from you than that. Word came in from a local source that this Monday night the Chiaras are brokering the sale of a submarine between the Russians and some bad-news Colombians. ICE wanted you to act as a bank insider and pinpoint the Chiaras' account in order to dissolve it and prevent the submarine sale. That's all off the table now that the mission's aborted, obviously."

She snagged his arm, stopping him. "So that's it? You're not going to try to convince me to help ICE catch the Chiaras or the RioBank insider? They don't want me to try to stop the submarine sale anymore?"

He lowered his knife and faced her. He wasn't going to tell her this, but it no longer mattered to him what ICE wanted from her. The mission ICE gave him was to protect Vanessa Crosby—nothing more, nothing less. The safe house ambush brought it home to him that Dreyer was rushing into a situation without a sound plan or an accurate understanding of the Chiaras' power and volatility.

He'd never expose an asset to that kind of danger. "This algorithm you created brought you to the attention of a lot of bad people. All that matters now is getting you as far from the threat as possible."

"Like where?"

"Probably somewhere in the States, in WitSec. I'm sure Uncle Sam will still want that program you made along with your testimony against whoever the Rio-Bank rat turns out to be."

Huffing, she wiped dirt and rainwater from her forehead with the back of her hand. "So they'll take what I created with a 'Sorry about your life'?"

She looked as irritated with the truth as he felt. He hated that it had turned out like that, too. Chewed up and spit out by a bunch of pale, pencil-pushing suits and criminal degenerates. "At least you still have a life. That's the silver lining, right?"

"Who's to say I would've told the kidnappers the access codes so they could destroy the program? That would've been my only leverage against them killing me."

"Leverage or not, it's almost eight o'clock. I'm thinking if my crew wasn't brought in when we were, they would've had you in their custody for nearly three hours. If you were still alive, they wouldn't be making it easy for you."

Her face blanched and she got real quiet, probably imagining the torture they would've put her through. Diego was visualizing it right alongside her and it made him sick. Whatever divine intervention sent him to her service today, he was grateful. The bitter truth that he'd railed against the assignment, that he'd considered quitting rather than debasing his worth by acting as a chauffeur, struck him like a punch straight to his heart. Vanessa would be dead—or worse.

This was why he didn't take days off—times like this when it hit him that the alternative to busting his butt on the job was that innocent people suffered. Vanessa, and civilians like her, was why he trained so damn hard.

He gestured north with his knife. "Let's keep walking. It's getting dark."

The jungle had opened up enough that he didn't need his knife anymore and they could hike side by side.

"Do you think the Chiara brothers were behind the attack on me at my apartment and the safe house?" she asked.

"Probably. What bothers me more is how they figured out where we were headed. Safe houses are supposed to be top secret. The only way it makes sense in my mind is if someone in ICE is a double agent, which increases the danger to you exponentially."

"What are we going to do?"

"Not sure yet. That's the beauty of a Leroy," he said. "Nobody knows where we are, so you're safe as long as we're here. I've got a way to communicate with my crew without revealing our location, and once we get to my cabin and regroup, I'll get on the line. Until we get an answer from ICE that makes sense, we can choose to either stay where we are or meet up with my crew and stay off the grid as a group. Either way we play it, we hold the power."

"Did you build the cabin yourself?"

"Yeah, but it's not a cabin like you're picturing. I know I call it that, but it's more like a glorified shanty. Don't get your hopes up that I'm taking you to my tricked-out secret lair or something. No sense building some sprawling mansion that's easy to spot from the air."

Despite the worry lines that seemed permanently etched on her face, she smiled. "In other words, no feather pillows?"

Thank God for that, because he could think of a hundred different ways he and Vanessa could make use of a feather pillow, and not one of them included sleeping. "Try no indoor plumbing. But the room's safe and waterproof, so at least we can regroup out of the rain."

"Do you own the land around the cabin? I thought most of the jungle in Panama is wilderness preserve."

"I don't own a single square foot of land in the entire world. Right now we're walking through Nobu territory."

She grabbed a fistful of his shirt and tugged, grinding them to a halt. "Seriously? I thought they shot trespassers. That's what the news stations are always saying."

"Yeah, they're pretty touchy about outsiders on their land, but I worked out a deal with them for access in exchange for the occasional crate full of firepower and ammo."

"So, what you're saying is that when they shoot at people, it's with guns you supply them? You're an arms dealer?"

"Sort of, I guess. But they're a peaceful people as long as the world leaves them alone. Everyone deserves the right to protect their land and families with the same caliber of technology their enemy would employ. Spears and knives don't cut it against poachers and corrupt government militaries."

"Do they know we're here right now? I mean, could they be watching us?" She glanced around, like she actually expected to see people in the trees staring at them from the encroaching darkness.

"I'm sure they heard the helicopter explode, and they probably went to investigate, but I'd like to think they have better things to do than watch us hike. I've been coming up here off and on for nearly a decade, so they know I'm not going to bother them."

She still didn't look totally convinced that there weren't a dozen tribesmen in the shadows with guns trained on them, especially when she rubbed her forearms and did one of her signature full-body shivers that tightened her muscles and skin everywhere.

Eyes on her face, horn dog.

Blood was pumping fast to certain spots on his body again, so he whirled around and busied himself slicing away at the vines on the edge of the trail. "Look, here's what you're going to need to get through your head— I know what I'm doing. I chose my Leroy location deliberately. And I keep the Nobu flush with weapons because it suits my purpose. Think about it. If anyone comes up the mountain looking to bother us, the tribesmen will stop them.

"That extra level of security is priceless, and today it might mean the difference between life or death, especially since the Panama army followed us halfway here in their chopper, so they have a general idea of the direction we were headed. But they can't get to us up here because it'd be a political nightmare for them to go charging through a protected indigenous people's territory."

"Okay, I'm sorry I questioned you."

He was sorry she kept questioning him, too, but he waved off her apology and kept walking. They were close to the cabin, and he wanted to take a good look at it while there was still a faint glow of daylight.

They reached the bottom of the ridge that marked the eastern edge of the cabin's clearing. He scaled the cliff of crumbly soil and reached a hand to her, hoisting her up without even trying to avoid looking down her shirt. A man could only resist so much temptation.

Atop the ridge, she shook the loosest pieces of mud

from her clothes and set her hands on her hips as she took stock of the cabin made from synthetic planks nestled beneath a rock overhang, set two feet off the ground to keep the rot, bugs and water out.

"Wait here while I check it over, make sure nobody or nothing's waiting to surprise us."

With that, he drew his gun and stalked toward the cabin, oddly anxious about her opinion of the place he'd built from the ground up nine years earlier, which was stupid. Sure, a woman like her deserved a four-star hotel room to recharge in after a long day of nearly getting killed over and over, but after the impressive way she'd sucked it up on the hike, he felt confident that she wouldn't surprise him by turning into a spoiled princess all of a sudden.

After all, they'd trekked uphill through thick underbrush in the rain, her clothes drenched and covered in mud, for nearly an hour, and she hadn't voiced a single complaint. Not even a groan of discomfort or sigh of fatigue. Hands down, she was the most badass civilian he'd ever met. Now that he thought about it, Diego didn't know many soldiers who could pull off a day like she'd had with half as much composure.

If he were to rank all the things he liked about her, her suck-it-up determination would edge out everything else, even the fact that she'd created a revolutionary anti-crime algorithm simply because she liked a challenge. Even the way her body curved and jiggled inside that wet, white T-shirt.

Well, that was a close second, but still, he stood by his ranking.

He approached the door of the cabin cautiously, his Sig ready for action. The possibility that any hostiles—from Chiara operatives or poachers, to rogue tribesmen—had breached his cabin was incredibly remote, but a false sense of confidence had felled better men than Diego and he refused to take any kind of chance with Vanessa's security.

Windowless, and with its rear wall flat against the rock face behind it, the door was the cabin's only access point as long as no one bulldozed through the wall or floor. He checked that first, then set his ear to the door, listening, before opening the combination lock chained to the bolt that served as a doorknob.

The darkness inside smelled musty, as usual. It'd been a month since his last visit. Whenever his schedule lightened up, he stole away here. It was one of the few places in the world he could scrounge a decent night's sleep anymore. Funny how living within striking distance of the scum of the earth messed with a man's ability to catch some z's.

Sleep, though, was nothing more than a pipe dream for the next few days. No way he'd leave an asset vulnerable by falling asleep. When they caught up with his crew, he'd succumb, but not a minute sooner. Good thing he was nowhere near drowsy.

Reaching his left hand onto his belt, he withdrew his flashlight and had a look around. The feather he'd set on the floor pointed south exactly as he'd left it and the synthetic floorboards were coated with a layer of undisturbed dust.

"We're clear. Come on in."

Without waiting for her, he lowered mosquito netting over the open door and crossed the ten-by-twelve space to flip on the electric lantern hanging on the far wall. The light made the space glow golden.

He kept it simple here: a cot, supplies loaded in plastic bins and two wooden crates he used as a chair and table. And tucked in a secret compartment between the wall and the rock behind it, an arsenal extensive enough to outfit a small country and enough rations to last a month.

He heard Vanessa enter as he shuffled plastic bins, digging for his stash of spare clothes, and that same ridiculous anxiety fluttered in his gut again. He'd never let another person into this place, much less a woman who set all his bells ringing like Vanessa did.

"This is the best-looking cabin I've ever seen." Her voice radiated relief, without the slightest hint of sarcasm. "You know what I like most about it?"

The joyful lilt in her voice snuffed his nervousness and tugged a smile onto his lips as he hauled the clothes bin onto the cot. "What?"

"That it's here and not another kilometer from here." She tapped her chin in mock consideration and rolled her eyes to the ceiling. "And the waterproof roof's pretty awesome, too."

"I built this roof myself. The rest of it, too." He registered the swagger in his admission and gave himself a hearty mental smack.

Did you seriously go there, man? As if the ability to erect a jungle shanty could possibly stir the interest of a woman with a PhD in applied mathematics from Princeton. Like construction skills were what she looked for in a man.

He swallowed hard, shocked by the direction of his thoughts. How had he allowed his lust to turn into fantasies of something more with her, when he knew good and well that was an impossibility?

Biting her lower lip against a smile that said she found his macho bragging amusing, she cocked an eyebrow at him. "Your Batman belt holds a hammer and nails? That is impressive. Now all we need to do is work on the belt's tissue-carrying capacity. You know, for all the ladies you steal away with to your bachelor pad in the jungle."

And there was his answer—because Vanessa Crosby was one of a kind. The smartest, toughest, prettiest woman he'd ever come across. With a sense of humor she held on to despite the trip she'd taken that day to hell and back.

He popped the lid on the bin. "It's time for you to get out of those wet clothes." Before he stroked out from the sight.

Her body tensed, not exactly a shiver, but a tightening everywhere, and he wondered if he'd gone and scared her again. He froze, replaying his words in an effort to figure out what he'd said wrong, but couldn't come up with anything, and so decided to proceed like he hadn't noticed. "None of these clothes are going to fit you worth a damn, but they'll do until yours dry out. Pick whatever you want and lay your wet clothes out on the cot. I'll string up a clothesline later."

"What about first aid for your neck? It stopped bleeding, but it needs to be cleaned."

"We'll do that next. You get dry first."

No sooner were the words out of his mouth than his inner horn dog got to wondering whether she'd leave her wet bra on or take it off to dry. With a low growl he prayed she didn't hear, he willed his feet into action and hustled through the door as fast as his legs could take him.

Chapter 7

From its place on the wooden crate next to the first aid kit, the lantern shone brightly against Diego's back, adding a glossy shine to his short, dark hair and glinting off the bits of glass and shrapnel peppered in his skin and scalp.

He sat on a second crate, hunching with his elbows propped on his knees, and didn't seem at all nervous about what was going to happen.

Unlike Vanessa.

She stood behind him, clad in a loose black T-shirt and the boxer shorts she'd settled on because of the heat and humidity, working to calm her nerves and steady her shaky grip on the tweezers. Having never been around blood much, she hadn't developed the stomach for it. Heck, she got squeamish when Jordan used a needle to pop a zit.

She picked gently at one of the larger pieces of glass right under his hairline, but it didn't budge.

"Don't be afraid to dig. You can't hurt me."

She paused, marveling at the statement. What would it be like to lose the capacity to be hurt—or at least the capacity to be afraid of it? Thousands of times over the course of her life, her decisions had been governed by fear of being hurt. How would her life story be different if she could've taken fear out of the equation?

She wouldn't be in Panama, that was for sure. And, though it wounded her pride to admit it, she might've been more successful in love, maybe married by now.

Sinking her fingers into his hair, she tipped his face down to improve access to the back of his scalp. She couldn't hurt him, he'd said. Why, then, did the idea of digging into his skin frighten her?

What a wimp.

After a fortifying breath, she chose a wound to begin with. And while her mind screamed in protest, she dug the first bit of glass from his neck.

Working steadily, methodically, she picked debris from the wounds and dropped each in the tin cup he'd placed on the crate. His neck and shoulders were tight with corded muscles, perhaps the only indication he felt any discomfort at all.

His earlobe caught her attention. Even on this iron-willed, ice-blooded man who risked his life for strangers, his earlobe was fine-honed, perfectly shaped. She wanted to skim it with her finger—or better yet, her tongue, to taste the sweetness in the delicate curl of skin, the only place of softness on his body she'd found besides his lips.

Those she'd noticed when he'd saved her from hitting the ground when she'd tripped over the log. Her body heated at the memory, not only of his lips as his breath fanned over her neck, but his body all around her. His strong hands on her, his hard, flat stomach under her palm.

If she thought too deeply about what had happened to her—and what else could've happened had Diego not been there—she'd be paralyzed with fright. To cope, she'd hang on to whatever positives she could, and Diego's body and testosterone-fueled confidence topped her list.

She picked the final shard of glass from his neck, then dropped her gaze to his shirt. Holes speckled the cotton from his shoulder blades to midback. More glass and shrapnel.

"You have to take off your shirt so I can clean the wounds on your back." Her voice was breathy. God, she hoped he had no idea how being this close to him was making her feel, the heat that had blazed to life inside her at the idea of seeing more of his bare skin.

He didn't make a move but stared at the ground beyond his feet, his hands clasped in a tight fist.

"Your shirt, Diego."

Without a word, he sat straighter. Grabbing fistfuls of material, he tugged his shirt over his head and tossed it next to the first aid kit.

His back was a darkly tanned map of muscle and scars. Vanessa set the tip of her finger inside a puckered patch of skin near his shoulder. "Were you shot?"

"Fourteen years ago. I took a bullet for Ryan, my second-in-command, while we were in Afghanistan."

Farther down, nearer to his spine, was a long, thin scar. "What's this from?"

"Knife fight with a pair of tribal leaders in Tunisia. I won, by the way."

"All that and a broken nose, hmm? That's one dangerous lifestyle you live."

He glanced over his shoulder, a sly grin on his lips. "Aw, now you're jumping to conclusions. How do you know I wasn't born with this ugly nose?"

"Call it instinct."

"I've broken it twice. First time was during training as a SEAL. Too much hooyah, the instructor said. I dove so fast into the pool I used my face as a brake when I hit the bottom."

"And the second time?"

"The second time, I got in a fight with my younger brother."

"That must've been a bad fight," she said. "Did you win that one, too?"

"No. I could've, but that would've upset our mom more. Plus, the family consensus was that I had it coming."

Her mood lightened, picturing a family of tough guys like Diego, with a no-nonsense mama at the middle of it all. "Did you?"

"From their perspective? Pretty much."

"Care to elaborate?"

"Nope."

She hadn't thought he would, but it didn't hurt to ask. She looked lower. Near his tailbone were four raised, crisscrossing scars like slashes that hadn't healed correctly, the skin roped and gnarled. She skimmed her fingertips over them. "What about these?"

"Those you don't need to know about."

"Why?"

"Because you're going to have enough nightmares once this ordeal is over without me adding to them any more than I already have."

That wiped the smile from her lips. "You've been through some bad stuff."

He sniffed. "And I've come out fighting strong, so no harm done, all right? Why don't you get busy on the last of that debris? I'm starting to feel modest without my shirt on."

She got the message loud and clear and pulled over a crate to use as a chair so the cluster of shrapnel in his midback would be at eye level. She allowed her legs to fall open so she could scoot as close as possible, and in the process accidentally pressed her knee into his outer thigh.

His gaze slid from the wall to where her bare knee touched him, a silent acknowledgment of her nearness that sucked the air from the room. Vanessa's breath froze in her lungs as they both stared at the point of their connection.

When she spread her legs wider to sever the contact, his arm shifted, and for a split second she thought he might drag her knee back up against him. Crazy, given everything that had happened to her, but she wanted him to touch her. She wanted his strong, capable hands on her body and those soft lips locked with hers. She wanted to be held tight and kissed until she could for-get—if only for a few precious minutes—that her life as she knew it had evaporated in a cloud of smoke and flame and violence.

Maybe that wasn't the correct response to having her life threatened, but so what? Fantasizing about the gorgeous, half-naked warrior assigned to protect her was a far better coping plan than cowering in a corner crying or shaking her fist at God.

Clearing his throat, he jerked his gaze back to the

wall. "I know it must've been in your file, but I can't remember reading about where you grew up."

She carefully worked the tweezers around a bit of metal. "I was born and raised in Nebraska."

"Nebraska? As in, *Children of the Corn?* That movie scared the crap out of me when I was a kid."

She dropped the extracted metal in the bowl and started on the next one. "Me, too. I was only three when the first movie was released, but when the second movie came out, the theater near my house played a midnight double feature. My best friend, Jordan, and I stayed for the whole thing. We were twelve."

"Hold on." He twisted to give her a skeptical look. "Your parents let you go to a midnight double feature of horror movies when you were that young? Unsupervised? Wish my parents had been that lax."

"My dad didn't exactly know about it. My mom died when I was two, so growing up, it was just me and my dad. He coached defense for UNL football—well, until he got a better offer from UCLA—so he was too busy to pay much attention to what I was doing. I snuck out all the time." She dropped another metal shard into the cup. "Didn't you ever do that?"

"I wish. I grew up in a typical, huge Puerto Rican family. Five kids. We couldn't get away with nothin'. We were lucky to get a minute of privacy in the bathroom. Forget about sneaking out of the house."

She'd done all right picturing him surrounded by family as an adult, but she couldn't imagine such a larger-than-life person as Diego being a child. She tried to visualize him sitting in a classroom or learning how to ride a bike but couldn't reconcile the image with the man before her.

She bent lower and studied his wounds. "I think I

got all the pieces back here. Do you want me to bandage them?"

"Nah. Use that rag on the bin to catch the drips while you flush them with water, then we'll let them air-dry. These kinds of explosion rashes are better off breathing."

Explosion rashes? As in, this sort of thing happened often enough in his world to be given a nickname? Unreal.

After cracking the lid on the new bottle from his stock in the corner, she dribbled water over his neck and back. The towel didn't quite soak up all of it, and drops raced down his back, trailing the curve of his spine. She loved that curve, framed on either side by ripple after ripple of muscle, and she especially loved the way it dipped in at his waist before flaring into his perfect, rounded backside.

She became well-acquainted with that backside while he'd thrashed a path for them through the jungle. Without it in front of her to focus her energy on instead of her screaming muscles and burning lungs, she would've never had the strength to make it.

And right now, she was straddling his backside with spread legs, her thighs only scant inches away. The hot, needy center of her open and empty. She had to touch him.

She set the tip of her finger on his spine and traced the path of warm, wet skin to the gray elastic band of the briefs peeking out from his low-slung cargo pants. He sat up straighter, his muscles tensing, and maybe she should've apologized, but she wasn't the least bit sorry.

"Are we done?" he asked, his voice gruff.

She fisted her hand and pressed it into her side. *No,*

that wasn't nearly enough. "Back here, yes. You have a few more spots on the front of your neck."

Tweezers in hand, she scooted the bin away and rose, careful not to brush against him as he rotated on the bin to cast the front of his torso into the light of the lantern. It was all she could do not to gape at the sight of his chest and abs. She'd thought his back was ripped, but it had nothing on his front. He was so carved of steel that it made it completely impossible to imagine him as a kid.

A sprawling black-and-red tattoo covered his left pectoral. The New York City Fire Department cross, a firefighter hat and a date—9-11-01.

Residual drops of water sprinkled over his chest and tattoo. She watched the trickle of a solitary drop curve around his hardened nipple, over his abs and lower, collecting in the dusting of hair surrounding his belly button. She pursed her lips against the ragged exhale working its way up from her lungs and forced her gaze to his tattoo.

His hands were clasped loosely between his spread, sprawling legs and when he figured out what had caught her attention, he tapped his thumbs together. "You want to ask about my tattoo, don't you?"

"Crossed my mind."

His gaze lowered to his hands. "My older brother was FDNY, died in the towers." His tone was flat, emotionless. Exactly the opposite of the deep, scarring pain that would drive a person to ink a memorial to a loved one directly over his heart.

She stared a long time and he let her without moving or saying any more. The urge to cover the image with her palm, cover his heart with her hand and connect with this vulnerable part of him, glowed inside her. But given the way he tensed every time she touched him, she thought better of it.

"What was his name?"

"I can't tell you that."

She gave her head a small shake, blinking in surprise. "Why not?"

"The less you know about me, the safer we both are."

"But you already told me your name."

His eyes, as intense and dark as ever, rolled up to meet hers. "You thought Diego Santero was my given name?"

In her stomach, she felt a yank. The rug being pulled out from under her. All the intimacy she thought they shared, the connection they'd forged in the eye of danger, it meant nothing to him. He was on the job and she was the asset. Diego Santero wasn't even his name.

"Pardon me for being gullible. I'm not used to all this black ops underworld stuff." Swallowing the bitterness in her mouth, she added quietly, "Was anything you told me real?"

Mashing his lips together in a tight scowl, he rubbed his hands over his quads. When he looked at her again, his gaze had morphed to one of challenge. "Look, here it is. I'm from a huge Puerto Rican family in New Jersey. My older brother died in the 9/11 attack, so when the Department of Homeland Security came sniffing around my SEAL team recruiting for a black ops unit to monitor U.S. security in the global theater, I was the first man in line to sign up. When I did, I changed my name to Diego Santero to protect my family.

"And, since you asked earlier, I'll tell you—when I went home and told my family about my choice, my younger brother broke my nose. He was scared because we lost one brother already and none of them understood that this was what I had to do. That's a lot of personal information, okay? A hell of a lot more than most people know about me, in fact. If that's not good enough for you, then forget about it."

His Jersey accent had gotten more pronounced with every word, belying the rush of feeling behind his admission. He was telling her the truth—as much truth as he was at liberty to share. The affection that had blossomed in the car at his reaction to her tears came back in full force.

So what if his name wasn't Diego? She was beginning to learn who he really was. He was someone whose voice glowed with love when he talked about his family and who tattooed a memorial to his brother over his heart. The person who'd killed to protect her and couldn't stand the idea of her crying.

She ran her fingers along his chin, then angled his face toward hers. The flickering, shadowy light of the lamp and flashlight highlighted the set of his jaw and turned his eyes to onyx. "That's good enough for me. Thank you for saving my life."

Bringing his right hand across his body, he tentatively cupped the side of her knee. "No need to thank me." His voice was little more than a low rattle. "It's my job."

There he went again, pushing away from intimate conversation, though his hand told a different story.

Right then and there, she made her choice. He'd sacrificed his safety and his identity to protect the country. The least she could do was help in her own small way, using her algorithm to put away criminals that threatened her homeland, even though it risked her life anew.

"I'm going to help you, help ICE, any way I can to stop the bulk cash scam and catch the Chiara brothers."

His hold on her leg stiffened. "No. Not a good idea. Something big and bad is going down with this operation. What you need to do is disappear. If you're not interested in WitSec, then I'll help you start over somewhere in the world with a new identity. I've got connections. You never have to put yourself in danger again, you hear me?"

She outlined the FDNY symbol with her finger. His already taut nipple beaded so tightly, the color leached from it. "I think this is all happening for a reason— finding the number patterns in the accounts, the kidnapping attempt, being here with you." She spread her hand flat on his skin. "I've never done anything that mattered before. I want to do what I can to stop the submarine sale. Let me help you."

His other hand found her forearm. His thumb stroked her. "I'm not letting you anywhere near the bank again, but if you think you can use that zip drive of customer data to pinpoint the account, we can make that happen at a remote location."

"I copied enough files onto the disk that if there's a lead to be found in the data, I'll be able to parse it out."

"Okay, but remember that my offer stands. You change your mind at any time or decide this isn't what you want for yourself, that the risks are too much, say the word. I'll get you out of Panama safely. I know how to make people disappear. That's my promise to you, understand?"

She leaned into the hand on her leg, coaxing him to strengthen his grip. When he did, wrapping his fingers around the sensitive hollow behind her knee, a charge of reckless desire lighted through her system.

It was that recklessness that goaded her to slide the hand on his jaw toward his ear, losing her fingertips in his thick hair. He closed his eyes but didn't stop her or tense at her touch like he had before. His hand moved higher, leaving her knee for the tender flesh of her thigh.

Just like that, she knew unequivocally that if they kissed, if their clothes came off, they'd burn the jungle down with the heat of it.

She lowered her head to his.

Chapter 8

With her forehead resting on Diego's and their mouths inches away from contact, she rubbed a fingertip over his lower lip.

"Thank you," she whispered.

His eyes still firmly closed, his hand moved from her arm to curve around her waist, pulling her closer until her legs straddled his thigh. "Like I said, it's my job."

Sure it is, tough guy.

Affection bloomed inside her with such force that her heart ached from it. She stroked his cheek. When he still wouldn't open his eyes, she asked, "What are you thinking?"

Stupid question, because she knew he'd never tell her, as guarded as he was.

After drawing a slow breath that filled his lungs, his eyelids cracked open. The look he leveled on her was so potent with hunger and need it made her toes curl. "You don't want to know."

"Maybe I do."

Their eyes locked, their hands froze on each other's bodies. A bead of perspiration slithered between her breasts, a cruel tickle that made her imagine Diego's mouth on her there.

She was pushing him too hard, coming on too strong. She knew she was. It was written all over his strained features, in his tight eyes and stiff hold on her. That was her self-defeating mode of operation when it came to men she was attracted to. Over the years, she and Jordan had analyzed and debated that truth ad nauseam, but knowing her problem and changing her behavior were two entirely different beasts.

She couldn't remember ever wanting a man as potently as she wanted Diego. But she'd learned the hard way that the more desperately she clutched at people, the faster they left. This time, though, there was more than her pride and her heart at stake. Her very life was in Diego's hands. It was a sobering realization.

Despite the wild temptation to straddle his lap and devour his lips, she eased her hand from his face and straightened. She adjusted her grip on the tweezers and shifted her gaze to his neck wounds.

Taking the hint, he dropped his hands, clasping them between his legs once more. His gaze returned to the wall. "Let's get this over with so I can radio my crew."

After getting Vanessa comfortable with a self-heating MRE of chicken with pasta and changing into a set of dry clothes, Diego opened a new untraceable satellite cell phone and called in to the voice mail line he and his crew used as a base of connection when they were separated. ICE wasn't aware of its existence, as Diego paid for it out-of-pocket, along with a second voice mail line he and his family used to exchange messages.

The family line he checked every Sunday if his work allowed. Invariably, there was a message from his mother, rattling on about the things the grandkids—his nieces and nephews—had done that week, the tinkering projects his dad was busy with around the house and how her garden was growing. He always left her a message in reply, telling her he loved her and that he was safe. Never where he was, never what he was up to. It was hard enough for her to know that every day of every year her oldest living son risked his life without him rubbing it in her face with unnecessary details.

Two messages had been left on the crew's voice mail line. Ryan and Rory. Both had reached their Leroys safely, and both left contact numbers. Like Diego, they probably kept untraceable, disposable cell phones on hand for situations like this. He scribbled their numbers with a pen onto his hand, then pressed buttons until he'd cued the voice mail up to record his message. He read the phone number off the cell phone's packaging and requested that Alicia and John phone him immediately upon hearing his message.

The first call he made was to Ryan.

"You safe?" Diego asked.

"Yeah, I'm good. Leroy was the right call. Panama's army descended on the safe house like a swarm. Nothing we could do to help without getting in the way, so we bailed. I connected with Dreyer tonight. No lives lost on our side, but the bad news is that no one knows who leaked the operation."

A glance in Vanessa's direction told him she was listening to every word he said, though trying hard not to show it. Her eyes shifted fast between the plastic rations bowl on her knees and Diego, and she actually tipped her ear toward him, her brow furrowed in concentration.

His lips twitched into a smile. Real subtle, Vanessa.

Thank God she'd never been pushed to act as an insider at RioBank. If some big shot from the bank was on the Chiara brothers' payroll, she would've been fingered as a spy immediately. And Diego wouldn't have been around to make sure no one laid a finger on her.

"Shouldn't be that tough to figure out," he said to Ryan. "Only so many people knew what was happening today."

"You've been around Montgomery and Dreyer more than the rest of us. You think either one of them is the rat?"

"I've been playing it over in my head all night, and I don't think so." He'd bet if he typed "straitlaced federal stiff" into an internet search engine, Dreyer's headshot would pop up. A former marine turned lifetime bureaucrat, the man might be humorless to the point that Diego often wondered if he plugged into an electrical outlet at night to recharge, but he never struck Diego as anything but a sworn patriot.

Montgomery was new to ICE this past year, transferring from his gig as a state park ranger. "Only time I've been around Montgomery was last year in Mexico."

"That was a fast, fun job."

"Yeah, but I'm thinking about how crazy scared Montgomery got because his woman's life was in danger. Remember that?"

"Definitely."

"If that broad's still in the picture, there's no way Montgomery would do anything to risk her safety, like jumping in bed with the Chiaras would do." Hard to forget the looks those two gave each other on the chopper ride after Montgomery and Diego's crew rescued the woman. Like no one or nothing else in the world mattered. He hadn't exactly been jealous, but more like fascinated. Wasn't something that came up all that often throughout his life.

His parents loved each other but never got all that intense about it, and they were the only example he could think of that came close. His sister Marisol's husband was a major jerk, and none of Diego's other siblings were married. Neither were any of his crew members.

"I'm with you on that," Ryan said. "Speaking of chicks, how's the asset?"

"Unharmed. She thinks we still have a shot at using her algorithm to track the Chiara brothers and stop the sub sale. Most of the computer work she can do remotely. So all we need is a safe house where Alicia can hook her up with the internet. Once we have the Chiara account pinpointed, we can pass that information to Dreyer to deal with while we escort Vanessa into protective custody."

Ryan's pause was too long. "That might not fly because Dreyer wants us to deliver her to a new safe house ASAP. He said the operation's back on for Monday, and he still wants to send her into RioBank to dissolve the account."

"Like the bank people aren't going to notice that her apartment blew up? I bet it's all over the news by now."

"I brought that up," Ryan said. "Get this. ICE wants her so bad they pulled strings at the hospital and with the police, faking that Vanessa's apartment went up in a freak gas explosion. The official line is that she was admitted to the hospital overnight under observation for a concussion, but her docs expect her to be back at work on Monday."

A burn akin to rage sparked to life in his lungs and throat. What a bunch of greedy suits, willing to risk her life all over again, like she was some worthless commodity. Over his dead body would that ever happen. "If you talk to Dreyer again, you tell him— Never mind. Let him stew for a while, then I'll call him myself after you pick us up."

"Roger that. When and where are we rendezvousing?"

"We had a small transportation issue getting to my Leroy." The explanation gave new meaning to the word *understatement,* but even though Ryan was the man Diego trusted most in the world, he still didn't feel right handing out details of his Leroy plan. Just wasn't done. "The place we are, it's going to take us two days hiking to reach the first road. If you and the rest of the crew want to meet up sooner, then pick us up as a unit, that'd be best."

"Name the place."

He gave directions to a mile marker along the unnamed one-lane road that skirted the edge of Nobu territory, then ended the call and repeated the pickup information to Rory.

Rory and John had come to his crew as a Green Beret sniper team five years earlier. Friends for life the same way Ryan and Diego were, they'd replaced Diego's last solo sniper. The job seemed to burn snipers out faster than the rest of them.

Something about the detachment of a calculated kill that the shooter couldn't see with the naked eye because he was so far away from the target beat even the most solid men into the ground after a while. He'd chosen a pair of guys this time, hoping their camaraderie kept them focused and stable for a longer stint.

After the call, he hauled the bin with bedding out from the corner and set it near the cot while Vanessa looked on. "You should get some sleep. We've got a long walk ahead of us the next two days."

"When are you going to sleep?"

"I don't need sleep."

She wrinkled her forehead in disbelief. "Everybody needs sleep."

He shrugged into his shoulder holster and grabbed his utility belt, struggling for the right words to help her understand. "You know how you can look at a page of numbers and know immediately what they mean? Equations no one else can do in their head, you can. Tell me how that's possible."

"Because that's what I do. It's how my mind works."

"Exactly. And this is how mine works. I've trained since I joined the U.S. Navy at eighteen for nights like this. I'm telling you, I don't need to sleep."

"What are you going to do, then?"

He cinched the belt and slung the rifle strap over his shoulder. "Stand guard outside." She hugged herself, so he added, "I'm not expecting any kind of trouble tonight, if that's what's got you worried."

Nodding, she got to work spreading blankets out, looking worn to the bone. He considered pitching in, but it was too much, the idea of doing something as intimate with her as setting up a bed.

Instead, he grabbed the first MRE his fingers touched and got the hell out of the room.

The night was dark as it always was in the jungle. Despite the clearing in which his cabin sat, not too much sky made it through the crowd of trees, and even less moonlight. At least the rain had stopped.

He stood still, just outside the door, until his eyes could make out the silhouettes of tree trunks and differentiate the ragged edges of the canopy surrounding the clearing from the sky beyond.

Birds, frogs and bugs did their noisy nighttime routine. Comforting, their sounds, because it meant nothing was out of the ordinary in the jungle. The real problem came when the animals and insects went silent. He'd been in that situation before. Been there at that moment when the silence rushed up like a wave of static in your ears and your gut dropped because you knew something ugly was about to go down.

But tonight, all was well. He had absolutely zero appetite, which wasn't unusual, given the day he'd had, and so chucked the MRE on the raised platform in front of the door along with his utility belt, and propped his rifle against the cabin's outer wall. He could get to it fast and he had two more guns on his body should trouble come calling.

He hopped from the platform and prowled the circumference of the clearing, finally ready to deal with the thoughts that had been waiting patiently in the background of his mind for him to have the time and space to acknowledge.

He'd killed today. At least eight men.

Never hit him until everything was quiet after a mission. Sometimes it wasn't until days later, but every time he took a life, he'd found it necessary to pause and get right with himself again. To remember why he led this life, and that he was one of the good guys, even though his fists and soul were stained with the blood of others.

He flexed his left pectoral, visualizing his tattoo, and

ran a list of the good he'd done that year, that month, that week. Today he'd taken eight lives but saved one. Probably saved more by snuffing the men he had before they got the chance to do more evil. *Wherever you are, Ossie, I hope you can see that the world's a little safer today.*

Meditating on the good he'd done only went so far to sever the dragging weight of the bloodshed, however. The rest, he had to work out in sweat.

That was Leroy Yarborough's idea. Nothing exorcised demons like exercise, he used to say. That certainly held true for Diego. From his utility belt, he pulled a climbing rope and wound it around his hands as a makeshift jump rope. He chose a spongy piece of ground that would muffle the noise, then started jumping.

About the time his leg muscles caught fire, all thoughts of death gave way to Vanessa's image.

He tossed the rope aside and dropped to the ground for crunches, ignoring the wetness creeping over his back and butt.

He'd been telling Vanessa the God's honest truth when he'd offered to get her out of Panama, either hide her somewhere safe or be the one to escort her into protective custody. If ICE demanded he hand her over in Panama so they could put her to work on Operation ICEWALL, he wouldn't do it. Going against them would mean his job, so he'd make sure his crew wasn't punished for his choice, but he hadn't saved her life only to push her into mortal danger again.

He rolled to plank position and held it for a count of one hundred. Then he hooked one ankle behind the other and got busy with one-legged push-ups. He was on his tenth set, with one hand behind his back and nothing on his mind at all except getting to twenty so he could start pull-ups on a nearby tree, when he heard movement in the cabin.

Maybe she was getting a drink of water or pacing around. Then he thought, what did he care what she was up to? She was safe, and really, that was the extent of his job.

He finished the set and stood, letting out a harsh exhale when he realized he was holding his breath, listening for more movement in the cabin and wondering why she was up when she should be getting the rest she needed. Okay, so he cared about her getting a good night's sleep. No big deal. Didn't mean nothing.

Determined not to think about her or puzzle over the reason for her restlessness, he worked out a comfortable grip on the limb of a tree along the clearing and started his set.

He was only on five when he heard the door open. The flickering glow of her flashlight caught on the trees to his right.

"Diego?" Her voice was tight with anxiety.

Like she was still entertaining the possibility he was going to leave her stranded. Un-freaking-believable. Someone had done a hell of a number on her, that was for sure. Whoever it was, Diego was working up the desire to deliver a smack down on them for damaging her like that.

"Over here." He dropped from the tree and walked her way.

"Where were you?" she asked.

"Doing pull-ups on the tree. Why aren't you sleeping?"

"I tried."

"You didn't try very long."

"I kept thinking about all the horror movies I've seen that take place in rickety old cabins in the woods. Can I sit out here with you?"

He didn't buy that lame excuse for a second. She was as transparent as her shirt had been after her dive in the lake. "You can sit out here, sure. But you'll want to turn that flashlight off. Lots of flying bugs in this jungle and, trust me, you don't want them dive-bombing the flashlight beam. That could get all kinds of nasty."

She sat cross-legged on the porch ledge, her back propped on the cabin wall. Diego snagged his MRE and settled next to her. One thing about Leroy's exercise strategy, it worked up an appetite. He felt around the box and brought up a two-pack of cookies, offering her one. He angled his whole cookie into his mouth and made short work of it. Chocolate. Not half-bad.

"Which movies had you spooked tonight?"

She took a nibble. "You name it. *The Blair Witch Project, Don't Go in the Woods, Cabin Fever.* Nothing good ever happens in a cabin in the middle of nowhere. I used to love scary movies, but they always seemed so unrealistic. Like you could be scared but could control it because you knew it wasn't real. And you could turn off the TV or walk out of the movie theater anytime you wanted, you know? But after what happened today, those movies don't seem so farfetched."

Ah. She needed to decompress from the day's violence as much as he had. Maybe he should put her to work on Leroy's plan. Ten sets of push-ups could cure anything. Then again, his sisters, aunts and mom weren't that way. They wanted to talk it out. Even Alicia was like that. Usually it was Ryan or John who acted as her sounding board while Diego got the hell out of earshot. But tonight, it was just him and Vanessa.

If talking was what she needed, he'd have to give it a try. Being the sensitive, articulate guy he was, that ought to go great. He cringed, but only because he knew it was too dark for her to see him doing it.

He cleared his throat. "I used to love scary movies, too, because the good guys usually won in the end. I've seen all those you mentioned. But I can't watch movies anymore, any movies."

In the MRE, he found the entrée and activated the heating fuel.

"What happened?" she asked.

"A couple years ago, I was in this hotel room in Egypt watching a movie on my computer because I couldn't sleep. *Friday the 13th.* That used to be one of my favorites, but that night it dawned on me what was happening. Sure, the chick kills that crazy woman at the end, but not before all these other kids were hacked up.

"The more I thought about it, the more I realized all those movies are like that. Whole families murdered, cities wiped out. Hollywood never talks about that. They play triumphant music during the end credits like the hero saved the day, and they never give a thought to all the people he didn't save.

"Even those big special effects films, like the ones where aliens try to destroy Earth. I hate those movies because I can't stop thinking about the millions of people who die during the special effects sequences when the aliens take out cities and landmarks before the heroes do their thing, and the Hollywood schmucks still play it off like something wonderful came out of all that bloodshed."

He filled his lungs, a little rattled by how easy it had been to tell her all that. Suddenly impatient to eat, he peeled the lid of the entrée and dug in. Beef stroganoff. Lukewarm, but edible.

Vanessa stayed silent for a while, then brought her knees up and hugged them. "I'd never seen a person die before today."

Damn. There it was.

He dropped his fork into the food and rested it in his lap. Appetite gone. "I hate that you had to see that. If there had been a way I could've prevented it from happening, I would've. But I didn't have a choice, and I'm not going to apologize because I don't regret it—not when your life was on the line."

"I don't think you should apologize or have regrets. I'm grateful for what you did. It's just that I'd never witnessed something like that before and I'm having trouble letting it go."

He poked at the stroganoff with the fork. "This probably isn't what you want to hear, but it's good that you're taking it hard. Means your head's screwed on straight and you've got a heart."

She humphed like she got what he was trying to tell her, despite the clunky way he'd said it. "Do you take it hard?"

"Yes. Never gets easier. And, honestly, I don't want it to. Scares me what that would mean."

"Good answer."

It was his turn to *humph*. He nudged her arm with his elbow. "I said the right thing? That's a first. I'm going to remember you told me that." He hoped the joke made her smile, or at least feel a little better, but it was impossible to tell in the dark.

"I'm curious about something," she said.

"Shoot."

"In the helicopter, you figured out that velocity equation fast. I was impressed."

"That was nothing special. I don't know a whole lot of math, but velocity is something I learned real quick in the navy. That and trajectory, force of impact, all those physics of warfare stuff they teach you as a SEAL in sniper school, jump school, weapons training and so forth. Everything you need to do the job and stay alive."

"Makes sense."

She was so close he could feel the heat of her. His arm twitched, wanting to touch her, give her a hug or something reassuring like that. A sure sign it was time to put some space between them. "You think you can sleep now? You ought to try because we'll be hiking all day tomorrow. Don't give me that horror movie line, either. I'm out here on guard, making sure you can sleep safe. Nothing's going to get to you when you're with me, got it?"

She stood and was halfway through the mosquito netting in the doorway when she stopped. "You're still going to be here when I wake up, right?"

She said it like she was trying to make a joke. It didn't work. If anything, it ticked him off more.

"How come you're so brave except about this? You're ready to risk your life to help ICE catch a bunch of violent criminals, but you're scared thinking I might abandon you in the middle of the night. I swear to God, Vanessa. Anytime now, you feel free to start trusting me to do right by you."

She squared her shoulders defiantly, but it was too dark to read the expression on her face. "You're right. Sorry. I trust you, I do. I didn't mean to insult you like that. Sometimes, even when I know it's irrational, I can't..." She sighed and shook her head. "Good night."

The second she disappeared behind the mosquito netting, he cursed under his breath and prowled to one end of the clearing and back.

He'd done it again. Flapped his lips and said the wrong thing. But over and over again she'd insulted his honor—the thing about himself he was most proud of—and he was tired of it.

She needed to get it straight in her head that when he promised something, he meant it. Then again, what should he care if she didn't trust him? He was supposed to keep her safe, and he would, but that didn't say anything about making sure she was happy and well rested. Beyond a lack of energy that would happen if she didn't sleep, what did he care if she exhausted herself imagining ridiculous scenarios? If she wanted to make herself miserable, that was her choice. It wasn't his job to talk her down from her irrational fears.

Then he thought about all she'd witnessed that day. Men had tried to kidnap her, then she'd watched her apartment blow up. She was out of a job and was going to be forced to leave the country, and she'd had no choice but to put her life in a stranger's hands— after she'd witnessed him kill a man and had gotten that man's blood on her clothes and skin.

Maybe he'd have trouble trusting, too, if he were in her position.

With another curse, louder this time, he stomped to the cabin door, grabbed his rifle and gear and threw the mosquito netting aside.

Chapter 9

Diego strode into the cabin. Vanessa's flashlight was on, pointed at the wall. She lay on her side on the cot, facing the door.

He couldn't tell if she was crying, and he wasn't sure what he'd do if she was. That was probably his least favorite thing in the world. Took him right back to his mom and sisters' grief after the news came that Ossie was lost when the Twin Towers had collapsed.

"Tell you what. I don't need to be outside to hear bad news coming." He cleared his throat. Why was this so hard? Wiping a hand across his forehead to swipe at the sweat, he crossed the room and loaded his gear on the lid of a bin. "So this is how we're going to do it. Sit up."

She pushed up on her hands. "You don't have to be in here. I was wrong before, what I said."

"Yeah, you were." He scowled and said a mental curse. That wasn't exactly the soothing statement he'd been going for. He tossed the folded blanket she'd used as a pillow aside, then sat where it'd been along the edge of the cot, propping his rifle against the wall. "Use my leg as a pillow. That way, you'll know I'm not moving while you sleep, because you'd wake up if I tried, right? So problem solved."

She stared at his lap and he could tell the wheels were turning in her head because she was gnawing on her lower lip. With a sigh, she nodded and clicked off the flashlight. "Thank you."

Her head found his leg no problem in the dark. She got comfortable fast, and while he was relieved that he'd found a solution she was okay with, the setup did nothing for Diego but cause him anguish. Because he had to rest his hands somewhere, but it was a mine-field of inappropriateness. Even in the pitch darkness, he knew the curve of her hip was nearby. He was a sucker for curves, and oh, man, did she have them in spades. He'd touched her there while she was cleaning his rash wounds and already knew how great her waist felt against his palms.

Then again, Vanessa had such pretty hair. He could settle his hands on her head and be happy for the rest of the night. He smoothed a hand over her hair once and she didn't seem to mind. In fact, her body relaxed. Good. They were finally getting somewhere. He stroked her hair again and she released a contented, resolve-melting sigh.

"Superhuman," she whispered.

"What is?"

"You. You're not scared, you don't feel pain and you don't need sleep. Do you have any weakness at all?"

On his next stroke of her hair, he allowed his fingers to keep moving down. He dragged them over the material of her shirt and curled them around the curve of her waist. Yeah, he had weaknesses all right. "I'm about as far from perfect as a man can get. I'm just doing my job."

"That's funny."

"What?"

"That you downplay it like that. 'Just a job' and all that nonsense. This isn't a job for you, it's who you are."

"Does your mind ever stop working at hyper speed? Because I thought the whole point of this setup was for you to get some sleep."

She burrowed her face into his leg and, Jesus Almighty, he hadn't realized something as simple as a woman getting all soft and cuddly would feel that good, that perfect. Until this moment, he hadn't realized he was missing out on something that pleasurable all these years. She hooked her arm around his knee in a kind of hug and he relaxed his hand against her waist. "Good night, Vanessa."

Then, just because he could, because he knew she wouldn't mind, he wove his other hand into her hair. And he thought, *Man, I could get used to this.*

There was a lot to be thankful for on the first day of their hike down the mountain. It wasn't raining, they were hiking downhill and Vanessa had benched the doubt and fear that had consumed her the day before. The circumstances surrounding the hike were dismal, but they were making the most of it.

"That depends," Vanessa called from behind him in answer to his question. "How long in kilometers is this hike, total?"

Her words were slightly winded, but seeing as how they were already four hours into their descent from the mountain, she was holding up fine. In fact, they were ripping along as fast as possible given the lack of trail and thick foliage.

"Thirty-three clicks, give or take."

She went quiet.

"Do the math out loud, would you? Come on and let me hear it."

"All right. This is a thirty-three kilometer hike and the average person's step distance is 0.67 meters, so we'll be taking nearly fifty thousand steps. Let me figure it out exactly."

He looked over his shoulder. Her lips were screwed into a pucker and her eyes were rolled up like she was literally looking into her brain as she rattled off numbers. Diego didn't usually think in terms of cuteness—there wasn't a whole lot that qualified for such a description in his world—but Vanessa doing math was pretty damn cute.

"Four-nine-two-five-three-point-seven-three-one."

Grinning, he set his eyes forward again and hacked at a tangle of vines blocking their progress. "Okay, then here's the next question—how are we supposed to walk the point-seven-three-one of a step?"

"No idea. I'm just the human calculator."

Diego had been shooting math problems at her for an hour and he figured he had at least another few hours left in him before he'd need a topic change. Maybe he should've been a math teacher because he could make up problems like that all day as long as nobody expected him to solve them.

"Okay, I've got another one for you. We started at twenty-eight hundred meters' elevation and the trail-head where we're meeting my crew is at, say, a hundred meters' elevation. What's the elevation change per step we take?"

"Easy."

"Easy? Gimme a break. All right, Miss PhD, why don't you go ahead and calculate the angle of our descent while you're at it?"

Before she could answer, lightning flickered, followed immediately by a roll of thunder.

Typical for Panama, the downpours happened almost daily and were especially torrential in late spring. About what someone would expect in a rainforest near the equator, and normally Diego wouldn't give a flying leap if it rained the entirety of the two-day hike or not. Problem was, Vanessa had changed back into the outfit Alicia had chosen for her, and walking in the rain wasn't going to make her clothes any less see-through than her lake jump had.

Groaning as a second round of lightning and thunder reverberated through the jungle and sent birds scattering, he pushed a dense bunch of fronds aside and nearly ran into a wall of rock taller than his head.

"Do you know what's on the other side of this rock?" she asked.

He shook his head. "This is my first time on this trail in a lot of years. GPS says this is the way we need to head, but looks like we'll be taking a detour."

He was in the process of searching for the best path down the drop-off, when Vanessa said, "The fastest way would be for us to go up and over."

"Depends on what's on the other side."

"How about you boost me up and I'll check it out?"

A roll of thunder cracked close by. Closing his eyes, he let out a dozen silent curses as the first drops of rain fell on his face. "Doesn't look like we're going to make it through the day without rain. We ought to hurry if we've got to get over this ridge." Squatting, he laced his fingers as a foothold. "Gimme your foot."

She slipped her shoe into his hands and turned toward the boulder, putting his face level with all her juicy curves.

With his eyes trained on the shoe he held, he decided the best course of action was to keep his mind occupied cataloguing everything in the jungle that might kill them. Number one for him was going to be a heart attack if she didn't get her derriere out of his face, stat. He gritted his teeth and got busy on his mental list of dangers—poachers, venomous spiders and snakes, pumas and jaguars, hypothermia, infection.

Infection was the nastiest, so he kept it in the front of his mind as he braced for her lift. "Okay, up you go."

She pushed against his hands and hauled herself onto the top of the boulder. And he didn't even peek at her backside as it accidentally brushed his cheek, just held his chin higher and thought back to the whopper of an infection he'd come down with on his arm a few years back in Somalia.

As soon as he got his body in check, he looked up. She was on her hands and knees, facing away from him. This time, he looked his fill.

"It's a drop-off. Steep. And I don't see any way around it."

"Do you see any water?"

"Um…yes. Oh, wow, that's pretty." She lowered her hip to the rock and twisted, flashing him a smile. "There's a waterfall in the distance. Looks like it feeds the river that cuts through this ravine."

"That would be the Rio Nobu. You're right. We don't have any choice but to rappel. I forgot about that part.

Luckily we're coming off the dry season so the river shouldn't be too high or swift to cross."

Another rumble of thunder shook the forest. The sky opened up with raindrops the size of marbles. In response, Vanessa let out a girlish squeak that just about stripped away the remnants of Diego's willpower where she was concerned.

The powers that be had a twisted sense of humor, that was for sure, because Diego didn't have the chance to avert his eyes before her clothes turned translucent again. He tried to remember the topic he'd been meditating on to distract himself, but the only thought in his head was wondering how he was going to survive his time with Vanessa Crosby without going insane.

Then she flipped to her stomach and slid to the ground, bouncing in all the right spots when she touched down, and he knew he was a goner.

Turning away from her, he dug into the backpack and withdrew climbing rope. He didn't carry a proper rappelling harness, preferring the fluidity of free-climb when possible and the versatility of knotting a harness out of rope when necessary.

As Vanessa watched, using her hands on her forehead like a visor to shield her eyes from the rain, he got busy with the ropes, fashioning them each a harness.

He looped a rope around each of her legs, tied the ends together at her waist with a water knot, then secured the straps with a carabiner. The situation shouldn't have been erotic. It was pouring rain in the middle of a two-day hike after a mission went FUBAR in a major way. Even without all that, his mind should've been 100 percent focused on Vanessa's safety, but the act of wrapping ropes around the wet fabric plastered to her thighs and waist only made the pulse of attraction buzzing between them hum like a live wire.

She set her hand on his back while he worked near her waist. "I'd tell you how scared I am, but then you'd accuse me of not trusting you."

He gave a tug on the rope to secure it at the place where her thighs met and stood, proud that his gaze hadn't lingered too extra long in that particular spot. "Don't go there. This is going to be a piece of cake compared to your jump out of the chopper. When you rappel, you control the speed."

"Control. I like the sound of that."

He liked the sound of her voice, husky and low in a way that got him thinking about pinning her to the rock and setting his mouth to work on the hollow of her throat, proving to her which of them was in control. Then again, feelings didn't get much more out of control than his were at the moment.

"You're going to be rappelling with me, aren't you?" she asked.

"Definitely. Rappelling in the rain isn't ideal. I'll be right next to you the whole time making sure you're safe." He fitted himself with leg loops, then crafted his own harness.

For makeshift rappelling devices, he used more rope and carabiners in a technique he'd learned as a SEAL, then took the time to double-anchor the ropes to trees and triple-check the strength of the knots. He boosted Vanessa onto the rock ledge again and followed her up. After a lesson on using the friction created by the rappelling device to control the speed of descent, he modeled the right way to back over the edge.

She was a trouper. Though her hands were unsteady and he knew from the chopper that she was afraid of heights, she put her back to the ravine and stepped off the edge. Hard rain pummeled their backs and heads, making footholds slippery and insecure. He kept up a string of encouraging words and positioned himself slightly beneath her in case she slipped. The descent was excruciatingly slow, but steady.

Her feet lost purchase once and she slammed into the rock.

He swung close and rubbed her shoulder. "You okay?"

"Never better. I'm a huge fan of scaling cliffs in the pouring rain."

Sarcasm was a good sign. It meant she was going to make it to the bottom without succumbing to her fear. They resumed their descent. Diego mirrored her speed, keeping as close to her as he could while still giving them each enough space to work.

"You know," he said, "there's some people that pay good money to go on a vacation that includes helicopter rides and rappelling through a rainforest."

"True, but I'm not one of those people. I like vacations where you can kick back on a tropical beach with a margarita. Do you take time off work to relax and recharge like that?"

The line had tangled around her foot. He shook it out and they kept going. Her question was probably a strategy to distract herself from what they were doing. He was tempted to tell her to be quiet and concentrate, but she was doing a terrific job for a beginner, and she hadn't complained once the entire day, so he didn't see any harm in playing along. "Not really. I try to visit my parents at least once a year, but that's about it."

"Don't you ever just want to be home, in your house or apartment or wherever you live?"

"I don't live anywhere. I have a couple P.O. boxes, one in Mexico City, the other in Jersey. When I'm not on a mission, I'm training. So either I sleep in base housing or hotels. And sometimes I go to my Leroy cabin."

They navigated over an outcrop in silence. When they were below it, she asked, "What about a vacation? Somewhere tropical."

He huffed. "Don't get much more tropical than this."

He didn't think it was possible, but the rain grew denser, surging down on them like sheets of water.

Vanessa's pace slowed. "No, I mean like Hawaii, at a resort."

"Um…last year, for my parents' fortieth anniversary, all us kids took them on a Caribbean cruise."

She cast him a sidelong look. "I can't picture you on a cruise."

"I know, right? I couldn't believe I was doing it, but that was my parents' big dream, so off we went. My brother and sisters, my middle sister's husband and their kids, the whole lot of us. It made my parents happy and that's all that mattered, but let me tell you, if I go to hell, it's going to look like the bingo hall of a cruise ship."

She laughed. "Were you able to relax at all?"

"Not really. The whole cruise, I didn't sleep a wink."

"What? Why not?"

"I couldn't stop thinking about what I should be doing, that while I floated on this barge of fake luxury, children were being sold into slavery, and I could've saved them if I was on the clock. I laid in bed and pictured boats of cocaine slipping into the country, and I thought, if me and my crew had been on it, we would've stopped all that from happening. I think, when you've seen the things I have and know what I do about how the world works, there's no such thing as a vacation."

The bottom four meters of rock were slick and flat and would be the most treacherous part for Vanessa. He eased the friction in the carabiners and sailed the rest of the way down to get himself in a position to help her should she need it.

"Every day, you wake up wanting to save people," she said as she negotiated the last few meters of the descent. "I know you don't agree, but you really are a real-life superhero."

She angled to look at him and her feet slipped. She yelped and her body twisted out. The rock was so slick that her arms, rather than grip the rope tighter, flailed as she fell.

Diego's instincts took over. He grabbed her waist with one hand and caught her left leg behind the knee with the other, stopping her fall with his body.

By the time he'd recovered enough wits to realize her arms were around his neck and she was straddling him, and that he was pressing her hips against the rock with his groin, it was too late to pretend that touching her like that didn't affect him in a fundamental physical way. Too late to deny that she fit around his body like she was born for it.

"You have to be more careful." Swallowing hard, he screwed up his mouth in a cringe, hating the telltale strain in his voice, praying she didn't hear it, too. So much for playing it close to the vest. He lowered his head to the rock above her shoulder, turning his nose toward her neck. Even sopping wet she smelled good. "I mean, what am I supposed to do with you if you get hurt up here in the middle of nowhere?"

She shivered from her legs up through her shoulders, and he felt like a total bastard because he'd probably gone and said the wrong thing yet again and scared her, like she was imagining that he'd abandon her in the wilderness if she sprained her ankle.

The rain pelted his head and back like pebbles. He hunched over her so it wouldn't beat her up as hard as it was him. "Forget I said that."

"No, you're right," she said. "We're a two-day hike from help, with at least twenty kilometers to go. Factor in elevation and the denseness of the undergrowth, rappelling and river-crossing, and I'd be useless if I got injured."

He didn't particularly want her factoring anything at the moment, but he was going to keep his trap shut until he thought of something harmless to say. Her grip tightened around his neck, which he supposed meant he wouldn't be setting her on her feet anytime soon. Not that he wanted to.

"You saved me again." The adoration in her tone frustrated the hell out him.

"You keep going on about superheroes and Batman, or whatever, but I'm no hero. I don't want you talking like that, romanticizing it like you've been."

"Explain to me how you're not heroic, when you wake up every morning wanting to save the world."

He wasn't exactly a dynamo in the verbal expression department, but he could tell she wasn't going to shut up about it until her curiosity was satisfied. "Saying I wake up implies that I sleep, but most of the time, I can't sleep at all. When I do, yeah, that's what I wake up knowing I'm going to do that day and every day for the rest of my life, but that's just because when I close my eyes, all I see is the evil of the world."

She stroked his hair. "When did you know this was the life you were meant to lead?"

"At my brother's funeral, I stood over his coffin and

looked at that American flag covering it, and I knew what I had to do. I made a vow to him right then and there that I'd never give up the fight to make the world safer for our family."

"Like I said…"

"Look, all it boils down to is that after 9/11, I was one of the few people in the country with the skill set and the drive to take a stand, make a difference. I only have this one gift—my guns and fists and the burn inside me telling me to use them. It's my reason for being on this planet. And it's a good thing I love it because I don't have the brains or patience for anything else but brute force."

She moved her hand between them, brushing her fingers across his collarbone. He ground his molars together and adjusted his feet, fighting the primal roar in his body urging him to find the way inside her and claim her for himself.

Her cheek touched his, and when she spoke, the corner of her moving lips tickled his skin. "How do you not realize how smart you are?"

He opened his eyes, blinking the water out of them, and was greeted by the sight of the downpour funneling between her breasts. Man, she was perfect. And he wanted her so damn bad it was killing him.

"Clearly I'm not that smart, or I wouldn't be standing here with you like this."

Beyond the fact that she was an asset, she deserved a whole lot more from a man than what Diego had to offer. Not just smarts-wise, but someone who could give her full-time attention, along with the home/kids/dog dream he'd bet a million dollars she harbored. That wasn't how Diego was made or how he lived. To change like that, to be what she deserved, he'd have to forsake the promise he'd made to Ossie—and that was the deal breaker.

Yet he couldn't bring himself to set her down and put some space between them. Couldn't stop blabbing about his life and his insomnia, about how much the pain grew inside him after Ossie died until the only way to deal with it was to throw himself into the fray. And the whole time, Vanessa's body was wrapped around him like she was the one doing the protecting. She was the one being strong as a shield while he stripped his life bare for her.

What was he thinking, doing that? How would he ever convince her to trust him with her safety if he kept showing her the weakest parts of himself?

Vanessa had no idea caring about somebody could feel like an umbrella. Sheltering, strengthening. The more Diego opened up to her, the safer she felt from everything.

In her mind's eye, she could picture him in the tiny stateroom of a cruise ship, staring at the ceiling, checking the clock and waiting for dawn. The weight of the guilt he'd brought on himself for taking time off from saving the world. He would've endured it silently on the cruise, to keep his parents happy.

Tenderness for him—for this man who was such a force to be reckoned with that he thought it was all he was good for—glowed inside her, bright and hot.

She wanted to kiss him. Needed him to understand that it was okay to hurt. That he hadn't lost any standing in her eyes, because she understood the bravery it took to be honest and open. Because she hurt sometimes, too. But somehow she knew he didn't give himself permission to feel it. He channeled the pain into action and never allowed himself the opportunity to process everything he and his family had been through.

With her fingers in his hair, she angled his face toward hers and pressed a kiss to his closed lips. His muscles tensed, his mouth became unyielding and his hands froze on her hips. She ran the tip of her tongue along the crease of his lips, seeking entrance. Finally his lips softened. He opened enough that she caught the faintest taste of him. A thrill of lust sizzled through her at the realization that his taste matched his scent—a masculine, sweet spice that called to her with its rightness, as if his taste and scent had been designed just for her.

Like he was meant to be hers.

She tipped her head to a steeper angle and opened, licking at the slight part of his lips, waiting for him to open to her, too.

Chapter 10

Vanessa closed her eyes. *Open for me, Diego. Kiss me back....*

But he didn't. He pulled his face away, twisting his neck to sever the hold she had on his head.

"Why did you do that?" he asked from behind clenched teeth, his nostrils flaring. It was a fierce look that might've sent her scrambling, except that he continued to clutch her like his life depended on it, holding her so tightly against him she couldn't draw a full breath.

Because I want you so badly my heart aches, and it's not because you're gorgeous and not because you've saved my life more than once, but because something inside you is calling to me.

None of that would do to say, of course. He was so skittish about intimacy, she didn't want to scare him away any more than she already was. She stroked a finger along his tight jaw. "Because I wanted to kiss you, and I think you wanted it, too."

He swallowed and dropped her legs to the ground. In a flash, he had her harness off, the rope untied from her waist. Gathering the rappelling gear in a haphazard bundle, he stuffed it into the backpack. "Don't let it happen again."

Without meeting her eyes, he sloshed through the knee-deep river to the other side. Vanessa scrambled to catch up.

Said in a harsher tone, the words would've stung, but Diego had said them like a plea. Like he was powerless to prevent them kissing again, so she'd have to be the strong one. Too bad for him because she couldn't think of anything she wanted more than to coax a real kiss from him.

"Why not?" she asked when they'd reached the other side of the water.

He continued to march at full speed, so that one of his strides equaled two of hers.

Into the jungle they went, Diego in front, hacking at the undergrowth with his knife, Vanessa behind him, wondering if he'd answer her. The canopy provided nominal shelter from the rain, but it still seeped through the trees in a kind of half mist, half shower.

When she couldn't stand it any longer and she thought her temper might explode if she held the question inside her for one more second, she repeated it. "Why shouldn't I kiss you again? Give me one good reason why we shouldn't do something we both want. And don't you dare deny it."

He whirled on her. The look on his face was dark, pained. "You need a reason?"

She raised her chin a notch. "Yes."

Three steps and he was before her, his hands on her shoulders. His eyes squeezed closed, and he lowered his forehead to hers. She wasn't sure if touching him would help or hinder his ability to get the words out, so she held herself still.

He brushed his thumb across her cheek. "Because one kiss with you wouldn't be enough for me."

"And that's a problem?"

"Hell, yes, it's a problem. Because..." He went silent.

"Tell me."

"Because all the things you deserve, I can't give you any of them. I can't even tell you my real name."

The loneliness pouring out of him made her want to wrap her arms around him and never, ever let go. She knew all about loneliness, about feeling like a ghost in the world. What it was like to have nothing to offer to keep the people you cared about from slipping away. She knew all too well that having a heart bursting with love wasn't enough to hold on to somebody, no matter how badly you wished otherwise.

She swiped water from her eyes, wishing the rain would stop so she could hold Diego's gaze without blinking a million times a minute. Risking his disapproval, she splayed her hands over his chest because it was impossible to say what she wanted to without touching him. "It seems to me it's the other way around. You're offering me everything I need right now—safety, the chance to do something that matters for the first time in my life, help for me to start over somewhere else afterward. But I don't have anything to give you in return."

Snorting, he rolled his forehead against hers. "That's a load of B.S."

She touched their noses together. "I don't even have

a P.O. box like you. Or guns or fists, for that matter. Nothing but this."

She slid her hands higher, clutching the back of his neck, holding him near. Then she leaned in, pressing her lips to his. As before, his body tensed, resisting.

"I know our lives are incompatible—heck, I have no idea what my future holds anymore, so I certainly can't make you any promises. But I'm not asking you for anything except a simple kiss," she whispered. "Would that be so bad?"

His hands moved up her neck to cup her cheeks. She parted her lips, vibrating with anticipation as his lips hovered over hers. She'd only known him less than twenty-four hours, so why did this feel like it'd been a long time coming? Like she'd waited her whole life to be kissed here, by this man, at this exact moment in time.

After a ragged inhale, his body tensed and gathered up like a wave building before it crashed to shore.

Then he kissed her. Took her mouth with a force that was fierce, wholly carnal. Every demanding stroke of his tongue dug the slow burn of desire deeper and lower inside her.

Rocking onto her tiptoes, she opened herself to him. His groan in response rattled up from his throat like a growl that turned the burn inside her into a blaze of heat. She loved that he was as ravenous as she, loved the sweeping sensation that they were becoming untamed together, as wild as the jungle around them.

She touched him everywhere she could reach. The rounded hardness of his biceps and chest, the rippled contours of his back, his thick, damp hair, until touching with her hands wasn't enough. She wrapped a leg around his thighs, arching her hips, desperate for more.

He took the cue, supporting her leg under the knee and grinding his hard length against the seam of her pants.

The friction obliterated her thoughts and nearly sent her over the edge despite the fact that they were both still fully clothed. She whimpered at the feel of his confined arousal, hating that layers of fabric prevented him from satiating the hollowness inside her core.

His body pressed her until her back flattened against a tree trunk.

Something blunt tapped the top of her head. But both Diego's hands were busy gripping her backside and holding her leg off the ground. The same something as before tapped her head again, then touched down across the yoke of her shoulders. She and Diego flinched at the same time, their lips wrenching apart.

His eyes widened. "Hold completely still," he said in a quiet, even tone.

"What is it? Feels like an animal. Iguana?" *Please let it be an iguana's tail. Don't let it be a snake, please, please, please.*

"Pit viper."

Oh, God.

"I'm going to let go of your leg to get my knife, but hold it steady."

Seeing as how she was paralyzed with fear, that wasn't going to be a problem.

"On the count of three, we're going to get you away from this snake. Did those self-defense classes you took teach you about controlled rolls?"

"Yes."

"Okay, good. You're about the last person in the world other than my mother that I want to give a hard shove to, but we need to get you out of striking range fast. So I push and you tuck into a roll, and just keep rolling as far as you can. You copy?"

Getting shoved away from a deadly, poisonous snake sounded like a perfect plan to her, except it would leave Diego vulnerable for a strike. "I got it. But what about you?"

"Don't worry about me. You do your job and I'll do mine. On three. One…"

Tucking her chin, she unlocked her ankles and arms from around Diego's torso. The snake was heavy on her shoulders, squeezing the back and sides of her neck.

"Two…three!"

He pushed between her shoulder blades so hard the wind knocked clean out of her as she angled toward the ground. Gasping for breath, she tumbled three times and slammed into a tree trunk.

Behind her, Diego let out a string of curses that might've made her blush if she hadn't grown up the daughter of a football coach.

She sprang to her feet. "Did it get you?"

"Yeah, damn it." He pulled up the sleeve of his right arm to reveal two small puncture wounds. "This is frea-kin' ridiculous. We don't have time for this crap."

To be bit by a venomous snake in the middle of the jungle without access to immediate medical attention was a death sentence. She supposed his grouchiness was a good sign because at least he was conscious, but that could change any moment. Lightheaded with fear, she rushed to his side. "What are we going to do? Will your cell phone work here?"

His legs folded and he sat where he'd stood. "Yes. It's a satellite phone, but I don't think we'll need it for this. Get the backpack off me. There's a first aid kit inside."

She slid the straps off his shoulders. "Where's the snake? Did you kill it?"

"Nah. Slithered off. I was ready with my knife in case it got aggressive, but I don't need to add killing an innocent animal to the list of my crimes."

"Biting you wasn't aggressive enough? What if it comes back?"

"It's not going to. Looked like it'd just fed. We just surprised it while it was digesting its meal, is all. There probably wasn't much venom left in its bite. You find that kit yet?"

She pawed through the pack. "Got it. What do you need first?"

"See that elastic band? Get it around my arm. Stop the spread of the venom."

With unsteady fingers, she pushed his shirtsleeve up over his shoulder and threaded the band around the top of his biceps.

"You know how you don't think I feel pain? Well, forget about that because this hurts like a mother—" He grunted and rolled his eyes skyward as she tightened the tourniquet.

"I can't let you die, but I don't know how to get you to a hospital."

"Vanessa, look at me."

She tore her gaze from the pile of cotton squares she was digging through.

"Do you honestly think I'm going to let a little snakebite keep me from doing my job? What good would I be to you dead? There's antivenom in the kit. Four vials of CroFab. You have to mix each one with water."

She found the vials in one of the pockets. Grabbing a water bottle, she got to work rehydrating them according to the page of instructions folded in the kit.

"It's been a lot of years since I've had a kiss like that."

She shook a vial to mix the medicine with the water. "For me, too."

"That's B.S. I bet that happens to you all the time."

She figured his strategy was to distract himself from the pain by talking, but her mind was spinning so fast it was hard to get the vials ready and think of anything to say. "No way. I'm a mathematician who yammers on about equations and calculations all the time. And I get nervous about people leaving me. Math and insecurity do not a good girlfriend make."

And why did she just tell him that? Oh, my God, how embarrassing. Maybe his pain would make him forget. Heat crept over her face. She finished mixing the final vial and laid it alongside the rest.

"The vials are ready. What do I do next? Do you drink it?"

"Not quite. Get some gloves on and open that sterile needle pack. Screw one on to the CroFab vial. Then come here. I got all sorts of fat veins ready for you to inject it into."

"You want me to give you a shot? I've never…"

"Well, you'd never flown in a helicopter or rappelled before, and you'd never been kidnapped before, so I'd say this is a week of firsts for you all the way around."

Scooting the pack over with the vials sitting on top, she knelt next to him. His forehead was beaded with sweat and his skin had gone pale. The arm infected with the venom had swollen and turned a splotchy red.

"Betadine first, right on the inside of my elbow." He draped his arm over her knees.

She scrubbed the area and took the prepared needle in hand.

"You see that vein running through the middle? Bring the needle up and I'll help you with the angle."

He guided her hand toward his arm but stopped an inch from his skin to rub the back of her hand, probably because it was shaking like mad.

"I like that you talk about math."

Her gaze flew from his arm to his face, questioning.

His lips curved in a lopsided grin. "How about these stats—my heart is going to pump the antivenom through my system at a rate of seventy ccs per beat. Since my resting heart rate is about forty beats per minute and my system has five liters of blood in it, how many different calculations can you do with numbers like that? Do the problems out loud. I want to hear them."

Crazy, to think about solving equations at a time like this, but the moment she saw the first numbers in her head, her nerves calmed. Maybe Diego was on to something with the math idea.

She rattled off figures as he guided her hand holding the needle to his vein. She kept pressing the tip of the needle forward, even after it dimpled his skin and her hand grew clammy. With a feeling like a pop, it broke through. Her stomach lurched.

"Nice work. Now depress the plunger, slow and steady."

With his guidance, she repeated the process with the remaining three vials, then removed the needle and tourniquet and repacked the needle in the sterile pouch it'd come in.

Mentally spent, she unscrewed a fresh bottle of water for Diego and collapsed against the tree trunk on his left side. "You're getting pretty beat-up for me. I'm so sorry." He filled his lungs with air like he was about to speak, but she held up her hand. "And don't tell me that's your job."

He draped his arm across her legs and hugged them. "How about I just tell you that you're worth it?"

She dropped her head to his shoulder. She'd never been worth it. Not to anybody, not really.

He rubbed his lips and nose over her hair. "I do have one point I feel obligated to bring up."

"I'm listening."

"If that was your idea of a simple kiss, then I'm going to need a bigger first aid kit."

Grinning, she curled her arm up and set her hand on his shoulder beneath her chin. "Consider yourself warned, then. I liked kissing you, and I'm going to do it again sometime soon."

He snorted. "Is that a fact?"

"Mmm-hmm. I'm going to have to kiss you a lot to get through the rest of this operation with my sanity intact."

He craned his neck to look at her, his expression bemused. "Kissing keeps you sane? Because for me it had the exact opposite effect."

She opened her eyes wide with fake incredulity. "You didn't find it calming?"

"Hell, no. That was the least calming thing I've ever done. Stealing you back from the Chiara brothers was more calming than that kiss."

"Then you'd better knock off all that grumpiness, because when you get all surly and serious like you're starting to right now, I only want to kiss you worse."

He sent her a bewildered look. "What are you, from another planet? Who thinks like that?"

"I do." Good God, she wanted to kiss him. She

wanted to wipe that scowl off his face and seek the soft gooey center inside him that was so irresistible.

"You're getting that look in your eyes like you might want to launch your lips at me—and I want you to, trust me—but we have a lot more ground to cover before we set up camp for the night. Kissing's going to have to wait."

That was the most ludicrous thing she'd ever heard. She pushed up to her knees and faced him. "You've got to be kidding. You were bitten by a poisonous snake. You need to rest. We're not going any farther today."

Exasperation crossed his face. "We're rendezvousing with my crew in twenty-five hours. We don't have time to sit around."

"I think they'll understand if it takes us a little longer than you originally planned. You're not superhuman."

His scowl intensified. "Yeah, I know I'm not. It's what I've been trying to tell you this whole time. And here's something else you ought to know about me. I don't share control of my missions. Not with my crew, not with the federal stiffs who pay my salary, nobody. Especially not a civilian like you. What I say goes, understand? If I say I'm okay to hike on, then that's the final ruling."

The tyrannical assertion was appalling. Offensive. It made her want to point out that they'd already had disagreements, and every time he'd conceded to her wishes. Except that she registered the fear behind his words. For a man who defined himself by his ability to protect others, having that ability stripped from him by an injury was a disaster of epic proportions.

It reminded her of her dad's football players, the ones who'd stayed in a game despite knee injuries or broken toes. Football players, soldiers, the more she thought about it, the more similar they were. Doing their job, playing the game—*winning*—trumped everything else: family, education and especially physical pain. The warrior mentality. Pain is just weakness leaving the body and all that macho B.S. she'd hear her dad say to his players at practice. It was a value system that defied logic, at least to Vanessa.

But because she was so familiar with men like him, she also knew there would be no changing his mind on this point. At least not through logic.

She leaned in and pressed a kiss to the corner of his closed mouth.

His hands fisted in the mossy earth. "You can't seduce me into agreeing with you."

Quirking a brow, she kissed her way from his neck along his jaw to the jut of his chin.

"Never gonna happen, Vanessa."

She slid a hand up his neck and lightly scraped his skin with her nails. "Diego?"

He grunted.

"I'll allow you to hike, but if you start to look sick or weak, we're going to stop for the night. And I don't want you to give me any trouble about it."

"Or else what? You think just because you've taken self-defense classes that you're capable of wrestling me to the ground with that puny little body of yours? I don't think so."

"Something even more effective. If I decide you've had enough and need to rest, then I'm going to sit down and refuse to continue." The words made fear coil in her throat. "And if I don't hike, then you'll have to stop, too, because you'd never leave me stranded in the middle of the jungle."

Then again, what if he did leave her?

Stupid, Vanessa. He'd never do that. Never, not in a million years.

But what if he did?

In a flash, she was on her back in the squishy, soggy moss, Diego over her. He stabilized himself on his left arm, allowing his right arm to settle limply on her ribs below her breasts. The rain dripped off his cheeks onto her.

His dark eyes were flinty and the scowl seemed permanently fixed to his lips. "Throwing down the gauntlet, hmm? Only problem is you don't believe your own bluff."

She swallowed hard as her heart squeezed with panic. Where was the gooey center inside all those muscles and guns?

He shook his head, his expression softening. "One of these days, you'll have it figured out that I'm not going to leave you in a lurch. How about I keep reminding you until then, deal?"

"Deal." It made her see red that she couldn't let go of the fear, but there wasn't anything she was going to do about it today. That die was cast a long time ago.

The therapists she'd seen over the years all agreed it went back to the sudden loss of her mother when she was two. According to her dad, she'd dropped Vanessa off at daycare, then was hit by a car that had run a red light. It had taken her a long time and a lot of growing up to articulate how frustrating and terrible it was that her emotional well-being was being held hostage by an event and person she had no memory of.

There simply wasn't anything about her mom for her to hold on to. Just a handful of pictures and stories, along with the imprint of loss on her heart and the awareness at too early an age about the fragility of human connection.

The events of the past couple days had issued a stark reminder of that fragility.

Diego's exhale fanned over her face. "You know why we need to keep pushing on, why I'm being such a jerk about it? Because my crew has extra vials of antivenom and I could use a few more doses to be sure I'm okay. And I need to get you somewhere safer than this jungle now that my shooting arm is compromised. A group of armed professionals can protect you better than me alone.

"And if we don't keep moving, we won't make it to a computer in time to stop the submarine sale because we'll have to spend a second night in the jungle, surrounded by friggin' pit vipers. In the rain. And I am sick and tired of the rain. I want to get a roof over our heads and dry clothes for you because I can see right through your damn shirt and it's driving me crazy."

It took her a second to process what he was saying. Then her arms flew across her chest, covering herself. "Oh, God. Seriously?" Apparently she'd been too concerned with staying alive and keeping up with Diego's pace to give much thought to the perils of hiking through the rain in a white T-shirt. "That's not so bad, I guess. I've got a bra on."

And he laughed. Raised his head to the sky and let loose with a chuckle that made his shoulders shake.

She uncrossed her arms and stole a peek. "My bra's see-through, too? Why didn't you tell me this morning before I changed clothes?"

"I thought maybe it wouldn't rain."

She swatted his good shoulder. "We're in a rainforest!"

He chuckled again and it stole her breath, how handsome he was. His face was strikingly masculine. Not perfect—his broken nose had seen to that—but powerfully rugged. Gorgeous. She reached up and touched the laugh lines on his cheek.

"If you get fatigued or start to feel ill, we have to stop. I'm not going to let you run yourself into the ground. All we have out here is each other, and the same way you're protecting me, I need to protect you. That's my job."

In his eyes, she recognized the same kind of affection blooming in her heart. He stroked her hair away from her face. Then he kissed her, slow and deep, without any of the desperate urgency of the first time.

He left her mouth to kiss and nibble along her neck. As before, the world around them narrowed until all that remained were the two of them and the swirl of energy and need stirring between them.

And she thought, maybe, just maybe, it was time to start trusting him to take care of her no matter what. If he said he was well enough to hike, then he was. Because, lying on top of her, he certainly felt potent, his body solid and thrumming with vitality.

She arched her chest and neck toward his exploring mouth. "I still haven't figured out what your weaknesses are."

He smoothed a hand to her hip and locked her more tightly against his hard length. "Really? Someone as smart as you are and you haven't figured that out yet?"

She tucked her hips, notching the juncture of her thighs around his arousal, rubbing on him in a way that had him hissing through his teeth against the skin of her neck.

"That doesn't feel like a weakness to me," she purred. "Quite the opposite, actually."

Laughter reverberated through his chest. "We have to get moving."

He lifted off her and stood, then took her hand and helped her up. She snuck a second look at her horrifyingly translucent shirt while he scooped up the backpack. How had she not noticed that? Had it been equally see-through after she dove in the lake? The question heated her face all over again.

"Vanessa," Diego said in a thin, worried tone.

She looked up in time to see his eyes roll back as he collapsed.

Chapter 11

Diego roused almost instantly after hitting the ground, but he was disoriented. His skin was cool and ashen, his eyes half-lidded. At his side, Vanessa was torn between wanting to scream or cry, but couldn't manage either.

Stroking his hair, she repeated his name over and over, but his eyes wouldn't connect with hers. He briefly muttered something that sounded like Spanish, but his words were too slurred for her to catch.

His bitten arm didn't look any worse than a few minutes earlier, but his breathing was coming in shallow gasps and she thought his tongue looked swollen.

What she needed was to try to connect with Diego's crew. They'd know what to do.

The disposable cell phone and satellite phone were easy to find in the small front pouch of the pack. The cell didn't have any service, but it had phone numbers.

He'd said to only use the satellite phone as a last resort. She glanced at his prone, semiconscious body.

A situation couldn't get more urgent than this.

None of the phone numbers he'd called the night before were labeled with names, not that their names would mean anything to her. She knew of Alicia and Ryan, but that was all.

Deciding it didn't matter which of his crew answered the phone, she dialed the first number she found. She was trembling so bad, she pressed the speaker to her ear with both hands. On the third ring, an automated voice mail kicked in. "This is Vanessa Crosby. Diego's hurt. We're somewhere near the Rio Nobu and I don't know what to do. I don't even know the number of this phone, so I hope you do. Please call me, and hurry."

Diego's breathing had turned into labored wheezing. Muttering a prayer, she scrolled through the cell phone for the next number. Again, it went to voice mail. By the third voice mail, all she bothered to say was, "Help. Diego's hurt."

She pressed the scroll button on the cell phone, but no more phone numbers appeared. Stunned, she stared blankly at the display screen. She had to do something, but what?

Out of options, she dialed Panama's emergency hotline.

A male dispatcher answered. Relief dropped her to her knees next to Diego.

"Yes, hello. I need help. My…my friend and I are hiking and he was bitten by a pit viper. I gave him four vials of antivenom and he was fine. But then he collapsed and he's having trouble breathing. I need to know what to do. Help me."

"Tell me your name and the name of your friend."

"Jordan. And my friend is Carlos." She'd blurted the first names that came to mind, thinking that was what Diego would do given the line wasn't secure.

"Is Carlos conscious?"

"He goes in and out."

"What's your location?" the dispatcher asked.

She pressed her fingers to Diego's neck, searching for a pulse. She found it and felt a little better. "Nobu territory."

"Do you have GPS coordinates?"

Her heart plummeted. "No. All I know is that we're near the Rio Nobu. But there's nowhere to land a helicopter and there aren't any roads. So I don't know how you're going to get to us soon enough to help him, but you have to try."

"Listen to me, Jordan. You need to stay calm. I'm alerting rescue services, but it takes time to get a helicopter in the air. You're going to have to help him. My name is Mario, and I'm going to walk you through it. First, I need you to give me some details about the antivenom and his symptoms."

She did the best she could, but staying calm wasn't an option. Diego's face had turned a shade of blue.

"Look in the first aid kit and see if you can find an EpiPen," Mario said. "I think he might be having an allergic reaction to the antivenom."

She dumped the pack and unzipped the kit. Her roommate in college used an EpiPen once after accidentally eating a bite of shellfish. Vanessa had watched, but she'd been too freaked out by the idea of someone sticking themselves with a needle to pay much attention to how it worked.

"Got it," she said.

"Good. Pull the blue safety release, then grip the

body of the pen like the handle of a tennis racket, the orange end down. That's the side with the needle. You're going to give him the shot in his outer thigh, right through his pants. Get in position to push it into his leg at a ninety-degree angle."

Being careful not to put any pressure on Diego's chest and lungs, she straddled his torso backward to get the best angle, all propriety gone. Who cared if he came to and the first thing he saw was her butt in his face—at least that would mean he came to.

"Okay, I'm ready," Vanessa said into the phone.

"Remember, ninety-degree angle. Hold it there and count to ten. Go!"

Gritting her teeth, she jammed the orange end against Diego's thigh and waited.

It was the longest ten seconds of her life. After the time was up, she tossed the EpiPen aside and scrambled off him. "Done."

"Give it a few seconds."

Gradually, Diego's breathing grew deeper, his eyes clearer. He looked her way and she thought perhaps he recognized her, but then he spoke in slurred, rapid Spanish and watched her like he expected her to respond. She had a fairly good grasp of the language, but her mind was spinning too fast to concentrate and she only caught a few words that didn't make any sense.

She held a hand over the phone so the dispatcher wouldn't hear her whisper, "Diego, it's me. It's Vanessa."

He licked his lips. "I said that in Spanish, didn't I?" His voice was scratchy and weak.

Relief made her wilt against him. "Yes. What did you say?"

"I said my dad used to tell me, don't let a woman

know she was right because you'll never live it down.
I think this might be one of those times he was talking about."

Tears crowded her eyes. She held the phone to her
ear. "Mario? He's awake again. Thank you."

"I heard. That's a good sign. Let him rest where you
are for at least twenty minutes, then I'm going to ask
you to get to the river so our rescue team can locate
you. Can you do that?"

"Yes. Thank you." Ending the call, she pinched her
lips together, stifling a full-out sob.

She threw her arms around Diego and rested her
cheek on his arm and shoulder, careful not to put any
pressure on his chest.

He smoothed a hand over her hair and settled it on
her back. "What happened to me?"

"You had an allergic reaction. The dispatcher said
that's a problem with antivenom sometimes."

"Guess you'll never think of me as a superhero
again."

"You're better than a superhero."

"Aw, now, I bet you use that line with all the guys."

Joking was a good sign, though his voice was still
weak and his eyes had fluttered closed. He was going
to be okay. She hugged him tighter. "Rest now."

"Good plan. Just for a minute or…" His words drifted
off.

She eased his arm away from her back and stood.
Mario told her it'd take a while to arrange help and that
she should let him rest. They were close enough to the
river that she could run to the bank at the first sound
of a helicopter.

Just in case help came before she could get Diego
to the water, she grabbed an orange emergency rescue

tarp from the aid kit and jogged to the bank. She secured the ends to the branches of two trees. There was no way the helicopter could miss seeing it.

The trees teemed with sounds of birds and the river gurgled by, but the jungle was otherwise still. She scanned the sky anyway but saw nary a dot on the horizon. With a quick prayer that help arrived soon, she beat a hasty path back to her dozing hero.

Hands on his chest shook Diego awake.

Groaning at the throb of pain throughout his body, he fluttered his eyelids open. Even that small movement ached. Vanessa leaned over him.

"How long have I been out?"

"About an hour, I think. You have to get up now."

That was easy for her to say. He could count on one hand the number of times in his life he'd felt this beat up. Like he was the coyote in those cartoons and he'd fallen off a cliff and landed flat on his back only to be run over by a passing car while the roadrunner pecked him on the head.

He'd readily given in to Vanessa's demand that he rest. She was right that he hadn't been in any shape to protect her. Still wasn't, given the pounding in his head and how heavy and achy his limbs were. The density of the surrounding trees made the spot he lay within relatively secure, all things considered.

He took a minute to register the urgency that had been in her voice.

Though his muscles and joints screamed, he levered up to an elbow. "What's wrong?"

"We need to get to the riverbank so the rescue copter can find us. I hear it coming."

That had him bolting upright. "Say that again?"

She slung the backpack strap over her shoulder and staggered under its weight. "I called all the numbers I found for your crew, but no one answered. I thought you were going to die so I called the emergency hotline. The dispatcher arranged for a helicopter rescue, and I hear it coming, so we've got to move to the river. Now."

"How did it know where to find us?"

"I told the dispatcher we were along the Rio Nobu. Come on." She tugged his arm by the wrist.

No way. No freaking way.

A spike of adrenaline shot him to his feet. Dispatching a rescue helicopter involved numerous alerts to the fire department, hospitals, police, aviation authorities—the works. Hell, the Panama army probably knew the score at this point, which meant the Chiara brothers knew their location, too, as well as whichever ICE agent was the rat.

"Don't go near that river, Vanessa. Gimme the backpack."

Vanessa looked confused and scared. "You don't understand. Mario, the dispatcher, arranged for our evacuation. We have to go right now."

"Listen to me. It might not be safe. Give me the pack. I need to make a call."

She looked longingly in the direction of the river but handed it to him without a word. He dug through it for the satellite phone and dialed the ICE attaché office number from memory.

To Yazmin, the office manager, he said, "This is Agent Santero. I need some information fast. Has an emergency rescue helicopter been dispatched in the last hour anywhere in Panama?"

He could hear her fingers clicking on the keyboard.

"The broadcast for a remote area medical rescue went out, but a helicopter hasn't been dispatched yet."

Diego dropped the backpack. He swung the strap of his rifle around and gripped the weapon, finger near the trigger. His arm throbbed, but he didn't have a choice except to fight through the pain because he was a lousy shot with his left hand.

"Sir, is there anything else I can do for you? Do you want me to tell Agent Dreyer that you called?"

He moved the phone away from his mouth and turned to Vanessa. "Grab the pack and get behind me." To Yazmin, he added, "Better not tell Dreyer, but cancel the chopper broadcast, would you? That was bogus. I've got to go."

He ended the call and shoved the phone in a pocket.

"What's going on?" Vanessa asked.

"That's no rescue chopper. Our location's been made."

A look of dawning horror crossed Vanessa's face. She stood frozen, so Diego opened his arms and ushered her into the cover of a thick cluster of trees.

"You needed medical attention," Vanessa said. "I had to get help."

He tucked her up near the tree with the thickest density of leaves and branches. "I know. You didn't do anything wrong. The helicopters are sweeping the river. If we stay out of sight, they should pass right by us. That river's more than a hundred miles long."

She muttered something Diego didn't have the time or mental space to process. All he could focus on was the sound of two choppers headed their way.

She grabbed the front of his shirt and shook it. "The emergency tarp."

"What emergency tarp?"

"From the first aid kit. I strung it out on the river bank so the helicopter could find us."

The bottom dropped out of Diego's stomach. He felt his pulse in his ears and head, in his injured arm. The sound blended with the roar of the approaching helicopters.

And then clarity struck, as it always did when his adrenaline levels peaked. The noise stopped. His vision tunneled. His body and mind aligned exactly as he'd conditioned himself to react to imminent mortal danger. "Get moving. Path of least resistance. We don't have time to hack at the vines. All we need to do is run."

He pushed her ahead of him, but it was too late.

The gunfire started. It tore up the trees around them, spitting leaves and splinters and bullets like a tornado had touched down.

Diego snagged Vanessa around the ribs and tossed her to the ground, threw himself over her and crawled them both to a fallen tree. He wedged her up against it and wrapped his body around her, his head tucked close to hers.

The gunfire stopped as abruptly as it'd started. But that didn't mean they were safe. He'd captained this sort of attack himself. After the gunfire came one of two things—explosives or ground troops. Either way, they needed to get the hell out of there.

"We're going to run, and we're going to do it faster than you ever have before. You're taking lead. Keep to the underbrush. Do not shortcut through any clearings in the canopy." He pushed a gun into the waistband of her pants, then transferred the phones to her pocket. "If I tell you to go on without me, you do it, damn it. You run until there's no daylight left. And then you call my crew. Understand?"

"I'm not going on without you if you get hurt."

"Yes, you will, if it comes to that. Don't make me fail at my job by doing something stupid like going against my command."

She drew an unsteady breath and nodded.

He bussed her lips with a kiss. "Here we go."

She ducked out the back side of the log and sprinted, crashing through the underbrush. Diego kept pace behind her, his ears tuned to the sound of the chopper. He kept one eye looking over his shoulder, waiting for round two of the ambush that was going to start any second.

Chapter 12

Ground troops it was. Over the continuing roar of the helicopters, he sensed men moving through the trees in pursuit, their gunfire blending with the noise of the helicopters' machine guns.

Now that it was clear they weren't in imminent danger of being bombed, rather than continuing to flee, which they had neither the resources nor energy to do efficiently or indefinitely, he needed a new plan. A plan that would equalize the power differential, being that there was only one of him and God only knew how many of his enemies or what weapons they carried.

He snagged Vanessa's arm and gestured for her to stop. They watched through a break in the canopy as the helicopters changed course, splitting up to circle over the jungle east of the river in different directions, covering a lot of ground. Neither had flown directly over them yet.

The sound of approaching ground troops grew louder.

He motioned north, toward a steep, rocky section of forest where plants with huge, green fronds grew seemingly from the rocks. This time, he ran point, picking a trail over the loamiest patches of soil to absorb the noise of their movement and obscure their footprints. A small alcove of rock and plants proved an ideal place to hide.

The crashing of troops through the foliage meant they'd burst into view any second. He urged Vanessa in, then crouched in front of her and wrenched a plant out by the roots for camouflage, easy enough to do given the loose, wet soil. He set the plant in front of him and threaded his rifle through the leaves.

As a final effort to camouflage himself, he smeared dirt over his cheeks and nose, turning himself as brown as the land surrounding him.

"Head down, Vanessa. Stay as still as you can," he said under his breath.

Not two minutes later, three men dressed in green camouflage and black ski masks prowled along the trail. One of the men pointed to the rocks near where they were hidden. He followed their stares to a scuff of dirt on the rocks that must've come off one of their shoes. The soldier got on a radio and reported the coordinates.

That gave Diego only one choice.

He squeezed the trigger and fired a succession of shots, felling all three men.

Pulling Vanessa's arm, he stood. "Gotta run again. They'll be coming for us fast now."

Sure enough, the roar of the helicopters grew louder.

Vanessa ran point, leaping over rotting tree trunks and dodging plants. Diego kept his focus jumping all around them. He didn't hear any other troops, just the choppers. Not a good sign.

He had a bad feeling about what was coming next.

"Faster, Vanessa."

"I can't go any faster."

Up ahead, he spied a dark, black gash in a wall of soil. A cave.

It was in the middle of an exposed cliff face, but if his instincts were right about what was going to happen, the cave was their best bet to stay alive.

"In there," he barked.

She twisted her head to see where he was pointing, but the next second, she was airborne, knocked off her feet as an explosion ripped through the jungle.

Diego fell forward, calling her name and eating the ground where he hit down. He spit the dirt out of his mouth and crawled on his belly to her. She was disoriented, so he stood and hauled her up, dragging her to the cave.

The entrance had partially collapsed and bats were streaming out by the hundreds, but he shoved her on the ground just inside.

Whirling around, rifle at the ready, he assessed their immediate danger.

The jungle was on fire, despite the lingering rain showers. Trees lay like fallen soldiers in a circle around the blast point.

The helicopters, green AW139s, were exactly the same look and model as the one that had trailed his helicopter. Could be the Panama army, or could be look-alikes, but whoever it was, they wanted Vanessa and Diego dead bad enough to destroy the protected land of Panama's indigenous people and risk inciting an international incident or starting a civil war between the Nobu and the government.

The only weapons Diego was carrying that were powerful enough to take down the helicopters were grenades. He loaded one into his rifle-mounted launcher and swung himself into view to get a clear shot.

"Diego?"

Vanessa sounded scared.

"Quiet a sec."

The helicopters spotted him and adjusted their course. He moved his finger to the trigger.

"You don't understand," Vanessa said, tugging his elbow. "We're about to be surrounded."

He raised his eyes from his sights and saw the troops, coming through the felled trees and jungle shrubs, close enough to tear them apart with ammo or a single, well-placed grenade.

He swung his rifle at them. "Get ready to move," he told her.

"Where?"

Her question smacked him into awareness like a slap. He glanced side to side, his thoughts turning black.

Damn it. She was right. There was nowhere to run. A ravine to the north, enemy troops to the south and west, and behind them the hill continued into the sky. Up there they'd be a perfect target for the helicopters.

He launched the grenade into the center of the troops and watched them scatter, moving fast to reload so he could strike the approaching helicopters before they were in range to fire their machine guns.

He muscled Vanessa back into the cave and took aim at the closest helicopter.

Then he held his breath and fired. He had to keep fighting. He had no choice, even though part of him already understood that this cave and this jungle was where it was all going to end. For both of them.

Diego could've rappelled down the ravine in a flash. Or he probably could've pulled a Batman and launched a grappling hook across it to use as a zip line to escape, but Vanessa could do neither.

Out of options, out of time, this was it.

She flattened her body against the earthy wall of the cave. "We're trapped."

"Looks like it."

"This is my fault," she breathed.

He pulled the trigger and a loud crack sounded. His eyes narrowed as he followed the direction of the shot. An explosion, far smaller than the last one, roared nearby.

"Not your fault."

Gunfire made her ears ache as bullets sent dirt flying on the cliff face way too close to Diego and the cave.

He returned fire.

Over the sound, she shouted, "You could make it out of here by yourself. I wouldn't blame you for it."

He ignored her. In fact, he probably hated that she'd said that. She hated it, too. She didn't want him to leave her and felt like the worst human being in the world for preferring him to die with her instead of saving himself. Guilt and fear churned in her stomach. She swallowed, fighting the rising bile in her throat. Then she gave it one more halfhearted shot to get him to leave her.

"You have to run," she pleaded, setting her palms and face against his back. "Or you're going to die."

And she hated herself anew for praying he didn't listen to her.

He pulled a grenade from his belt. From what she could see, it was his last. "I know. So let's see how many hostiles I can take with me into hell."

Chapter 13

Diego was going to die for her.

No, not for her, but for the life and career he'd chosen. He was going to die for his principles, exactly as he'd told her he would. How had she ever doubted him?

Yet maybe the real question was what was she going to die for?

It was too much, that question. Evoked a panic in her that she'd never had the chance to stand for something, to live by principles as Diego did.

She tipped her face around the corner to look over his shoulder.

Only one helicopter was in sight. From the opening on the passenger side of the remaining helicopter, a machine gun aimed in their direction. In front of her, Diego sprayed gunfire at the trees.

The ground troops shot back. Diego ducked into the cave and snapped a fresh magazine onto his rifle, his face etched with steely purpose. He didn't once look her way.

Suddenly, nothing seemed as important as atoning for her mistake. "I'm so sorry I didn't trust you."

"Forget about that."

He pivoted into shooting position and took aim at the helicopter. Vanessa reached for the gun he'd tucked in her waistband. She'd only ever shot hunting rifles, years ago, and had never hit anything but trees. The same would probably prove true today, but she refused to stand there idly and watch Diego give his last breaths in defense of her without doing something.

She didn't think he'd noticed that she'd taken it out until he said, "Rest your arm on my shoulder to help your aim."

With an unsure grip, she stood on a rock behind him and propped her forearms on his shoulder, stretching the gun out in front of her. Then she aimed at one of the men wearing a ski mask and squeezed the trigger.

Nothing happened.

"Safety," Diego called over his shoulder.

"What?"

He reached over the gun and flipped a small switch on the far side.

Ah.

The helicopter inched nearer, its machine gun pivoting to correct its aim at them. Diego fired a volley of shots at it and it swerved out of range once more.

Vanessa resumed her aim over his shoulder, but shadows on the rock above the cave caught her attention. Before she could turn to search for the source, a shot rang out from atop the rock face. A line of heads behind a line of rifles appeared along the ridge.

They were surrounded.

Gasping, she took aim at the new intruders.

"Don't shoot," Diego said.

Her gun arm dipped. "What?"

He pulled her into the cave. "I know those rifles. I gave them to the Nobu." She searched his face. His expression was still serious, but lighter. He swapped out his rifle's magazine again and met her gaze. "Took them long enough."

He swung back into firing position and continued his assault.

Eyes wide, she risked a glance up the hill. Dark complexions, dark hair and shirtless, the men on the ridge certainly had the look of Panama's indigenous people.

A whooping war cry made her flinch. Then the Nobu started shooting.

In the jungle, men fell at a fast rate. More Nobu warriors appeared along the ravine, herding the enemy front and center, lining them up for the warriors on the ridge to cut them down. It was a bloodbath. Vanessa burrowed her face into Diego's shirt, the images of death and violence too stomach-turning to watch.

Diego continued to fire. She felt the power of the rifle through his back, as hope for their survival washed through her for the first time since the buzz of the helicopters first broke the peace of the jungle.

At the sound of movement behind her, she raised her eyes. The Nobu warriors descended the hill, continuing to fire into the trees. But from what Vanessa could tell, no one was returning their fire anymore. Still, the warriors poured into the jungle, amid the smoldering trees and smoke.

Diego stopped shooting but kept his rifle poised to fire as the helicopter rotated south. It paused midturn and the pilot sneered at them through two curtains of chin-length brown hair.

"Nico Chiara," Diego growled.

He looked down the sights of his rifle, but before he could get a shot off, the chopper lifted and flew away.

The Nobu trickled out of the forest in twos and threes, relaxed in a way that told her they'd slaughtered every intruder and the danger had passed.

She wrapped her arms around Diego's ribs and took a deep breath, letting her cheek rest between his shoulder blades.

He stroked her arm. "I let you down."

He sounded so tormented, she tightened her hug. "You don't look dead to me," she said, echoing his words from the day before.

His only response was a derisive huff.

She walked around to face him and stretched her arms out wide, attempting to look as tough and confident as he had while the bag of her work clothes burned in the street. "The fact that you're standing in the middle of this God-forsaken jungle with me means you have a perfect record when it comes to protecting people."

He shifted his gaze to her, looking unconvinced.

She swept a smear of dirt from his cheek. "You were the one who provided the Nobu with guns and built your Leroy in their jungle as an added layer of protection. What happened just now, it was part of a plan you spent years designing—and it worked. You kept saying one of these days I'd figure out that you knew what you were doing." She nodded. "Consider me schooled in the matter."

His features softened. His shoulders eased down. "Let's go thank the Nobu."

* * *

The Nobu spoke their own language, defiantly refusing to add a single word of Spanish to their lexicon, but as best he could given the language barrier, Diego offered the Nobu warriors his gratitude for coming to their aid. Smiling, he bowed and gestured his thanks. Shirtless and barefoot and dressed in ill-fitting cotton slacks of various colors, the warriors returned his smile and petted their weapons, a gesture Diego interpreted as "Just returning the favor."

While Vanessa looked on, he sought out the leader and offered him the gun from his ankle holster along with a spare magazine.

The warrior, dressed as his soldiers were but with swipes of blue paint on his cheeks and arms, accepted the gift and launched into emphatic chatter. He gestured northeast in the direction of the river, then to Diego's snake-bitten arm. He'd forgotten about that injury. It looked puffy and, now that he was thinking about it, hurt like hell. He let his rifle hang loosely by its strap and shook out his arm, trying to loosen the tight, swollen flesh.

It soon became clear that the leader and his men wanted Diego and Vanessa to join them. If it had only been him, Diego wouldn't have gone because his presence made their people a target for the Chiaras. But the opportunity to have Vanessa guarded by a village of armed warriors was an offer he couldn't refuse.

They trod a well-worn path to the river, buffered on all sides by the Nobu.

Diego slung his left arm around Vanessa's shoulders and tugged her close to his side as they walked, establishing his claim on her. Maybe that was a sexist way to think, but most of the world still worked that way, especially pockets of people as far removed from the influence of first-world modernism as the Nobu were.

Diego hadn't spent much time around the tribe's village, so he didn't have an accurate picture of their culture's treatment of women, but he wasn't taking any chances. Luckily, it was a universal truth that soldiers didn't mess with another soldier's woman. And though the Nobu probably already figured it out, it was critical that they understood in no uncertain terms that she was off-limits to them in every way.

They were escorted to one of a series of flat boats lining the bank of the Rio Nobu. For the hour it took the Nobu to paddle south, Diego was happy to let someone else work while he caught his breath and processed the truth that he and Vanessa were still alive and unharmed.

The village sprawled over a grassy lowland along the east bank of the Rio Nobu and filled the air above it with the inviting scent of cooking fires and freshly chopped wood. Houses here were painted white or blue to combat rot and termites and built on stilts to weather the frequent floods that plagued the area, a strategy Diego used in designing his Leroy cabin.

He and Vanessa were marched through the center of the village, dodging chickens, stray dogs and curious children. Their mothers, equally curious, stared up from their chores or babies while Diego and Vanessa passed.

Though the Nobu were one of the most isolated native peoples in Panama, signs of Western influence were still present in the occasional pair of sneakers, cotton T-shirts and modern tools. Some Diego recognized as gifts he'd thrown in along with the weapons. It was gratifying to see them put to good use.

They were directed to the same thatch-roofed blue hut on the edge of the village that Diego had stayed in during his first visit to the tribe ten years ago. His first exchange of artillery for access and safe passage through their land. The hut sat two meters off the ground and was walled only waist-high, with mosquito netting covering the opening all the way around.

Shortly after the warriors deposited them in the hut, a tribal woman dressed in a colorful skirt and woven halter top appeared. Smiling broadly, she held a bowl he soon discovered was a poultice for his snake bite.

He sat on a long bench along the wall and pulled his shirt off to let her tend him. Vanessa hovered nearby, looking curious and grateful for the help. The woman then smoothed the medicine over the explosion rash on his neck. He probably looked like he'd gotten in a mud fight, but all that mattered was his arm felt markedly better.

Soon after the medicine woman left, a second woman arrived with a plate of rice and plantains. Vanessa accepted the food graciously and they both dug in.

Finally, as twilight descended on the village, they were alone in the hut. Diego checked the disposable cell phone. He had a few bars of service and had missed thirty-three calls. Time to touch base with Ryan.

"What the hell," Ryan said by way of a greeting. "I've been out of my mind. We all have. Are you okay?"

"Yeah. Vanessa is, too, but we almost weren't." He gave Ryan an abbreviated version of the truth.

Ryan sighed. "Anyone could've intercepted that emergency call she made."

For reasons Diego didn't understand, Ryan's comment triggered an illogical defensiveness of Vanessa's choice. "She did what she had to do, okay? If she hadn't made that call, I would've died and left her in the middle of freakin' nowhere by herself."

"I know she didn't have a choice. I get it. Doesn't make it suck any less."

"True. But we're living large now at one of the Nobu villages, and even if the hostiles get it in their heads to take a second strike at us, there's no way they'd risk going to war with the tribe. Vanessa and I will be safe for tonight."

"Good to hear."

His eyes stayed on Vanessa, futilely trying to be subtle while listening to the conversation as she washed in the water basin. "Did everyone in the crew join up already?"

"Just about," Ryan said. "Rory's not due in until later tonight."

"We have a new pick-up point, but the road's a mess and there's no reason for you to make the drive in the dark. If you're here tomorrow morning, that gives us twenty-four hours to stop the sub sale."

"And put an end to the Chiara brothers," Ryan added.

The man had a one-track mind. "We'll see what Vanessa and Alicia can do when they put their heads together."

He gave Ryan directions, along with his assurances that he'd do his best to convince the Nobu not to attack their van. At least he and Vanessa had the good fortune of being brought to the Nobu's southernmost camp, which was one of two that had recently been outfitted with a crude dirt road.

After the call ended, he walked to the Nobu warrior stationed as their guardian at the edge of the walking path leading to their hut. Using gestures and crude pictures drawn in the dirt with his finger, he did his best to explain that his crew would be there with the morning sun and would he and his fellow warriors please refrain from blowing them up.

When Diego returned to the hut, Vanessa was done at the basin, so he took her place. He dunked his hands, then scrubbed them over his face and through his hair. He'd killed again today, but he'd have to wait to get right with himself until Vanessa fell asleep. He could feel her eyes on his back and figured she was waiting for him to finish everything he needed to do so she could talk her way through processing the day's events.

Unlike yesterday, the prospect of sitting and chatting with her sounded like the best idea he'd heard in a long time. She could talk all she needed to as long as he could pull her near and let his hands do some PG-rated exploration. She might even get all soft and cuddly like she had before.

If fact, he really hoped she would. It'd been a long pounding of a day. All he wanted to do was get close to Vanessa and stay that way for the rest of the night.

When he turned to reach for a drying cloth, he caught her in the act of watching him. She smiled, not attempting to hide her bold appraisal. His eyes holding hers, his body tight with anticipation, he tossed the cloth aside and walked to her.

Chapter 14

The sunset over the Nobu village lit the sky with vibrant reds and oranges, but Vanessa couldn't tear her eyes away from Diego as he washed at the bowl of water. And not only because of how magnificent he looked without his shirt on, which he most certainly did, despite the mudlike medicine coating his arm and neck.

She couldn't stop staring at him because he'd almost died that day, more than once. From a venomous snake bite, anaphylactic shock and then at the hands of vicious criminals. He'd almost slipped through her fingers like so many other people she'd cared about. And it scared her all over again to realize how important he was becoming to her.

She already felt herself falling in love with him and knew it would be easy to fall the rest of the way. They were opposite in so many ways, but it was the kind of difference that was balancing—her softness with his steel, his instinct and her logic. He was teaching her by example to have courage in the face of fear, and she badly wanted to help him give voice to his grief and understand it was all right to feel pain.

Yet even if he felt the same way, even if he wanted her back, she did not want the kind of life she'd lead with him. She'd always come second to his career and would be alone all the time, like she had been as a child during football season when her dad was too busy to notice her. But this would be so much worse.

Although she'd finally internalized today that he'd never purposefully abandon her, the hard, cold fact was that his job of protecting people with his life wasn't limited to Vanessa. Once she was safe, he'd move on to new assets and new life-threatening dangers. The scars on his back were a vivid testimony to the kind of risks he undertook on a regular basis. She'd die a little every day knowing he was off somewhere putting himself in harm's way, never knowing when or if she'd see him again.

Sometimes being courageous meant saying no to something that wasn't good for her. It meant loving herself enough to walk away from a situation that would hurt her. She hadn't had the strength of character to do that in the past. This time, though, she was going to take a stand—for herself.

When Diego finished at the wash basin, he lit a lamp and walked her way. He sat next to her on the bench and pilfered a bite of food off the plate she'd set aside. "You enjoying your jungle shanty tour yet?"

Picking at the mosquito netting that lined the structure's windows, she attempted a smile. "Parts of it, absolutely. But it's a little too adventurous for my taste. Were the Chiara brothers behind the attack today?"

He nodded. "I recognized one of the Chiaras in the helicopter. Nico. He's the youngest. Leo is the oldest and Vincenzo—Enzo is what he goes by—he's the middle brother. Heartless bastards, every one of them. My crew's been tracking them for going on ten years."

"Then I hope I can get you the information to help you catch them."

"Me, too."

"What's going to happen after I pinpoint the account being used for the Chiaras' submarine sale?"

"I pass that information on to my boss, Thomas Dreyer, then escort you into protective custody or help you get lost somewhere in the world, if you'd prefer. All you have to do is tell me what you want and I'll make it happen."

"I'd like to go into protective custody," she said. "I want to be there to testify against the bank and the Chiara brothers when that day comes." She might even change her identity, as Diego had.

Diego dipped his head in a slow nod. "That'll go a long way toward helping the Feds put the Chiaras behind bars along with anyone else who's been helping them."

After a brief mental debate, she took the plunge on a question she'd been chewing on since the night before. "You don't have to tell me if you can't, but I've been curious. How did you come up with the name Diego Santero?"

He lounged back against the wall, a hand propped behind his head. "Diego was the name of my great-grandfather on my mother's side. One of my great-aunts, when she got dementia, started calling me Diego because I guess I look like him. Santero was one of my nicknames when I was a SEAL. That got started when we were training in Puerto Rico. One of the guys showed up for breakfast with a Santeria doll. Santeria is like Puerto Rican voodoo."

"Let me guess—you were the only SEAL there of Puerto Rican heritage."

"Exactly. They started razzing me about using Santeria magic to disappear into the jungle because I was so good at it. A santero is a Santeria priest."

"I like that story."

"I haven't thought about it in ages. I'd forgotten what a fun time that was." He took her hand. "Ask me something else."

He probably hadn't intended for that to be a loaded question, but she still felt like she was navigating a minefield. She didn't want to ask the wrong thing and watch the window to his soul slam shut. It would be too stark a reminder that he'd never fully share himself with her. Better to stick with the safe questions. "What's your favorite food?"

"My mom's *arroz con gandules*." At her questioning look, he added, "Rice, beans, pork and peppers mixed with this Puerto Rican sauce called *sofrito*. It's out of this world. She makes it for me every time I visit. What about you?"

"Papaya."

"Just papaya?"

She nodded. "I'd never had it until I moved to Panama. There was a vendor at the outdoor market near my apartment who saved me the best papaya every Tuesday. I can't get enough of it. I think when I'm back in the States it'll be nice to eat papaya and think of my years in Panama. I'll miss this place."

"Why'd you move to Panama?" he asked.

"My best friend, Jordan, followed a guy here, and I

followed her. She's like my family and I couldn't stand the idea of being…" She swallowed.

He hummed deep in his throat, a sound she had no idea how to interpret, but then he slid his shoulder over until it touched hers. "You didn't want to be alone."

The fear of being without Jordan, without anyone, had been suffocating. Even the four-month wait after Jordan had left Nebraska, before Vanessa had secured a job in Panama, had devastated her.

And her life was about to come full circle. Back in the States, alone.

But she was determined that this time around was going to be different. This time, she was going to be all right on her own. She had a higher purpose now, a plan for herself that was totally self-generated and self-sufficient. One that didn't involve chasing loved ones who were slipping away from her. One that didn't involve fear.

She nestled into Diego's shoulder, not because she was feeling weak or scared, but to be inspired by his strength and let it flow into her. Thanks to his example, she was more and more ready to stand on her own two feet, brave and sure.

She still had a small, private smile on her lips when he asked, "You said Jordan's like your family, but what about your dad? It was just the two of you while you were growing up, right? So then, you and he must be close."

Her smile faded. "We were never close. My dad's career as a football coach had him working most nights and weekends. My house was so lonely and quiet. I hung around school or the library or friends' houses all the time to avoid being in the empty house by myself."

"You mentioned that he moved to California to work

at UCLA. I'm assuming that happened after you moved to Jersey for college?"

"No. My senior year of high school. I refused to go with him because I knew what would happen. I'd be alone in a brand-new empty house, but this time with no friends to take my mind off it. Jordan's parents took me in. I went to visit my dad a few times, and he came to visit me. My freshman year of college he remarried and his new wife got pregnant. They didn't have room for me after that. Turned my bedroom at his new house into a nursery."

"Ouch. Then again, I never had my own bedroom. Shared one with both my brothers."

"I always wanted a brother or sister."

"So then you got one when your dad remarried. That's good, right?"

"They had three kids, actually. But I don't think of them as half siblings. Not really."

He released her hand and plopped his arm across her shoulders, tugging her close. "Help me out here. I'm scrounging for a silver lining."

She huffed and allowed a bit of sarcasm to seep into her tone. "Good luck with that."

"Didn't that make you happy, not to be lonely anymore? To have a family? I bet holidays were more fun than ever. In my family, the holidays are manic. My parents' house is so stuffed full of people on Christmas that my sister's husband parks their trailer on my parents' lawn."

She jumped on the chance to refocus the conversation on him, away from her sorrow. "You go home for Christmas?"

"I try to. Missed it four years in a row, though. One

year soon, the bottom-feeders of the world need to cool it in December so I can sneak to Jersey for the day."

The more they concentrated on his life, the easier it got for her to shed the melancholy that had settled over her while talking about her family history. Desperate to keep him talking, and without thinking it through, she asked, "Have you ever been married or engaged?"

He snorted. "Not even close. Longest relationship I've had was in high school. When 9/11 happened, I'd been dating some girl in San Diego for a few months, but when I joined ICE I gave up everything—my apartment, my car, my girlfriend. 'Eye of the Tiger' and all that stuff. What about you?"

Yikes. They were back to her, and he was asking about the worst part of her life. Worse than the day her dad had come home and told her about the UCLA job. She hated talking about this particular topic, about Dave, enough that she almost lied. But that didn't feel right to do with Diego. "Engaged," she said quietly.

His arms and back went rigid. "You don't say."

She nodded, hoping that'd be enough. Time for a redirect. "How long did you live in San Diego?"

"Oh, nuh-uh. You're not weaseling out of this one. Spill it. What happened? Who was the idiot who let you get away?"

No such luck. Sighing, she pulled away from him and sat forward, rubbing her legs. "It was a few years ago. Dave was an investment banker at RioBank. At the time, I thought I loved him, but I didn't have a clue what I was doing. I know better now what real love is like, and that wasn't it. We dated for two years. When the bank transferred him to Brazil, I pressured him to get engaged."

She rolled her eyes, her face flushing with residual

embarrassment she still couldn't shake after all this time. "So stupid, I know. I thought if we were engaged it'd help me hang on to him after he left Panama. Immediately, I put in for a transfer within RioBank so I could follow him. But while I waited for the transfer to go through, I decided to surprise him with a visit."

He twisted, hitching his knee on the bench to look at her, and held up a finger as a gesture of caution. "Do not tell me what I think you're about to or I swear to God, I'm going to fly to Brazil and go all black ops on this guy for cheating on you."

His indignation on her behalf was sweet and reminded her of the long-winded rants Jordan indulged in for months to come after the fact. She snared his hand out of midair and twined their fingers. "He didn't cheat on me, or at least, if he did I never found out. What happened was I got there and took a cab to the address he'd given me, but it was vacant. He wouldn't answer his phone, and it was getting late, so I had to get a hotel room and wait at his work in the morning. That was pretty humiliating."

"Did he ever show up at work?"

"Yes." She swallowed. The memory still hurt. "He said he forgot to tell me the apartment hadn't worked out and that he'd moved in with two other guys. I was too shocked to be mad right away. I said, 'But we're getting married. We can't live with roommates.' And he said, 'What's the rush? We don't have to live together right away.'"

"Like I said, an idiot...."

She flashed her eyes his way, but she was too deep into the memory to quit. "I begged a little. It wasn't good. And then he said maybe the engagement was a mistake. Maybe we needed to take a break. I remember standing there in his office, looking at a beetle crawling on the outside of the window, feeling about as insignificant as it was. He asked for the ring back and I set it on his desk and walked away. At least I still had time to withdraw my transfer request at the bank."

She stared out at the darkness, fiddling with the hem of her shirt, feeling tiny—thin and fragile and so much smaller than she wanted to be, than she'd vowed to be from this point forward.

Diego closed the space between them and wrapped his arms around her. "I'm not big on jumping to conclusions about people I've never met, but I kind of hate your dad and Dipstick Dave."

The fitting moniker hit her straight in the funny bone. "Jordan would approve of that nickname. She never liked him."

Diego couldn't believe the way laughing erased the pain from Vanessa's features and made her seem stronger from the inside out. At least he was starting to get a picture of why she had so many hang-ups about trusting him to stick around. For about the millionth time since he'd met her, he wished he were better at saying the right thing. Would've been nice if he could've told her something comforting.

Screw it, he thought, scooping her up and hauling her onto his lap. "So you remember earlier, how you were kissing me?"

She smiled at him, and, oh, man, it did a number on him, the way it reached all the way to her eyes and turned the skin beneath her freckles pink. Reminded him of how she looked after they'd kissed that afternoon and got him wondering all sorts of dirty things, like how she'd look after a night spent in his bed.

"We were interrupted by a snake," she said.

"And I told you we had to stop kissing because we had a long way to hike before nightfall, so we had to keep moving?"

She toyed with the strap of his shoulder holster. "I remember that, too. And then you went into anaphylactic shock."

"Okay, so I'm not in shock anymore, and nobody's trying to kill us at the moment, and we're done with hiking for the day. Frankly, there's nothing left to do. I wonder how we could pass the time until we're tired?"

She was still smiling, but her eyes turned hungry.

He captured her jaw in his hand and lowered his lips to hers. With a breathy little moan, she brought her leg across his body to straddle his hips, melting into him, surrounding him with all her soft curves and sweetness.

His hands explored the shape of her while his tongue dipped inside her mouth with slow, deep strokes. He drank in the details of her like a starving man, and in some ways, he probably was. This easy, tender intimacy was something he never knew he needed. But now that he was experiencing it, he couldn't imagine going the rest of his life without Vanessa to touch and kiss and talk to. To temper the vileness of his job with the peace and pleasure of holding her in his arms.

Nothing he'd experienced with other women had compared.

In the past, the superficial, temporary nature of the relationships he'd shared with his bedmates never entirely left his mind, and it never bothered him in the least. But with Vanessa, there wasn't anything he wanted to forget more than the responsibilities that prevented him from being the man she deserved. From taking her hand and hanging on to it forever.

But forget his responsibilities, he could not. Their time together was fleeting at best. As soon as she no longer needed his protection, he'd move on and so would she. She had to know that, too, but all they'd done was talk around it. She hadn't brought it up directly. Maybe she was working as hard as he was to ignore the truth that soon they'd be saying goodbye.

He must have had some kind of physical reaction to his wayward, unpleasant thoughts because she ended the kiss. "Does your snake bite hurt?"

"Not at all. I can't even feel it."

She stroked his cheek, her eyes searching his face. "Then what's wrong?"

"Nothing. I was thinking about how I almost never met you. I fought hard against taking this assignment because I was insulted by how easy a job it looked like it was."

"You mean, being a chauffeur?"

"Yeah. How am I doing with that, by the way?" He squeezed her backside. "Am I chauffeuring you okay?"

She splayed her hands over his chest, a wicked gleam in her eye. "You're chauffeuring the hell out of me."

It was his turn to laugh. Couldn't have said it better himself. Threading his fingers through her hair, he coaxed her face nearer. "Come here, you. I wasn't done kissing you yet."

She opened for him, kissing him back, demanding it harder this time. No problem, he could do that, too.

He kissed her so long it left him dizzy. Must be all that blood rushing away from his brain, he figured, but eventually he regained the willpower to stop, using the excuse that his arm was starting to ache.

The truth was, though, that if he ever took it further with Vanessa, if he ever had the chance to lay her back and make love to her like he was crazy with need to, it wasn't going to be in the middle of the jungle under mosquito netting after he'd gone two long days without a shower. She was worth so much more than that.

She slept with her head on his lap again and this time, he wasn't shy about putting his hands on her. He rested his back against the wall of the hut and kept his mind sharp until the sky lightened by puzzling out a way he could prevent Vanessa from getting caught up in the dangerous world he lived in, yet keep her in his life.

It was an impossible fantasy, but the part of his brain that loved solving problems wasn't ready give up strategizing a way to guarantee she'd never feel lonely again.

An hour before the sun crested over the trees, the sound of a car engine broke the relative silence of the waking village. Good. Hopefully it meant the Nobu let his crew pass into their territory peacefully. He ran his hand along Vanessa's side to rouse her.

She rolled to her back and smiled at him with sleepy eyes.

He smoothed a strand of hair away from her face. "Morning, sleepyhead. I hear my crew's car getting close. Time to get up."

She touched his shirt. "I'm going to miss being alone with you."

He folded over and kissed her, not a fireworks kind of kiss, but the kind he hoped told her how much she'd come to mean to him. "Me, too."

A boxy, brown van rattled up in front of the hut, Ryan at the wheel. A parade of Nobu tribesmen, women and children jogged alongside and behind the van, curious and smiling, probably thrilled for the diversion from their morning chores.

Vanessa stood and stretched her arms up. "That's what your crew drives? Guess the Batmobile wasn't available, eh?"

He pushed up from the seat and shook out his legs, chewing the inside of his cheek to fight a grin. "Around these parts, we call a van like that camouflage."

She smiled. He nodded toward the stairs. "Come on. Time for you to meet my crew."

Ignoring the crowd of Nobu who watched them like they were the day's entertainment, he introduced each agent as they piled out of the van. Ryan first, then Alicia and Rory.

John was the last man out, and when he zeroed in on Vanessa, he whistled, strutting forward. "Vanessa Crosby, it is a pleasure to finally meet you. And, may I say, you're even prettier than your pictures."

Then he gave her body a brash, intentional once-over.

A potent, primal emotion Diego didn't take the time to name struck him like lightning. Before he knew what he was doing, he'd sprung forward, curling his hand into a fist.

Chapter 15

Scattered, volatile anger tore through Diego's system like the explosion of a dirty bomb.

He stormed up to John, shoving him in the chest until he back-stepped behind a cluster of trees, out of sight and earshot from Vanessa. In his periphery, he saw Ryan, Rory and a whole slew of tribesmen had followed. He knew Ryan would stop him from doing anything too stupid, but he hoped he'd get to make the point he needed to before Ryan stepped in.

"What's wrong with you?" John said.

Diego twisted John's shirt in his fist, the welling of emotion so hot it boiled inside him. "The woman I'm about to introduce you to? She matters. A lot. You don't get to talk to her like that and you don't get to look at her like that, understand?"

John held his ground. "Who, Crosby? I was just being friendly. She's had a tough couple days and a little harmless flirtation might make her feel better." He smoothed a hand over his shirt. "Relax, man. I'm in this mission as deep as you are."

Not even close, pal.

He got in John's face. "If you so much as breathe wrong in her direction, you don't want to know the wrath I'll bring down on you."

Rory huffed and stood with John. "Overreact much? The Diego I know would never threaten one of his crew members. And over an asset? Makes me wonder exactly what happened in that jungle between you and the broad."

The way he said it crawled right under Diego's skin. Like he was picturing Vanessa doing something cheap and nasty. He cracked his knuckles, ready to brawl. The whispered commentary of the Nobu cranked up to an excited racket. They knew someone was about to get a beat down. "Got something you want to ask me to my face, Rory? I dare you."

Ryan sauntered into view, his expression blank, taking it all in. Not many things in this world rattled Ryan. "She's watching," he said just loud enough to be heard over the noisy Nobu.

As if on cue, he heard "Diego?" from somewhere behind him.

He inhaled deeply, fighting to douse the flare of anger still burning bright in his veins, and turned toward her. Alicia stood next to her, frowning, but Vanessa wore the same look of calm as Ryan.

She walked into their circle, Alicia following, and took in John's wrinkled shirt and Diego's clenched fists. He flexed his hands and shifted, putting her behind him. Holding himself as a shield between her and his crew.

It wasn't until he'd moved that he realized the significance of what he'd done. Nothing ever came between him and his crew. But it hit him in that moment that if it came to a choice between Vanessa and the four members of his team, he'd choose her.

My God.

He'd never felt like that before about a woman—a protectiveness that was levels beyond professional, levels beyond anything but his own driving need to make sure she was safe at all costs from anything or anyone coming at her, even his closest friends.

Maybe his crew realized it at the same time he did because Alicia stepped back, her eyes wide. Rory and John exchanged a look of concern. Only Ryan seemed unfazed. He met Diego's goading, violent stare and gave him a subtle nod of understanding that eased the fight in Diego's heart just enough for him to take a breath and relax his posture. Ryan's loyalty stood, as it always had, with Diego.

He twisted his chin over his shoulder toward Vanessa. "We were on our way back," he said lamely.

She nodded. "Alicia got the first aid kit out. I need to take a look at that snake bite."

She didn't wait but pivoted on her heel and headed back to the van.

Diego shot John and Rory a final warning look, then strode after Vanessa.

Vanessa wasn't stupid. She knew Diego had been fighting with his crew member John—as he was introduced to her after they emerged from the trees. Hard to miss the obvious when he bullied the man out of sight. Diego's body had vibrated with fury that he worked futilely to mask.

When her dad's football players started posturing

and fighting, her dad used to wave it off and say, "Don't worry about it. All that testosterone has to go somewhere." She wasn't sure what John had done wrong, and she didn't care. Diego's snake bite had swollen again during the night, and all she could think about was getting him the medical treatment he needed.

Alicia didn't think it would hurt to administer more CroFab, as long as they preempted it with antihistamines and had an EpiPen standing by. When Vanessa suggested they take him to the hospital, Alicia explained that was out of the question for a lot of reasons, the most ardent being that Diego would refuse and then they'd be back to square one.

She and Alicia had laid out the kit and the CroFab on the floor of the van just inside the open door. Diego eyed the setup and cringed. "We don't have time for that right now. I'm fine. I told you, I don't feel—"

"I know you don't feel pain." Vanessa didn't consider herself much of a taskmaster, but she wasn't going to take no for an answer. She took a vial of the CroFab in hand. "But too bad, because you're going to get an injection of antivenom or I'm not getting in the van."

The tribespeople chattered, their smiling faces showing their delight at the exchange. But she didn't care who was watching, not with Diego's health at stake.

He rolled his tongue along the inside of his lip, then gave her a look of intimidation that had probably made many a soldier quake in his boots over the years. "You don't get in the van, I'm throwing you in, you hear me? You want to play dirty like that, you don't know what you're up against." His Jersey accent ramped up, sending a shot of pure lust right to the center of her. Inappropriate timing for sure, but she couldn't help it.

She got nose-to-nose with him and tried out an intimidating stare of her own. "I don't care how many guns and knives you've got stashed in your cargo pants, soldier, you don't scare me." She pointed to the floor of the van. "Sit down and be quiet."

His expression was fierce. The lust that had kicked to life along with his accent started spreading to all the places that counted. Probably, it wasn't the best idea to lay a big, wet kiss on him in front of his crew, but she was headed down that road if he kept up his churlishness. It was the only way she knew how to strip away his macho defenses and access that gooey center she loved.

A spark of understanding flashed across his features. "Oh, no. No, no, no." He held his hands out in front of him like a buffer. His eyes were wide and panicky and shifted to his crew, then back to her again. "I see that look on your face. Don't you dare. Not here."

Guess she was right about it not being a wise idea to kiss him in front of his subordinates. There was a name for knowledge like that—leverage.

Gazing longingly at his mouth, she hummed and tugged her lower lip with her teeth.

"Vanessa, I'm warning you."

She tore her eyes from his lips and drilled him with a look of sharp determination. "Then you'd better sit and let Alicia and me tend to that wound, pronto."

She pressed on his shoulder and he submitted, sitting in the open side doorway of the van with a sullen "Fine. Have it your way."

While Alicia prepared Diego's arm, Vanessa doled out antihistamine, but Diego was looking past her. She followed his gaze. Ryan, Rory and John were staring, dumbfounded, with Rory and John sporting amused grins. Behind them, the Nobu were laughing.

"Any of you say one word," Diego said in a menacing voice, "I'm going to kill you."

Vanessa rolled her eyes. Ugh, men. How could he care about looking tough in front of his crew when he obviously needed medical attention?

Once Alicia administered the doses, Diego scowled at Vanessa. "Satisfied?"

"Almost." She tucked an EpiPen in a leg pocket of his pants, then helped Alicia repack the aid kit. "You haven't gotten a wink of sleep in days. Are you planning to nap in the van?"

"I might be."

"You'd better."

"Will you stop with the third degree and get in already?" He waved his hand toward the van door in invitation.

She pretended to consider the question. "Yes. I do believe I will."

In the van, she watched Diego bid farewell to one of the senior Nobu who'd been watching them, a stout man Vanessa remembered from the previous day's battle. Surrounded by his crew and a cluster of tribespeople, Diego presented the leader with his rifle and spare magazines, much like he had with his handgun from the day before. Then he and his crew nodded in gratitude before turning to the van.

John took the wheel with Rory riding shotgun. Alicia sat next to Vanessa into the forward-facing bench seat, leaving Diego and Ryan to take the backward facing bench that abutted the driver's seat.

After several long minutes of awkward silence, Rory cleared his throat. "Okay, fine, I'll ask since you're both being so quiet. How did you two end up in the middle of Nobu territory? They hate outsiders."

"En route to my Leroy we crashed a helicopter, then hiked for two days. When we got attacked by Chiara operatives, we found out the Nobu don't take kindly to battles being waged on their land. They helped us escape the hostiles and took us in."

John darted a quick look over his shoulder. "Good thing you had Vanessa with you or they might have turned you into Swiss cheese along with the Chiaras for trespassing," John said. "The Nobu have rules against hurting women, I've heard."

"Yeah, that must be it." Diego met her gaze and winked.

"Whatever the reason," Alicia said, "you're lucky you made it out safely."

"Where are we headed?" Vanessa asked.

"We have orders about a new ICE safe house location to deliver you to immediately." Alicia smiled at Vanessa. "I'm sure Diego debriefed you."

Her gaze dropped to her hands as her pulse picked up speed. No, he most certainly had not.

"Give it a rest, will you, Alicia?" Diego said, sounding annoyed. His boot tapped the side of Vanessa's shoe. "I didn't mention it to you because I knew that wasn't the way it was going to go down. Nothing's happening until I have a chance to assess the situation properly."

They'd discussed this on the phone, he and his crew, yet he hadn't filled her in. Why not? Probably because he thought she'd fly off the handle given her abandonment issues.

Time to prove to him she'd changed from the meek, fearful woman she'd been that first day. She was going to face her future, however out of her control it was, with her chin held high, her newly acquired bravery firmly in place. Even if she didn't trust herself to keep a neutral expression if she looked at Diego.

She attempted to return Alicia's smile instead. "These people you have orders to deliver me to, they're your bosses, right? So I'm guessing that going against their direct order would get you all in trouble?"

Diego leaned forward. She glanced at his hands folded between his knees but still couldn't muster the bravado to meet his gaze.

"Don't go filling your head with things that aren't your problem." He patted the seat next to him. "Come here."

And now he was patronizing her, like she was a child that needed talking to. But the truth was she'd brought it on herself with her constant need for reassurance. She'd made the man sit with her while she slept, for pity's sake.

"Here is good. I'm fine. Really." She forced her eyes to his face in order to prove it to him. "And it *is* my problem. You and your crew saved my life and I'm not going to repay you by getting you in trouble with your jobs. It's okay to deliver me to the new safe house like you're supposed to. I bet ICE is going to be extra cautious this time not to leak the location, so there's no reason not to comply with your boss's orders."

"Move it, Phoenix." Diego just about tossed Alicia out of the way. Taking her place, he crooked his knee on the seat and cupped Vanessa's chin in his hand.

"Do you think I spent the last three days keeping you safe just to deliver you somewhere and say 'See ya and good luck'?"

"That's what would happen if you were to escort me straight to WitSec, so I don't see how this is any different. I'll be on my own eventually, so it might as well be now."

Something flickered in his eyes and tightened his jaw. Frustration, if she had to name it. As though he hated knowing what she said was true. That made two of them, but hating the facts didn't change them.

She wrenched her chin from his hand and looked at John, ignoring Alicia's, Ryan's and Rory's stares. "John, go ahead and deliver me to ICE's new safe house." The words left her breathless and her heart aching so bad she couldn't believe it was still beating. She was determined to face her future with her chin held high, but that didn't mean it wouldn't hurt like hell.

"John only takes orders from me." The calm authority in Diego's tone left no room for challenge. He took her hand in his. "You're not going anywhere, so relax."

Relax? Maybe that would've been possible if they were alone and she could kiss him to forget her worries, but with so many eyes on her and so many people's lives and jobs at stake, relaxing was out of the question.

Still, she attempted a deep, calming inhale and nodded.

Diego squeezed her hand, then released it and looked across the seats to Ryan and Alicia. "I told you guys to figure out a place for Vanessa to work, so where's it going to be? Somebody give me some answers I'm gonna like because Vanessa's been harassing me for days about getting some sleep and I'm about ready to take her up on the suggestion."

Despite everything, she felt the slightest tug of a smile on her lips. "I've hardly been harassing you."

He darted an "Oh, please" look at her.

Alicia raised an index finger topped with an acrylic French-tip nail. "How about my Leroy?"

Diego's brow wrinkled. "Why would you give up the location like that?"

"It makes the most sense," Alicia said. "I already have the computer equipment Vanessa and I would need to hack in to RioBank, along with a change of clothes for Vanessa and a working shower."

Geez, that sounded good. The last real shower she'd taken had been Thursday night. She didn't exactly have a vote but decided to put her two cents in anyway. "That would be divine."

"Where's this Leroy?" Diego asked.

"Near the Costa Rica border. John knows the way," Alicia said.

Rory twisted in his chair. "How does John know the way? You two have something going on we need to discuss?"

John kept his eyes on the road, quiet, but Alicia snickered. "In his dreams. No, he knows because I'd already decided to look into a new Leroy, so I asked him to pick me up there on the way to this rendezvous."

"Sounds great to me. Let's do it," Diego said.

"Hang on, everyone, because the road's about to get bumpy," John called. He waved a cassette tape. "Now that we've got that all settled, it's time for some tunes."

Everyone groaned. Vanessa did, too. She didn't see how it could get any bumpier. In fact, the strip of packed dirt they were bouncing over could barely be called a road. Already she'd gone airborne several times and had to brace her legs wide to keep from crashing into Diego.

The opening notes of Michael Jackson's "Bad" sounded from the stereo.

"At least he didn't start with 'Man in the Mirror,'" Diego called to Vanessa over the music. "I've heard that song so many times it's like the soundtrack to my nightmares."

Alicia and Rory chuckled. Even Ryan looked like he found it funny, but it was hard to tell.

Of all Diego's crew members, she was having the most trouble putting her finger on who he was. He'd barely said a word, and his smiles and facial expressions were of the blink-and-you'll-miss-it variety. Compared to Diego's caged-animal energy, Ryan was the black ops equivalent of a statue. But she'd seen him in action in the alley behind her apartment. She'd watched him shoot to kill and knew he was as skilled and lethal as the rest of them.

Unbelievably, the rattle-bounce got worse, as John had warned. Diego's head hit the ceiling once, much to the delight of Alicia and Rory.

Vanessa gripped the armrest more firmly so she wouldn't go flying. "I take it he plays Michael Jackson a lot?"

"How do you think he got the call name Thriller?" Diego asked.

The volume dropped. "I'm telling you, Vanessa," John called over his shoulder, "most people think love is the international language, but they're wrong. Michael Jackson's what it's all about. In fact, this album saved my life ten years ago in the Czech Republic."

Alicia rolled her eyes.

Diego shook his head. "Hell, no. I'd rather listen to 'Heal the World' on repeat than hear that story one more time. Vanessa and I've been through the ringer, so how about you do me a favor and save it for after I'm asleep?"

"You got it, boss. Stay tuned, Vanessa. You're going to love that story, guaranteed."

John's good mood was infectious. She loved his jocularity, but it was also the aspect of his personality that made it difficult to picture him as an effective black ops agent. Nevertheless, they rocked and bumped over the jungle road, the tension that had crackled through the air in the van virtually gone. Maybe Michael Jackson was the international language after all.

Yawning despite the jostling car, loud music and John's even louder off-key singing, Diego settled his head in the corner of the seat back and the window. "Time for some shut-eye. You sit here with me and take deep breaths. Try to relax. Everything's going to work out because I'm going to make it work out."

She nudged his thigh with her knuckles. "Because that's your job, right?"

With eyes half-lidded and drowsy, he grinned and twined his fingers with hers, then pulled their joined hands on to his lap. After another huge yawn, he closed his eyes.

Vanessa looked around. Everyone, even John through the rearview mirror, was gawking at her. She offered them a tentative smile and decided to bulldoze through the awkward moment with levity. "No big deal. I'm sure he holds all the assets' hands, am I right?"

"Oh, yeah," Alicia said. "He's real touchy-feely that way."

"Still awake here," Diego grumbled without opening his eyes. "And I can hold whoever's damn hand I want. Get over it."

That settled that. Vanessa gave his hand a little squeeze and bit her lip against an affectionate grin at his grumpy declaration. "So, John, back to that Michael Jackson story. You said this album saved your life?"

Chapter 16

"Your Leroy is a timeshare?"

They stood in the shadow of a high-rise beach resort, watching tourists lug beach gear and children through the parking lot toward the sand. He should've guessed Alicia wouldn't scrimp on luxury even in an emergency situation.

Alicia shook her hair back. "Damn right. In the full-time vacation condo section of the resort. Think about it. Vacationers don't notice if I haven't been around for months or years, and they don't bat an eyelash if I come and go at odd hours. It's the perfect setup. I can't believe none of you ever thought about doing the same."

"Nope," Diego said. "But I like the way you think. I can hear the shower calling my name all the way from here. Lead the way, Phoenix."

Alicia's one-bedroom condo sat on the corner of the third floor off a private hallway with a nice patio area at the front door. The inside was classy in a beige furniture and fake palm trees kind of way. Usually places where the ambiance seemed tailor-made for a mobster's mistress or a corporate stiff's extended stay at a convention hotel gave Diego the willies, but he liked that Vanessa would have every amenity she needed, including a bed and a fresh change of clothes.

With directions from Alicia to pick anything she wanted from the closet and use whatever toiletries she needed in the bathroom during her shower, Vanessa disappeared into the master bedroom clutching one of the new toothbrushes John had detoured to the resort's general store to buy.

It was useless to try to stop himself from picturing her getting naked. That was a given, seeing as how he'd spent the better part of the past few days fantasizing about her in much the same state—sopping wet and naked. The real problem now was that he was imagining the other men on his crew picturing her like that.

Nobody had said anything or indicated in any way that's what they were thinking—they were all too smart to pull that kind of bonehead move—but he couldn't stop the jealousy, however irrational it was. He prowled to the kitchen and got a drink of water, at a loss for what to do, feeling cranky and filthy, totally out of place in the sterile condo.

He considered timing his phone call to Dreyer with Vanessa's shower to keep her in the dark so she wouldn't worry, but he thought better of it. He wanted her to hear him tell Dreyer he could take his demands about handing her over and shove them where the sun don't shine. That way, maybe she'd take another step toward trusting him. He could hope, anyway.

The shower water turned off. He braced his hands on

the counter and listened through the wall to her moving around, ticking off all the reasons he wasn't storming in there to towel her dry and toss her on the bed. Topping the list was the fact that she deserved a whole lot more than a one-night stand and that's about all he had to offer.

He'd racked his brain, but it was impossible to keep his promise to Ossie and still make Vanessa number one in his life. A week or two together at the most would be all they'd have, then he'd be off on another mission, leaving her alone, as she'd reminded him in the van.

See ya later and good luck.

He hated the idea.

"Hey." Alicia's voice made him jump. "Finding everything you need?"

"Yeah. You have a secured internet connection in this place?"

She nodded. "My encrypted internet link is set up and ready to roll in the living room."

"Good. As soon as Vanessa's out of the bedroom, dial Dreyer. Get him on video phone. I want to see the look on his face when he explains to me why his operation went FUBAR."

Ten minutes later, Vanessa emerged dressed in black stretchy pants and a tank top, looking so pretty and comfortable that he nearly lost his resolve to keep his distance.

Alicia set her laptop on the coffee table and tapped on the keyboard. "Good morning, sir," she said into the computer's camera. "I've got Agent Santero here, ready to speak with you."

"Put him on," Dreyer said.

Diego rolled his shoulders back, then took Alicia's place on the sofa. "Sir," he said. He never could muster anything friendlier than that when it came to the pencil-pushing Feds.

"Agent Santero. Glad to see you and your team are alive and well."

Diego frowned, irked by the man's insincerity. "You mean, you're glad Vanessa Crosby's alive and well. Because honestly? Forget about us. We're not what this mission is about. She is."

Dreyer's expression was instantly weary. So he didn't care for Diego. That feeling went both ways.

"With all due respect," Dreyer said, "this mission is about stopping the sale of a narco-submarine to a Colombian cartel and putting a stop to a bulk cash smuggling scam. Vanessa Crosby's safety is one component of the mission's success—a large component, mind you—but not the primary objective."

Wrong answer. "Screw the submarine sale and bulk cash. The mission you assigned me and my crew only has one objective, and that is ensuring an asset's safety. That's what we're going to do, and that's all we're going to do. While we're on the subject, how about you tell me what happened that compromised the safe house? If we'd delivered Miss Crosby to you a few minutes earlier, she'd be dead. No doubt in my mind."

"We haven't yet determined the cause of the security breach. Either someone leaked the information or we were followed," Dreyer said.

Diego made a fist, then flexed and drummed his fingers on his knee. Dreyer's lack of information and condescending answers were making his blood boil. "How do you not know? What have you and your ICEWALL team been doing the last three days?"

"Stand down, Agent Santero. I am your superior and you will show me respect."

Pretty much, Diego wanted to punch Dreyer's face through the computer, then quit his job. Might've even done it had Vanessa not been there.

Not only was she in the room, but the minute he started unleashing on Dreyer, she transferred next to him on the sofa out of the camera's range and touched her knee to his. He draped his arm over her leg, hooked his fingers around her knee and let a stream of air out through his nose, slow and steady.

"Respect is a two-way street, Dreyer. And I'm not seeing a whole lot coming our way lately."

"I understand your frustration. You and your team have my blessing to take a long furlough after you deliver Vanessa Crosby to us. I'll find another unit to escort her to the bank."

Her leg went stiff. He rubbed it, trying to get her to relax. "Vanessa Crosby isn't getting anywhere near your Operation ICEWALL lackeys or the bank. She has enough data with her to follow the money trail for the sub sale from our remote location. After I pass you the account information you need to stop the sale, I'm delivering her straight to the U.S. Marshals Service for WitSec placement."

"No, you're not. Let me lay out the facts for you. The Chiara brothers are in Panama purchasing a Russian-built submarine that they're planning to turn around and sell to a group of Colombian narco dealers. Our informant has reason to believe the sub's coming loaded with human cargo. The Chiaras negotiated some kind of package deal."

"Human cargo?" Vanessa whispered.

Diego shifted his focus to her. "Girls that are going to be sold into prostitution."

Her eyes widened, horrified. And she was right. It was horrifying.

"We don't know where the sale's going to take place," Dreyer continued. "But we do know the Chiaras are holding the money in RioBank and using the help of an insider to complete the transaction. There's no way to dissolve an account of that size remotely, and we can't go through legal channels to freeze the account because it would take too long and tip off whoever the insider is."

The prick was breaking the details down into digestible pieces like he was performing a rehearsed act for Vanessa. Like she'd get swept away by his talents of persuasion and volunteer to put herself in mortal danger again.

"This sale is happening tomorrow night," Dreyer continued. "Vanessa Crosby is the only person with the power to prevent dozens of young girls from being sold into sexual slavery, stop a submarine that will be used to smuggle millions of dollars of cocaine into the United States, and shut down the Chiaras for good. This is our one window of opportunity and she's our only hope."

The melodrama made him want to puke. "Not a chance."

Vanessa leaned in front of him and looked at the camera. "I'll do it."

Like hell she would.

He snapped the laptop's lid closed. "I am not risking your life for this half-baked, piece-of-junk operation."

"When you got involved with this mission, you knew I'd be asked to go back to the bank. That was the plan all along and you were on board with it. What changed?"

What changed? Was she kidding with that question? Everything had changed since those first few hours when he was nothing but a chauffeur and she was nothing but an asset.

Somewhere in the jungle, doing his job got tangled up with his need to protect one beautiful, brilliant woman at all costs. "You want to know what changed? I got a clue about how screwed up this mission is and how much I don't want you part of it. I got a clue about the loss it would be to the world if something bad happened to you." *The loss it would be to me.*

The kind of loss a man didn't recover from.

John cleared his throat. "I don't see how we have a choice."

"We always have a choice," Ryan said.

John shook his head. "If we go against Dreyer's direct orders on something this big, we're risking our necks. I know the argument was shot down in the van, but the truth is, if they label us rogue agents, we're not talking about getting fired, we're talking about being arrested or worse. We're talking AWOL-type stuff."

Diego rocketed to his feet. "Then you can leave, John. That goes for any of you. You don't like the choices I make, get off my crew. Nobody's forcing your allegiance to me."

The tense silence stretched on until Vanessa set her arm on his. "For the first time in my life, I have the chance to do something real. Something important. This operation is bigger than me. I honestly believe all this has happened to me for a reason—and stopping this submarine deal, saving those girls from prostitution, that's part of the reason. I didn't realize I had a gift that could help people until this weekend. I could never live with myself if I don't do everything I can."

She wasn't getting it about the danger, and it scared the crap out of him. "You might not live at all if you went through with Dreyer's plan. Then what good would your gift be for the world?"

"That's a risk I'm willing to take. You of all people understand what it's like to have a talent you can use to save people."

"It's different with you and your gift."

"Why?" she asked.

"Because you're not trained for this kind of mission like I am. My crew and ICE can still stop the sale of the submarine and the human cargo without putting you in danger."

"How, if you can't block the money and you don't know where the sale is going to take place?"

He scrubbed a hand over his mouth. Good question. "We'll figure it out."

"One way or another, I'm going to see this mission through." She pulled herself up tall, and if he hadn't been in the middle of negotiating against her for her life, he would've admired her courage. "If you and your crew aren't on board with it, I'll leave this place right now and call Dreyer from a pay phone. I'm sure one of his ICEWALL lackeys would come pick me up."

"Like I would let you walk out of here unprotected."

"Then I'd sneak out. That's how determined I am."

Her expression held no hint of a bluff, and that rattled him to his core because it meant she didn't think he was serious about going after her. God, he hated all the people in her past who'd made her feel expendable.

He set his hands on her shoulders. Though he was aware of his crew's undivided attention, it was more important that he get his message across to Vanessa. "I would chase you to the corners of the earth to keep you safe if I had to. Doesn't matter if you believe me or not. That's what would happen. There is no scenario you could dream up that won't result in me protecting your life with my life."

Maybe it was an illusion because he wanted to believe it so badly, but she looked like maybe she was starting to trust him on that point.

She covered his hands with hers. "Then help me do this."

Vanessa doing hard core math was the most erotic thing Diego had ever seen. While she worked, she rolled a pencil eraser over her lower lip and let out girlish squeaks when she came up with answers.

He'd been hard and needy ever since that first day with Vanessa, and now his nerves were strung taut as a wire. He escaped to a cold shower and stayed in there as long as any respectable man could without risking getting razzed about acting like a prima donna. God knew he smelled like one after using Alicia's ritzy chick shampoo and soap.

After the shower, he'd managed his arousal all right until later that night when Vanessa confessed it was the longest she'd worked on a computer without glasses since high school and her eyes were starting to hurt. That was when, in an incident that was later dubbed Operation Spectacle, Alicia and John discovered the resort's store was closed and had to run to town and scour the shops in search of reading glasses.

Diego had thought he might combust, watching her do math in glasses. Partly because of that and partly because he had no freakin' idea what she and Alicia were talking about and therefore couldn't offer even a modicum of help, he tried to stay out of their way. But it struck him, from watching her across the room, what an unprecedented maneuver Vanessa was spearheading. And all by using an algorithm she'd created in her spare time—because she'd wanted a challenge.

She blew his mind with her smarts and courage.

Who would've guessed that the rules of counterterrorism would be revolutionized in a timeshare condo in Panama by a young, beautiful woman?

He and the other men on his crew retired to the kitchen to plot their infiltration of RioBank and catch Dreyer up on their plan, but they could only get so far without finding out from Vanessa what and where she needed to be within the bank.

Once she and Alicia had determined which offshore account the Chiaras were using—a shell company called SPB Investing—they all gathered around the coffee table to finish their plans for the next morning.

By eleven, the planning was done, but Diego was too content to move. Next to him on the sofa, a dozing Vanessa had worked her way against him little by little, snuggling into his side. He'd eased her glasses off and she'd cuddled closer until her cheek was on his shoulder, her hair tumbling over his shirt in a way that got him wondering again what it'd be like to wake up next to her in a soft bed.

When everyone rose and began preparing for sleep, picking corners of the room to bunk down and using the hall bathroom, she stirred and rubbed her eyes.

She was so sleepy-sweet, he wanted to drag her onto his lap and kiss her. "Time for you to catch some z's. The bedroom's all yours."

She straightened and looked around, getting her bearings. "I'm comfortable here. Alicia can take the bed."

"Give me a break. You're the asset."

"Does someone else already have dibs on the sofa?"

Sighing, he stood and scooped her into his arms, then headed in the direction of the bedroom. "You haven't had access to a real bed in a couple nights. You're going to need to be at the top of your game tomorrow. A great night's sleep will help with that."

"You're quite the 'Vanessa needs her sleep' task-master."

"Someone's got to be, and it sure ain't you."

In the bedroom, she trailed kisses up his jaw to his cheek until he laid her on the bed. Damn, she'd felt perfect in his arms. So perfect that he wanted to drop on top of her, sink into her and not let go until duty pried them apart with the arrival of dawn.

But even if he decided to throw his vow to Ossie out the window so he could make love to her without feeling like he was denigrating her honor with a one-night stand, it wouldn't be respectful to put her in the position of having everyone in the condo knowing what they were up to. And it wouldn't be ethical to make the crew deal with the knowledge that their boss was in the next room screwing the asset, although he no longer thought of her as merely the asset and what he wanted to do with her was far more meaningful than a screw.

So he'd have to be the superhero Vanessa thought he was and find the strength to walk away.

"Good night," he said, clearing a strand of hair from over her eyes.

She was wide awake now, watching him. "Good night."

He couldn't even kiss her, knowing there wasn't enough willpower on the planet that would allow him to stop at a kiss.

He stood outside her closed door, his eyes shut tight, visualizing all the things he wanted to do with her. In his mind's eye, her clothes were gone. Her supple body stretched out on the bed, her legs open to let him get up close and personal with the sweet, wet heat between her thighs. It was easy to imagine what it would feel like to push his body inside her, what sounds she'd make when she found release.

The thought brought his mind around to the contented sighs she'd made in her sleep the past two nights. He'd been lucky to have had the opportunity to spend those nights watching her, learning about her sounds and the feel of her. Lucky that he'd found a way to ease her fears of being abandoned.

His mouth went dry.

Maybe it wasn't the right move to have stuck her away in the bedroom by herself. Maybe she'd wanted to stay on the sofa so she wouldn't feel alone or get nervous about waking up to find them all gone. He wanted to believe she knew better now that he'd never do that to her, but her fear wasn't exactly logical.

Damn, was he confused. What if she didn't sleep at all because she was afraid of waking up alone? What if she spent the whole night scared and all he had to do to prevent it was stay with her?

He didn't realize he was still standing outside her closed door until John said, "You okay? You look like you're trying to do some of Vanessa's math."

He gave his head a shake, attempting to rid himself of the feeling he'd made a mistake walking away from her as he had. He returned to the sofa and cradled his head in his hands, working to get a grip.

"You sure you're all right?" Alicia said from the corner where John was helping her unroll a sleeping bag. Rory was making a bed in front of the TV. Ryan was cleaning his firearm in preparation for the first guard shift.

"I, uh, I don't know—" Geez, he sounded like an idiot, stuttering and dumbfounded. But what was he supposed to do when where he wanted to be was behind the door he'd just closed?

The living room was stuffy; everyone was too near. He couldn't breathe and couldn't figure out how to get his libido to take a break so he could think straight. Shoving up from the sofa again, he bolted for the door, desperate for a little fresh air and perspective.

Chapter 17

No matter what happened with RioBank and the bulk cash scam, Vanessa's life would never be the same. She'd thought about that before, but it hadn't truly hit home until tonight when she realized that as soon as she finished doing all she could at the bank, her life sentence as a nobody would begin.

New name, new place of residence, new job.

The ghost she always felt like she was to her dad, to all the men she'd dated, would become literal. Being brave, she was discovering, wasn't about gaining control over her life. It wasn't even about risking death over a noble cause. It was accepting that the world was built on quicksand and yet still retaining her hope and her capacity for happiness.

She sat in the middle of the bed in the dark, girding herself for the days and weeks ahead.

No matter what happened or where she ended up,

she'd always have math. Numbers and the rules that governed them were constant, unshifting. In mathematics, there was always an answer, and once you determined it, it never changed. Math was the only part of her life that couldn't sift through her fingers.

Somehow, when the dust settled, she'd use her gift for math to do good. Though she'd enjoyed working bank security, it had never occurred to her until this week to explore the world of national security. But now she couldn't get it out of her head that the perfect place for her would be in a government job writing algorithms to stop criminals and track illegal behavior on a global scale.

Maybe ICE would hire her. Or maybe the Pentagon.

A job like that would help her get out of her head. Girls being sold into prostitution certainly lent perspective on her own petty problems. They were the real ghosts in the world. It'd feel fantastic to be the one saving people, rather than the one left behind feeling like a victim.

There was another selfish reason to choose a government career should she be given the opportunity. Going into the business of protecting the innocent would afford her a connection, however nominal, to Diego, even though the two of them didn't have a future together.

It would break her heart to say goodbye to the best man she'd ever met, but she'd realized yesterday that she wasn't willing to settle for less than a man who would look at her and say, "Yes, you. Forever. No matter what, you're the most important part of my life." Corny, perhaps, but that's what she wanted.

That's what she deserved.

And it didn't do her any good to wish that man was

Diego. Or whatever his real name was. Even if she'd fallen in love with him.

The old Vanessa wouldn't have taken the goodbye with Diego well. She would've licked her wounds and wondered what was so wrong with her that she fell for men who weren't emotionally available and willing to put her first.

New Vanessa, however, was going to pick herself up, dust herself off and get on with creating a new life. She was done chasing. Let a man chase her for a change.

Smiling into the darkness, she felt her newly tapped resolve all the way to her toes.

She was going to save lives tomorrow. She could hardly wait.

Bracing a hand on the stucco wall, Diego drew a huge gulp of air into his lungs and held it there until it burned.

The doorknob turned. Someone was following him out. If it was Vanessa, he was going to kiss her. He was going to crush her to the wall and let her know in no uncertain terms how crazy with need she was making him. Then he was going to march her past his crew's overcurious eyes and straight to the bedroom, their opinions of his actions be damned.

Ryan raised his eyebrows in greeting and closed the door behind him.

Drawing a tremulous breath, Diego kicked the wall, regrouping. "Hey."

Ryan perched on the top of the raised planter. "Everything okay?"

"Just ducky, can't you tell?"

"I noticed. Thought you might need some advice."

He and Ryan had been through it all over the years, ex-

perienced things together—both terrible and wonderful—
that had bonded them for life. No one could read him
like Ryan, but that didn't mean he wanted to discuss his
woman troubles with the man.

"Oh, hell, no. Not only is you and me talking about
that stuff ten different shades of wrong, but you don't
know jack about the kind of situation I'm in."

"There's nobody in the world who's going to give it
to you straight except me. Well, and Gabriela, but she's
not here." Gabriela, Diego's youngest sibling, was single, Newark P.D. and tough as nails, the most like him
out of any of their siblings.

"Plus," Ryan added with a shrug, "I know a few
things about women."

Oh, please. "What could you possibly know about
women that I don't? You're married to the job as much
as I am. Always have been."

"I know you should go for it."

"Go for what?"

"Life with her. Go for it with Vanessa."

"It's not that easy."

Ryan cocked his head. "Seems like a no-brainer to
me."

"I never took you for a romantic."

He shrugged again.

Ryan shrugged a lot, now that he thought about it.
Shrugged his way out of all kinds of conversations, side-
stepping the pressure to come up with the right words or
take a stand. The ultimate way to play his cards close to
the vest. Diego ought to take a page from Ryan's book.

"Putting the moves on an asset is completely unethical."

Ryan raised an eyebrow. "Maybe you need a reminder of why you switched from the navy to black ops."

"That's not fair."

"Go on, say it."

He chewed the inside of his cheek. Sometimes it was a pain in the butt to have someone around who knew him so well. "Because working outside the lines and trusting my instincts almost always gets better results than playing by the rules. But that doesn't mean I can do something dishonorable."

"Does being with Vanessa feel dishonorable?"

Hell, no. It felt more genuine and right than just about anything else in his life. "It's not that easy because if I went for a life with her, she'd be a sitting duck for all the scumbags who have grudges against me."

"That's only half-true and you know it. There are measures we can take to secure her safety. Stop it with the B.S. excuses. This is the only life we got and we're not getting any younger."

Ryan was right about that, but what he didn't understand was that Vanessa wasn't built to be alone. If he were her man and he stayed on the job, she'd be miserable. He would've saved her life over and over, only to ruin it in the long run. Because with his job, there was no gray area. If he wasn't putting work first, he wasn't doing it right—and that put people's lives at risk. His crew, the assets, civilian bystanders. That was the reason almost every SEAL and black ops agent he knew was single or divorced.

He sighed and picked at the stucco. "She has a thing about people leaving her, about being alone, and with this job, that's all I'd do. I could be gone from her for months at a time. It wouldn't be fair to ask her to sacrifice like that. She'd be better off without me."

When he put it that way, the decision sounded easy…
until he thought about Vanessa's next Christmas in Wit-
Sec, alone.

Thinking of her alone for the holidays actually made
his heart hurt, something he hadn't experienced since
the weeks after Ossie's passing. But if he chose to be
with her—if she let him—he knew he could make her
happy and keep her happy for the rest of her life. He
didn't know why he was so sure about that because he
knew zilch about being in a relationship, but he knew
it as a fact. He felt it in his bones.

Ryan rubbed the scruff on his chin. "Maybe you
know more about women than you're giving yourself
credit for."

"Women, no. Vanessa, yes."

"So don't make her sacrifice. You do it. Choose to
be what she needs. Tell ICE to pound sand."

"You mean give up the job? How can you suggest
that? My brother—"

"I know all about Ossie. I was with you when he
died, bro. But this job, you said it yourself, it's not what
it used to be. The world's changing. National security
isn't the same game it was ten or even five years ago."

"Definitely not, but you, Alicia, John and Rory,
you're family to me. As much as I couldn't leave Vanessa if I committed to her, I can't leave you stranded
like that. Wouldn't be right."

"All four of us, we'd follow you off a cliff, but the
job's wearing on us, too. Might be time for all of us to
move on to other things."

Diego chortled. "Says the man with the Chiara brothers obsession."

Another shrug. "I'm going to see that goal through,
then think about making some changes to my life, too."

Diego scrubbed a hand over his face. Give up the career that defined him, along with the adrenaline rush he thrived on? Then who would he be? Could he still be happy?

He'd buried the idea of having any semblance of a normal life a long time ago. After 9/11, the thought of getting married or starting a family had been unfathomable. Every day around the world people suffered at the hands of tyrants, and he was one of a select few with the skills and drive to fight for them. He'd made the choice and had never given it another thought.

Then, boom.

Without trying, without knowing she was doing it, Vanessa had him rethinking everything he thought he was at peace with—the constant risk of death, the toll his job took on his body and spirit, the loneliness.

Maybe the better question was, could he be happy without Vanessa, now that he knew what he'd been missing? No matter what choice he made, he couldn't stuff the new awareness she'd triggered into a box and ignore it.

"I take it you like Vanessa for me?"

Ryan didn't hesitate. "Yeah, I do. I'm not going to lie, you caught us all by surprise, but I like her. And more importantly, I like the way you are around her. She's good for you. Alicia and I talked it over. We're going to support you in whatever you need to do so you can be with her. This thing you two have, it doesn't happen to everybody, especially guys like us. You got to run with it. Like I said, a no-brainer."

"The only way this is a no-brainer is because my head's going to explode." Because the way he saw it, his choice came down to either the woman he could see himself loving with a selfish kind of happiness or his vow to Ossie that he'd never stop fighting for the world to be a better, safer place. There wasn't a choice in the universe more difficult than that.

Ryan slugged him on the shoulder. "Naw, man. You're psyching yourself out. You know what you need to do, so make it happen."

"I had no idea you had so much advice inside you, waiting to get out."

Ryan grinned. "Got to live up to my nickname."

Diego managed a chuckle. "If only Magic Eight Balls gave great advice, you'd be right." He'd issued the nickname to Ryan when they were eighteen and barrack roommates. At the time, Ryan's quietness drove Diego nuts. One night, he was extra pissed about Ryan's silence and told him he'd be better off buying a Magic Eight Ball to have conversations with. Usually the memory made him happy, but tonight he was too pent up with confusion to enjoy the nostalgia.

"Don't go knocking Magic Eight Balls. They really work," Ryan said.

Diego scoffed. "No, they don't."

"Sure they do. They give you a push to trust your instincts. Like I've been doing with you since we were eighteen."

"And here I thought I called you that because you rarely say more than two words at a time."

"That's the magic part."

Maybe he was overthinking it, at least for the time being. Maybe tonight was as simple as Vanessa being in a room by herself, probably nervous about being alone, and him wanting to be in there with her. "I'm going to stay with her tonight, see if it helps me figure out what to do long-term. Thanks for this."

"You bet." They knocked forearms, then Ryan

snagged his shoulders in a one-armed hug. "You need protection?"

It wasn't the first time the topic had come up over their seventeen-year friendship, but it felt wrong to talk about Vanessa that way with another man, even Ryan. He'd stumbled on a stash of condoms in the bathroom after his shower while looking for toothpaste, and though he didn't want to meditate for even a second on the intimate details of Alicia's private life, they'd been kind of hard to miss. "I'm good."

Ryan gave him a hard shove toward the door, then pulled his rifle around from his back, grinning. "Then get out of here. I'm trying to start my guard shift and you're distracting me."

"See you in the morning."

Wiping his hand on his pants, he walked past Rory, John and Alicia without looking their way. He stood and stared at the closed bedroom door for a beat. What was he going to say to her? Did it matter? What if she was already asleep and he'd be disturbing her?

Screw it.

He turned the knob and stepped into the darkness. The shaft of light from the door illuminated the room all the way to the bed. Vanessa was sitting up, her back against the headboard, her arms hugging her knees.

He was right to return.

Closing the door, he took a tentative step closer. Knowing he was right didn't make him any less jittery.

"Hi," she said, turning on the bedside lamp.

He opened his mouth but nothing came out. How come he never hesitated in battle, but this soft, pretty creature brought him to heel with one simple word?

Come on, Slick. You've got to have the perfect words floating around somewhere inside your thick melon.

"I thought…I thought you might need me. I mean, so you can sleep. I could stay with you if you want." What was he, an eighteen-year-old virgin? "I'd like to stay with you, if that's okay."

She scooted to the edge of the bed and dangled her legs over the side, a serene expression on her face. "It's more than okay. Come here."

He walked to her and stood, totally blanking on what he should do next. Take off his shoes? Sit down?

Kiss her?

That's what he wanted to do more than anything. Hell, he'd wanted to kiss her constantly for the whole day, but the presence of his crew rendered that impossible. While he was still contemplating his strategy, she slipped her fingers behind his belt and pulled him between her knees.

She pressed her face into his shirt, grazing her nose and lips across his stomach, and all he could do was dig his hands into her hair and hang on for dear life.

Then she turned her big blue eyes up at him and smiled. A sultry, confident invitation.

Just like that, his future came into focus. Ryan was right. This was a no-brainer. Being with Vanessa was going to be as easy as breathing.

He still had no idea how he was going to reconcile his promise to Ossie with this new, selfish need to keep Vanessa in his life, but he'd find a way to make it work. He had to.

Emboldened by the realization, he dropped to his knees.

Chapter 18

Vanessa had been debating strategies to get Diego back to the bedroom.

Although they didn't have a future together, her new, bold self decided she wanted one night in his arms. So she gave herself permission to ask for what she wanted. She hadn't quite figured out the details of how to entice him to let down his guard and give himself to her when he appeared at the door as if she'd conjured him.

Even though he'd been his typical brazen self to walk right into a sleeping woman's room without knocking, once there he was uncharacteristically nervous. As if they hadn't spent every moment of the past three days together and they were back to being cautious strangers.

Diego was a natural leader and an alpha male through and through, but if he needed her to take the lead tonight, she was prepared to. She was determined to create a memory of the two of them together—not just a fantasy—to carry her through the scary days, weeks and months to come.

She had a hand on his belt, ready to show him exactly what she had in mind for the night, when he lowered to his knees between her legs, his hands spanning her ribs. Nervousness had vanished from his expression, replaced by eyes that glimmered with tenderness and perhaps even a hint of joy.

Stroking his hair, she leaned in and brushed a kiss across his lips. "I want you."

It made her feel strong, asserting herself, saying aloud what she'd been thinking every waking minute. Strong and proud of the person she was evolving into.

The corners of his lips curved into a smile. He touched his forehead and nose to hers. "Like breathing."

Her fingertips danced over the stubble on his cheek. She knew exactly what he meant because it was the same for her. "Yes. Like breathing."

Then he pulled her down to straddle him and crushed his lips to hers in a kiss loaded with the promise of incomparable pleasure. Forget about creating a memory of sensual lovemaking—she wanted Diego to ravish her.

She grabbed her shirt and tugged, but his hands shot from where he cupped her backside to clamp over her wrists. "Not yet."

Openmouthed and breathing hard, she tried to make him understand. "I need you right now, here on the floor. I don't want it soft and slow on the bed."

He rose up, pinning her torso against the side of the mattress, and kissed her again. "Not on the bed, not on the floor. Come with me."

He strode to the bathroom, guiding her by the hand into the shower. Showering was fine with her, as long as he was with her, both of them naked. She reached for the hem of her shirt again.

"Your shirt stays on." His words were gruff, clipped. He stripped off his own shirt and stepped in. "You drove me crazy for days in your wet clothes. I couldn't stop thinking about putting my hands on you, peeling your shirt off, wondering what your rain-soaked skin would taste like on my tongue."

She hadn't thought it was possible to be any more turned on, but his words made her dizzy with arousal. She'd been fantasizing about his mouth on her skin, too.

He turned the faucet on and scooted her out of range of the spray. The water was straight-up cold. It licked at her feet and sprinkled over her arms, making her skin tight and her breath catch in her throat.

But then Diego pulled her against him and all thoughts of the cold vanished. Her hands smoothed over the bunched muscles of his shoulder and chest, exploring the harnessed power of his body as she'd longed to since watching him emerge from the lake after his dive. The moment she'd stopped thinking of him not only as a stranger who'd saved her life, but also as a man in his prime.

"You're so beautiful," he rumbled low as his hand found her breast through the cotton.

"I was thinking the same about you." She pressed her lips to his tattoo and licked down. Her tongue captured his nipple and flicked it. As if in answer, his hand tightened around her breast and rolled her taut nipple between his fingers.

Steam rose up around them as the hot water kicked in. He lowered his lips to her neck and nibbled a path behind her ear.

"Diego," she whispered on an exhale.

"No." He jerked back. Clasping the sides of her face, he urged her gaze to his and she wondered what she'd said or done wrong. Then she registered the look on his face. The intensity of the adoration in his eyes made her legs weak. "Not Diego. Marcos. My name is Marcos Aponte."

Her mouth fell open with a soft gasp. But before she could recover her wits, he spun her into the stream of water, wrapped her hair around his hand and seized possession of her body with his lips and tongue and hands.

He was everything she needed—urgent, demanding, hard in all the places it mattered. Every spot of skin he unwrapped from the drenched cotton, he laved with kisses, working his way down her body until she stood before him in nothing but a pair of white satin panties, drenched and translucent.

Whispering words of reverence about her body, he turned his hand palm-up and fluttered the pads of his fingers lightly over the wet material. A touch so light and teasing, she could hardly stand it.

Her need for him was primal, her thoughts nothing but *More. Harder.*

With a wicked grin, he indulged her, pressing his index finger along the crease of her folds. He swallowed her whimper with a kiss as he gathered the satin in his hand and gave a gentle tug. The satin lodged between her folds, shrouding the epicenter of her nerve endings.

He jiggled the material, brushing her with delicate wisps of friction until her knees buckled and she had to brace her shoulders against the tile wall.

Stepping back, he drank her in, his gaze lingering on the cling of the satin as his hands reached for his belt.

The clang of the metal buckle opening was the most erotic sound she'd ever heard. She stepped forward and shooed his hands out of the way so she could have the pleasure of unzipping the cargo pants and unleashing his straining erection. The anticipation of seeing him naked for the first time had her breathing shallow and her hands trembling. She felt nineteen again, alive with wonder and want. Fearless.

The thick curve of his erection was molded by his wet, black briefs and wrapped around his hipbone. A sound of admiration bubbled from her throat. Being with him was going to feel magnificent. She stroked up the length of him, relishing his hiss of breath and the way he arched into her hand.

His cargo pants, as wet as they were, required some oomph to push down. He kicked them into the pile of clothes and reached for the waistband of his underwear.

It was her turn to clamp her hands around his wrists. Time for him to experience the same rapturous agony as he'd put her through. "Not so fast, soldier."

Tamping her impatience to see him, she knelt and cupped her hand around him, then drew up the side of the leg hole. She filled her mouth with him, savoring the salty spice of his flesh.

He groaned and twisted. Out of the corner of her eye, she watched him open the same drawer she'd inadvertently discovered condoms in before her shower. He must've come across them earlier, too, because he pulled one out and ripped the wrapper open.

The thought of what they were about to do sent a pulse of exhilaration through her core, even if she wasn't ready to quit her exploration of his body. "Right now?"

He hooked a hand under her arm and hauled her up. "Yeah, right now." His voice was gravelly, his eyes dilated. He stripped her panties off without ceremony and burrowed a finger in her folds. The move elicited a sound like a purr from her chest. "Right now" was sounding better and better.

He swirled his finger. She looped an arm around his neck to steady herself as she was rocked with sensation.

"This night's not going to end without me putting my mouth on you here," he said. "I've been dreaming of that since the first time we kissed. But if I don't get inside you right the hell now, I'm going to have a heart attack."

She loved that she drove him as crazy as he drove her. The head of his erection jutted over the elastic band of his briefs. She bent and pushed her lips over it, sampling him as she slipped the water-soaked fabric from his hips.

With a growl, he took a firm hold of her hair and lifted her away. Then he pinned her to the wall, his hand roving over her body, his erection a hot, hard force between them. "Damn, Vanessa. You're going to kill me."

She'd never seen a condom go on so fast.

Faces close, they breathed into each other, their bodies slick with water and sweat. Stroking himself with one hand, he grasped the back of her leg at the knee and jerked it up in a dirty, functional move to open her that proved he understood as well as she did that they were beyond tender caresses. The burn of arousal they'd suffered for days demanded to be quenched at the same frenzied speed with which it had blazed to life. To be eviscerated by a hard, reckless crush of flesh on flesh.

She rolled the back of her head along the wall as he stretched her with that first thrust. A tuck of her hips slipped him deeper. He gripped the backs of her thighs and her second foot came off the floor, driving him deeper still.

His stubbled jaw rasping over her cheek, he pumped

into her again and whispered a curse that sounded like a prayer. Vanessa couldn't make a sound. The rapture was too powerful for her to do anything but succumb, to let herself be taken. With his strong arms holding her up and the confident control he'd taken of her pleasure, there was nothing left to do but bury her face in his neck and lose herself in the relentless rhythm of his thrusts.

Release started way deep down in her belly, a gathering pressure that drew a deep inhale from her. She held the air in her lungs, felt her abs clench, then every muscle squeezed. Her hands pushed against his chest. Her knees drew up.

His movement froze, hanging her on the edge. Her head tipped back and she moaned around gritted teeth. Impossible, impossible…

With long, smooth thrusts, he finally let her go. The bliss turned her vision white. Maybe she was noisy, because he covered her mouth with his, but she couldn't tell and didn't care. Her body pulsed, over and over, outside and inside. She rode it all the way through, meeting him movement for movement.

She knew when he'd joined her in the fall because his body quaked and his face twisted into a sneer that could've been pain or pleasure. Cursing again, his head dropped to her shoulder and he held himself inside her, merging them to their pelvic bones until nothing was between them, not even the steam from the shower.

"Oh," she sighed with a shudder. She wove her fingers into his damp hair as residual pulses of bliss fluttered through her. "That was…"

He nuzzled the hollow of her throat. "Yeah, it was."

She nibbled his earlobe, right at the curl at the top. She loved his ears. The incongruity that something so delicate could exist on a man who'd dedicated his life to being strong for those who couldn't made her ache with love. She hugged him tighter. "Like breathing," she said.

He raised his head and melted her heart with a lazy, sated smile. "Better than breathing." After a languid kiss, he smoothed her hair away from her face. "It's time."

"For what?"

"For me to take you to bed and let my mouth get to work. Hold on to me. I'll carry you."

But she was already holding on, and though she knew she'd have to soon, she didn't see how she'd ever be able to let go of him.

"Marcos Aponte," Vanessa whispered as her finger traced the outline of the muscles on his chest and stomach. It was at least the tenth time she'd said it, like his name was a new term in a foreign language she was trying to memorize.

He nuzzled her hair. "I like the way it sounds coming from you."

"I like it, too, but I'll still call you Diego. It's safer for your family."

"Yeah, that would be best. The only people outside my family who know my real name are Ryan, you and the ICE director who hired me. I'd like to keep it that way."

They lay in the bed skin-to-skin, the sheets kicked down, their bodies spent. Diego could lie like that with her forever, but dawn was coming too fast. Dawn and a million dangers Vanessa was determined to walk into. He still didn't understand why she had to do it.

He tightened his arms around her. "Tell me how I can convince you not to do this bank job."

"My mind's made up."

"You don't have anything to prove, you know. Not to anybody, and especially not to me."

"I do, actually. To myself. I've spent most of my life chasing people I love who've left me. I don't want to be that person anymore. I finally feel like I'm coming into my own. This is what I'm supposed to do with my life. Use the gift I was given to help people. This is my chance to prove to myself that I can be somebody who makes a difference in this world."

Absolutely killed him that she was only now beginning to understand her worth. "You've made a difference to me, more than you'll ever know. And with that algorithm you created, you don't have to risk your life to do good in this world."

"Today I do. I couldn't live with myself if I didn't do everything I could to keep those girls from being sold. My long-term plan, when it's safe for me to come out of WitSec, is to see if the U.S. government might be interested in hiring me to run the algorithm to track bulk cash smugglers. You said ICE has a whole division devoted to that, right? So obviously there's a need. It's time for me to step up and fill that need."

Wasn't a bad plan, even if it was still way more dangerous a career than he wanted for her. He made a mental note to call his contact at the Bulk Cash Smuggling Center. There was no doubt in his mind they'd hire her in a heartbeat, but he wasn't going to suggest it until he had a handle on the security precautions the department took for its employees.

"You start shutting down cartels' and smugglers' money supply, you'll land yourself on the kill list of a lot of bad people," he said. "What you're experiencing this week is only the tip of the iceberg."

"I know, and I'm at peace with the risk. If I change

my name and keep a low profile, I don't see how the criminals I stop will ever find out my identity."

"You'd be surprised."

"That's probably true, but I'm going to do it anyway." She splayed her fingers over his tattoo. "You opened my eyes to what I could be and there's no going back."

"The path I chose, I don't want that for you. It'd damage you. The scars I have inside and out, they'll never go away."

She slid her hand up his neck, behind his ear. "Scars never do. But you taught me that somebody has to take a stand and do what's right."

Rotten trick, using his own words against him. They probably taught her that in chick school. "Yeah, but that somebody doesn't have to be you."

She levered up on her elbow. "You want me to start singing 'Man in the Mirror'?"

A laugh rumbled through him. "Please, no." Wrapping his hands around the juicy curves of her backside, he pulled her on top of him. "For a math geek, you sure do play dirty."

She settled her thighs over his hips, rotating a bit. Unbelievable, because he'd thought he was all tapped out, but his body stirred to life again.

Leaning forward, she set her hands on either side of his head, caging him. "You know what they say about math geeks, right?"

"They're great kissers and have a soft spot for black ops soldiers with bad attitudes?"

She grinned broadly. "We're a calculating bunch."

He laughed, though he had no idea why. It was a terrible joke. "Oh, my god, woman. That's painful. I'm going to have to kiss you to recover from that."

He guided her lips to his and before long, they were both breathing hard again.

Vanessa pulled her mouth away and drew circles on his cheek. "I have something I want to talk to you about before I forget."

"It's not another bad joke, is it? 'Cause I'm still smarting from the last one."

"I love that joke." He groaned and she pressed a finger to his lips. "Anyway, as I was saying, I need your help. I've decided I should have a Leroy plan before we go to the bank, but I don't have the slightest idea how to go about it."

He still hated that she was determined to go through with the bank operation despite the danger, but he knew now there would be no changing her mind. "You're right. You do need one. Since you know the bank layout better than we do, figure out how you'd get out of the building and I'll plan the rest."

She kissed him. "Thank you."

His body was getting restless with all the talking they were doing. "If I help you with your Leroy, then you've got to do something for me."

"Name it."

"Scoot up a little higher, would you?"

With his hands on her waist pulling her, she inched her knees up near his ribs. "Like that?"

"Not quite. Higher."

More scooting, this time hitting her knees on his armpits.

First one side, then the other, he snuck his hands under her knees and lifted them above his shoulders as he slid down, lining his mouth up exactly where he wanted it to be. "That's more like it."

Her hands tangled in his hair. "You're insatiable."

He planted kisses on the silken skin of her inner thighs. "Only with you. No one but you."

Then he set his hands on her hips and guided her onto his waiting tongue.

Vanessa didn't know where to look. She felt awkward, but clearly she was the only one.

She leaned against the kitchen counter, sipping coffee and staying out of the way. The bank operation might hinge on her, but all the planning and prep work fell on the shoulders of Diego and his crew.

Alicia wandered in to refill her mug. Vanessa wasn't a prude or anything, but she still averted her eyes. Weird to see a near-stranger drinking coffee in hot pink panties and a matching bra with a silver-handled knife sewn into the band.

"What's up?" Alicia asked.

"There's a lot of men here walking around in their underwear. I don't know where to look. I'm trying not to check them out, but it's not working. I think the combined body fat percentage of all the men in the living room would be less than one percent."

Alicia chuckled. "Yeah, they're all pretty hot, aren't they?"

"Are you guys always this free and easy before an operation?"

"It all boils down to common sense. You can't strap a knife to your thigh while your pants are on."

Vanessa sipped her coffee. "Words to live by."

Alicia dropped a heaping spoonful of sugar into her mug. "Look, these are the people I risk my life with every day. Modesty flew out the window years ago. When we run covert ops, like today, we've got to be discreet. Weapons go under the clothes as much as we can."

John wandered in, clad in skimpy red briefs, two thigh holsters, and two leather straps across his chest, one that sheathed a long-handled knife and the other with a gun. Of its own volition, her eyes darted to his bulge. She caught herself looking and flicked her gaze to the wall, her face heating. Oops.

Alicia sputtered her coffee. "A red bikini, John? We have a civilian present."

"Pot and kettle, Phoenix. You're wearing fluorescent pink." John grabbed a mug and reached for the pot.

"Yes, but I can get away with bright colors and pretty underwear because I'm a woman."

He slammed the pot down with a bit too much gusto. "Trust me, I noticed." He turned his back on Alicia. "Besides, you can take it, can't you, Vanessa?" He arched an eyebrow and struck a pose. "Or am I too much man for you?"

Diego prowled up behind him and shoved him in the back, sloshing coffee onto the floor. Vanessa couldn't decide if he was being playful or tapping into residual anger from their argument the day before. "Give it a rest before I confiscate all your banana hammocks and burn 'em."

Diego, dressed in black boxer briefs and socks, with guns and knives strapped around his body, was about the sexiest thing Vanessa had ever seen. A rush of pride crashed through her at the realization that, at least temporarily, he was hers. And in her heart, he always would be.

"You can't go bagging on my personal style when you don't have any," John said with mock indignity.

"I have a style. It's called 'what can I grab that's clean.'" He slid his arm around Vanessa's waist and nodded toward the bedroom. "Can I talk to you alone? I've got something for you."

"Hey, now. You can't have her for too long," Alicia said. "I want to go over our strategy one last time."

"I'll be fast. Ten minutes, tops." He ushered her down the hall.

"I've got a comment I could make to that, but I'm gonna refrain out of respect for the lady," John hollered after them.

"Smart move," Diego called back. To Vanessa he added, "I swear, every sniper I've met has been off his rocker in one way or another. John's a little nutso, but he's the best at what he does." Shaking his head, he closed the bedroom door behind them.

Chapter 19

"I like John," Vanessa said after the door closed.

Diego scowled. "You should be careful about saying stuff like that, because—and I never knew this about me—but it turns out I'm the jealous type."

Vanessa faked some surprise. "You don't say."

But all she could think about was the wild nature show she saw about wolves and how there was only room in a pack for one alpha male, which meant that every so often he had to reestablish his dominance when another male got too big for his wolfy britches.

"Big shocker, I know. I pretty much want to blindfold you until John, Ryan and Rory put their clothes on. Then I want to take some of Alicia's vampy lipstick and write 'Don't even think about it' on your chest."

"I don't think my chest is big enough for all those words. Besides, after the things you did to me last night, I hadn't even noticed there were other men in the condo." She felt none of her usual guilt over lying. A little white lie to massage a male ego was perfectly permissible, she and Jordan had decided shortly after her marriage.

He smiled. "My fib detector's going off, but I still like your answer." From on top of the dresser, he picked up a fold of cash. "Here's the best I can do for your Leroy on such short notice. This is all the money I have on me."

He set it in her hand, then added a scrap of paper on top. "Here's the combination and number of a locker at the Colón train depot. There's more money in there and extra cell phones. You don't have a passport, so leaving the country without help is out of the question. If you get to the point where you need your Leroy, that means I'm either dead or incapacitated, so I'm also giving you two phone numbers."

He removed the lid of a ballpoint pen and took her arm, turning it to expose the inside of her forearm. "This first one is for the head of ICE, Richard Piastro. He's my boss's boss's boss and the man who hired me. Name drop Marcos Aponte and he'll get the point that you're an important caller. The second number is my crew's private voice mail line. If we get separated, you call this number and I'll come get you. If I'm dead, someone in my crew will get you."

"I don't think that's going to happen."

"Neither do I, but a Leroy's a last-resort option, so we have to consider the impossible."

"You're right. Thank you." She secured the money and paper in her skirt pocket and pulled out the note she'd scribbled that morning. "Here. The web address where my algorithm's stored and my access code. In case the unthinkable happens."

His eyes tight, he ripped the paper in half and stuffed the code in his sock. After a cursory second look at the web address, he walked to the bathroom and flushed it down the toilet.

"There's one more part to your Leroy." Back in the room, he motioned to the bed where a small handgun and holster sat. "It's time to teach you how to handle a firearm. Other than yesterday, had you ever shot a gun before?"

Her mind balked at the notion of using a gun. Not that she was scared per se, but there was an inherent volatility in guns that intimidated her. Statistically, mathematically, guns weren't a safe bet.

"Growing up, I used to go hunting with Jordan's family, but I've only used a hunting rifle, and only a few times." Those trips with Jordan's family were more about pretending to be part of her friend's loving clan than killing birds and rabbits.

He nodded while doing a safety check to make sure the gun was clear of ammo. "We can work with that. At least you already know about the kick and the noise. Let's get you outfitted. Take off your shirt."

While she unbuttoned the silky turquoise dress shirt Alicia had provided her with that morning, Diego removed the gun and strapped the holster around her ribs above the seam of her black pencil skirt.

"I'm going to do everything in my power to make sure you never need to consider pulling your piece. If you get to the point where you have to think about your gun, then I've failed you. And I never fail. But I'm not sending you in unarmed."

"I understand." She took the gun when he offered it, holding the cold metal and plastic at the end of a limp grip. It felt heavy and awkward, though it couldn't have weighed all that much.

"We're going to see if we can plant the seed of some muscle memory in your body, because if something goes wrong, you're not going to have time to figure it out." He took the gun from her and secured it in the holster. "Draw your piece and aim it at the lamp shade. Let me see your form."

She reached behind her to draw, but she had to torque her body at an odd angle to get her hand around the gun handle.

Diego adjusted the holster nearer to her side. "Try that again."

This time, she cleared the gun from the holster and brought it around to aim at the lamp shade.

Behind her, Diego adjusted her grip and stance. "Don't tense your shoulder. Arm loose."

She exhaled and worked to relax. He put his hand on her hips. "Shift one leg back to make an upside-down T. It's more stable than parallel stance." She swung a leg back. "There. You got it now. Holster the piece and draw again."

She did. With his hands on her hips, he mirrored her movement, then made adjustments.

"Better. This time, start facing forward. Pull and pivot at the same." He waited until she'd returned the gun to its holster, then, "Draw."

She stepped back and drew the gun, aiming at the lampshade. But it seemed the more she did it, the more nervous she got. Her hands were sweating, her heart beating fast. The danger of her situation was becoming more real with every pull of the weapon.

"That's better. You're on your way to earning a spot on my crew."

She tried a smile. "I don't think I'm cut out to be a black ops agent."

"Like it or not, that's exactly what you are today."

Her stomach dropped, erasing the tenuous smile from her lips. She holstered the gun and wiped her hands on her skirt. He must have sensed her rising anxiety because he moved behind her again, one hand spanning her hip, the other her shoulder.

"Draw."

He rotated her, moving his hand with hers as she pulled and aimed the gun.

"Arms straight, but not locked, legs braced. You're gripping the gun too hard. Relax your hand."

"It's a little hard to relax knowing in a couple hours we're going to be risking our lives. I know you do that all the time, but I don't and I'm scared."

The hand on her hip curled around her waist, pulling her close. "Am I going to fail you today?" he asked in a low voice close to her ear.

"No."

"But you have to prepare for it anyway. You came up with your own way out of the building if all hell breaks loose?"

"Yes."

He brushed kisses along her shoulder. "You have the cash I gave you?"

She nodded. His lips reached her nape. The slightest feel of teeth nibbled up her neck.

"You have my voice mail numbers and the locker code?"

"I do."

"That means you can take care of yourself if it comes to that." He suckled her earlobe.

Tingles of pleasure rushed all over her skin. She

reached her chin over her shoulder, all the way back until her lips found his and captured them in a kiss. "It's not going to come to that," she said.

"How do you know?"

"Because you're not going to let it."

"Damn right, I'm not." Determination, ferocious and unyielding, emanated from his eyes and voice.

She hooked an arm around his head and pulled his lips to hers. They kissed deeply, evoking memories of the way he'd made her feel the night before. His hands traveled over the front of her, from her breasts to her belly.

When she ground her backside into his erection, he spun her to face him and continued their kiss. Everywhere her hands explored, she hit a weapon—a knife or gun, grenades and ropes of muscle.

He pulled away, his breathing labored.

"Tonight, after we're done with the bank, we're going to finish this. Somewhere it's just the two of us. But if I keep kissing you right now, I'm not going to have enough blood left in my brain to keep you safe at the bank."

It was a reasonable request, and yet his erection was still pressing into her belly, calling for her to touch. A quick fondle to whet her appetite for later, she decided, reaching her hand between them.

Fast as lightning, he captured her wrist and brought it to his lips, pressing a kiss to her pulse point. "Tonight."

She played up a disappointed sigh as he lifted her blouse from the bed and helped her into it. "Once you get your top and jacket on, practice pulling your firearm again. It'll be harder with your clothes on."

While she buttoned it, he put on a white undershirt, then a white dress shirt. All she'd seen him in were form-fitting black T-shirts and black cargo pants, but she liked him looking all Tom Cruise in *Risky Business,* with the shirt and underwear.

Shrugging into her suit jacket, she couldn't take her eyes off him.

"Let me watch you draw your weapon now."

She drew and stepped back into the position he'd taught her. It took longer to remove the gun from its holster, and when she did, it snagged on the jacket.

"Again," he said.

She glanced at his reflection in the closet mirror. He was tying a burgundy tie. Man, oh, man, did he look fine. Like the world's most lethal businessman. His raw, primal power civilized, but barely. She drew, aiming at her reflection.

"Better." He flipped the ends of the tie, knotting it with a deft skill that caught her by surprise. "Again."

She was feeling more confident with every pull. This plan had to work today. Nothing was going to go wrong. She wouldn't need to shoot a gun or put her Leroy plan in action. Diego was in charge, and he never failed. She was going to be fine.

Vanessa saw the mission laid out in her head like a grid.

Rory and John were somewhere outside, working the lookout points. Ryan sat in the lobby, playing it cool while pretending to wait for an appointment. An ICE unit was on standby at the attaché office, ready to move when she pulled up the locations of any people accessing the Chiaras' account in the last several months.

She had a plan to get into her office with Diego and Alicia, a plan to make the fifty million dollars in the Chiara account disappear and more than one plan to leave the building. Everything was laid out in a perfectly logical, mathematical grid. Grids, she could handle.

What she was having trouble with, what she was notoriously terrible at and had been her whole life, was lying. Trotting Diego and Alicia up to the ground-floor guard, she thought she might start hyperventilating, she was so paranoid about getting caught. And she'd thought the guilt from copying client account information onto a zip drive had been overwhelming.

But Alicia had told her on the drive that morning that in covert ops, confidence was everything. Act like you know what you're doing and people will believe you.

So she offered the incessantly brutish guard a smile. "Good morning."

He grunted. Friendly as he ever was. Today, though, she was grateful he wasn't chatty.

He cast a distrustful look at Diego and Alicia. "Manuel Rodriguez and Natalie Callahan," she said by way of introductions. "They're visiting from the Venezuela branch for training and should be on your list." Because Alicia had planted the names there the night before.

The guard read the fake names off the bank IDs she and Alicia had created, then buzzed them through the door. One bridge crossed and many more to go. The next one being to get to her office without running into any supervisors, who'd know right away that there weren't any inter-branch bank employee training sessions on the books.

The ground floor was Monday-morning quiet, thank goodness. Vanessa kept her head down and avoided eye contact. The three of them fast-walked over the marble floor to the elevator landing on the far side.

"Vanessa?"

Vanessa froze, simmering behind her smile. Drat. It was Carol, an investment analyst she was friendly with.

Diego and Alicia stepped out of the way as Carol pulled her into a hug. "I heard about the gas leak in your apartment complex. That's horrible. Are you okay?"

"Perfectly fine. But I'm due in a meeting. Let's get together for lunch and I'll tell you all about it." The lie made her face hot and had probably turned her skin tomato-red.

She mashed her thumb on the elevator button. Diego and Alicia flanked her.

"You're doing great," Diego whispered, his eyes scanning the room.

His praise calmed her twitchy nerves and helped her stand still until the elevator chimed and the doors opened.

Inside, Vanessa punched the button for the ninth floor. Another hurdle cleared. But before the doors closed all the way, a man's arm popped through and wedged them open.

"Going up?" Mr. Tavares said, like they weren't already on the lowest level. He squeezed in and beamed at Vanessa, tapping a file against his left palm. "Well, look who it is. Terrible, about your apartment fire. It was an answer to all our prayers that you weren't seriously injured."

"Thank you, sir."

"Do you have a place to stay until you get settled in a new apartment?"

She cleared her throat. "I do. My best friend lives in the city. Thanks for asking."

The elevator chimed at the ninth floor and they all stepped out. For the first time, Mr. Tavares seemed to notice Diego and Alicia.

"These are visitors from our Venezuela branch, in the mortgage lending department." The heat rose on her face again as her voice cracked. She cleared her throat. Mr. Tavares and the manager of the mortgage lending department hated each other, so there was no way he'd call to double-check her story. "I'm giving them a tour, but I'm taking them to my office to show them the new customer service interface on our website first." Confidence was everything, she reminded herself.

After introductions and handshakes, Diego and Alicia followed Vanessa through the hall to her office. She made to close the door, but Diego stilled her with a head shake.

"Don't close it. He's still watching," he said in a low voice.

The words made her stomach churn. Maybe this wasn't going to work, not with Mr. Tavares buzzing around. Was it her imagination or did he have a glimmer of awareness in his eye that she was up to no good? She was about to scold herself for acting paranoid like she had on Friday with the zip drive, but then, hadn't her paranoia been justified? Who was to say it wasn't right now?

She shook off the questions and drew a fortifying breath. Nothing was going to happen to her at the office on a work day—especially not with Diego and Alicia in the room. Calmer, she walked to her chair. Time to get this mission over with before she lost her breakfast.

Diego positioned himself on the far side of the room in front of the windows that looked out on the street and the Pacific Ocean two blocks over.

"We're in," he said into the wire masquerading as a cell phone ear piece. Vanessa heard his words through her ear piece as well as Ryan's, John's and Rory's responses.

To Vanessa, Diego added, "Your boss is creepy" under his breath.

"Creepy, but harmless."

Alicia sat in a chair along the wall and drummed her fingers on the armrest. "Let's hope so." A laptop rested on her legs with a cable running between it and Vanessa's computer so they could both look at the same screen.

Vanessa pulled up her log-in screen for the bank's system. "Let's make fifty million dollars disappear."

She tapped in her password, but the computer dinged. Access denied.

"Try again," Alicia prompted.

Typing slower and more deliberately, she reentered her name and password. Again, the Access Denied pop-up screen appeared with a ding. "I don't know what to do. Someone must have locked me out of the system."

Diego peered out the inside office window. Vanessa followed his gaze to Mr. Tavares, who was talking with another man. Every few seconds, his eyes shifted back to Vanessa's office. "I don't like this. It could mean the bank insider knows our plan. I'm giving this five minutes, tops, and then we're out of here."

"I'll get us in the system," Alicia said. Her fingers flew over the keyboard. They sat in silence as they waited. Vanessa watched Alicia's handiwork through her screen as she hacked the system. "We're in."

Thank God. Her heart thumping like mad, Vanessa pulled up the SPB Investing account. She stared at the account total. Fifty million and change.

Then the screen refreshed. The total had dropped by a hundred grand.

Alicia sat straighter. "Wait a sec…"

Her hands unsteady, Vanessa clicked over to the account's withdrawal history. What she saw stopped her cold. She met Diego's searching stare. "Someone just withdrew a hundred thousand dollars cash using one of the tellers on the ground floor of the bank."

Diego was mid-stride toward Vanessa's desk when he abruptly stopped and relaxed his posture. "Incoming," he whispered.

"Vanessa's words were muffled. Repeat, please," said Ryan's voice through the wire. "Is there a problem? Please copy."

The next second, Mr. Tavares was in the doorway. "Say, Vanessa, I thought you were supposed to be leading our visitors on a tour of the building. They didn't come all the way from Venezuela to sit in your office."

He let out a hollow, forced laugh.

"We're about to start the tour, but first we're going over some of the bank's security features." Her throat was impossibly dry and itchy. She tried in vain to ease the itching by clearing it. "Is there something I can do for you, sir?"

Mr. Tavares toyed with the wand that opened and closed the blinds to the window that bordered the hallway. "Actually, I do have a quick question, if our guests will indulge me the interruption. Regarding the matter we discussed on Friday, you have something to give me. A program. I know you went through a lot this weekend and probably didn't have time to work out all the kinks, but I need it, finished or not. Okay?"

Play it cool, Vee. Close to the vest. She smiled at him. "Yes. I'll drop it by your office in a few minutes."

"How about I take it right now?"

* * *

The second that Tavares twisted the rod and closed the blinds, Diego plunged his hand into his jacket and settled his palm on his Sig. They hadn't crossed the line to where he was going to start knocking heads and abort the mission, but they were at the threshold.

Someone presently inside the building had withdrawn a hundred grand in cash—a Chiara brother with the help of a dirty bank employee, most likely. Diego's instincts were throwing up all sorts of red alerts on Tavares, but seeing as how Diego had maintained a visual on the guy while the transaction had gone down, he definitely wasn't the Chiara insider.

That didn't mean he wasn't guilty of something else, though.

What Diego needed to do was get the information to Ryan that a Chiara brother or representative was somewhere in the building, but Tavares wasn't going to leave the room and Diego wasn't about to take his eyes off the man to send Ryan a text or leave Vanessa vulnerable so he could step out to the hall to explain the situation over the wire, even if it meant a Chiara slipped past their defenses.

Then again, Ryan, John and Rory should have all the exits covered. They'd recognize Nico, Enzo, Leo or one of their men in a heartbeat. How had a Chiara gotten into the building if his crew were doing their jobs?

As Tavares settled into the chair next to Alicia, Ryan's voice came over the wire again. "Devil, there's another problem. Ghost Rider is M.I.A. His wire's been disconnected."

Where the hell was Rory? More importantly, why? Actually, scratch that. Didn't matter why. Rory's disappearance was one suspicious circumstance too many. Time to leave.

"Eight Ball, get the van," he said into his ear piece, no longer concerned if Tavares heard. "We're aborting."

"Copy that," Ryan said.

Alicia shut her computer and stood, her face and posture a picture of tranquility, as was her usual game face.

Vanessa, who'd heard the update right along with them, was trying and failing not to look rattled as she gawked at Tavares. He made a mental note to never let her play poker with his sister Gabriela, then got in her line of sight.

"I could use a smoke break. You have a smoking lounge in this building?"

Vanessa blinked at him as his request sank in. "No. Most people smoke in the plaza out back. I'll take you."

Tavares leapt to his feet as she rose. "Not until you get me that program." He planted his feet in the doorway, blocking their exit. Like Diego couldn't lift his sweaty, paunchy body out of the way with one hand tied behind his back.

"Yeah, well, I get cranky when I need a smoke, so your little program's going to have to wait."

He had a hand on Tavares's shoulder when the peal of the smoke alarm sounded and everyone in the room jumped. Outside the door, workers shuffled by in the direction of the stairwell, grumbling about another unannounced fire drill. Leroy's first rule when a mission went FUBAR was to know what's still in your control and give up everything else.

The first thing Diego was giving up was the charade. He brought his Sig out and shoved it into Tavares's neck, strong-arming him against the wall.

Alicia kicked the door closed.

He jiggled the muzzle of his gun against Tavares's jugular. "Who's got you fishing around for Vanessa's program?"

Tavares stammered, nervous. Diego didn't have time for nervous. He brought his left fist into the man's gut, then raised the gun to his temple. No more deadly a position, but there was something about the person actually seeing the gun that has the potential to blow their brains out that convinced them to cooperate.

"You gotta speak up so I can hear you over this fire alarm. Who's using you to get to Vanessa? And it's the last time I'm going to ask nicely."

Alicia patted Tavares down for weapons but came up empty.

"U.S. Immigration and Customs Enforcement," Tavares squeaked. "Don't kill me."

Not the answer Diego was expecting. He exchanged a look with Alicia. She shook her head and Diego had to agree. No freaking way that was possible.

He slapped his Sig across Tavares's cheek. "Try again."

"N-n-no, I'm telling you the truth. Immigration and—"

"Yeah, I heard that part," Diego said. "Who's your contact there?"

The door banged open and hit the window behind it, cracking the glass. Rory stood in the doorway, his prized Kimber .45 in hand.

In his periphery, Diego saw Alicia move into a shielding stance in front of Vanessa, her gun drawn. She nailed Rory with a look of distrust. Come to think of it, Diego was starting to feel that way about Rory, too.

Maintaining his hold on Tavares, he turned his focus on Rory. "What are you doing out of position?"

"You sounded like you were in trouble. Thought you might like some help."

He crowded into Rory's space. "Did I ask for help?"

He was too close and too pissed to see it coming. The jolt of the stun gun on his gut zapped him into the worst pain he'd endured in several years. His gun fell from his hand as he hit the ground.

Rory ripped Diego's ear piece off and crushed it with his boot.

Gasping for breath, Diego couldn't make his twitching muscles function properly. All he could do was bellow when Rory raised his gun and fired a shot in Vanessa's direction.

Chapter 20

Vanessa saw the stun gun before Diego did, but not with enough time to warn him. She reached behind her and drew her gun, her world slowing down and coming into crystal-clear focus while she watched him collapse.

Rory raised his weapon. He was going to kill them all and she couldn't let that happen.

Before she could aim, Alicia swept her legs from under her, knocking her to the ground as a shot exploded.

She looked up in time to see Alicia stagger back and collapse to the ground behind the desk, her chest bloody.

Oh, God. He'd killed Alicia. She or Diego would be next.

Rolling to her hands and knees, she found the gun on the ground and clutched it with both hands.

The zap of the stun gun sounded again, followed by Diego's groans. She clutched the gun like a lifeline.

Rory was a far better and faster shot than she'd ever be. Surprise was her only hope. Instead of leaping up while shooting and getting herself killed, she held her position under the desk.

"This isn't what I signed up for," Mr. Tavares said, sounding fearful. "I thought you worked for ICE."

"He does," called the voice of a man she didn't recognize over the incessant din of the fire alarm. "But he also works for me."

Another shot fired, this one breaking the outside window. *Diego.*

She chanced a look out the back of her desk.

Mr. Tavares lay on his side, his shirt stained crimson. "Vanessa," he said in a sandpaper voice.

She covered her mouth with her hand to stifle a gasp of horror...and a twinge of relief, though she hated that she felt that way when her boss lay dying.

Behind her, Alicia stirred with a groan. Vanessa whipped around. Staring at the ceiling through half-lidded eyes, Alicia rasped, "John, Ryan, help."

"John won't be coming to your rescue," Rory said. Vanessa peered from the desk in time to see his gun aimed in Alicia's direction, but he was stopped by the other man.

"Don't shoot again," he said, his accent European though she couldn't place it specifically. "My brothers might want to have some fun with her before she dies. Enzo loves blondes."

Shuddering, Vanessa drew herself into a ball in the center of the desk and clutched the gun between her stomach and knees.

"This must be our eager beaver." The new man's boots appeared next to the desk. He bent to look at her, wearing a malicious smirk on his lips. And then it hit her who it was. She'd seen him in the helicopter over the jungle. Nico Chiara.

"Don't get shy, eager beaver. Come up and say hello. Or I might shoot your friend." He motioned with his gun to Diego who lay prone on the ground, Rory's gun trained on him.

He'd found her weakness right away. Maybe that was a cold-blooded criminal's gift—to hit where it hurt the most. Before rising from under the desk, she slipped her gun back into the front waistband of her skirt and fluffed her shirt over it as she stood.

"Take a seat. It's time for you to destroy the algorithm."

There was that malicious smile again. When she sat, Nico brought forth a pair of handcuffs and locked her left wrist to the desk leg. He removed the wire from her ear and crushed it in his fist, then stood behind her and watched her work.

She touched her keyboard, fighting to still the shaking in her hands so she could type.

It took less than a minute to destroy her masterpiece.

"Good work, eager beaver. We have an important meeting to get to in Colón, so we must leave you now."

He set a metal box on the far side of the room and flipped a switch. A digital display lit on the front of the box. "Enjoy your last five minutes of life."

A bomb. Vanessa felt bile rising in her throat. At least it would be quick. *Please, God, let it be quick.*

Rory sent another charge through Diego's system, then lugged his limp body up. "Do you see that, Devil? Your girl's going to die and there's nothing you can do."

Diego flailed his arms. She saw him dig deep for strength that would not come.

"Lucky for you, I'll make more money handing you over to the Chiaras alive than if you were dead."

Diego roared.

Laughing, Rory pressed a pressure point in his neck until his eyes rolled back and he went unconscious.

Nico slung an unconscious Alicia over his shoulders. "Let's load them into the elevator and get out of here." He flashed his ugly smile at Vanessa. "Time's a-ticking."

Diego came to on the sidewalk as he was being dragged toward a car in front of the bank. Careful to stay limp, he blinked and flexed his fingers. Good enough. All that mattered was getting to Vanessa before that bomb went off.

He curled his hand into his pocket for his knife, but it wasn't there. Good thing he knew Rory kept a knife strapped to the small of his back.

No time to get fancy, he dug his boots into the ground and came up swinging, catching Rory in the gut with an uppercut. Rory doubled over, giving Diego the perfect angle to rip the knife from its sheath on his back and jam it into his kidney.

Growling in pain, Rory latched his arms around Diego's legs, but Diego was feeling his full power now and nothing or no one was going to stop him from saving Vanessa. He broke Rory's stronghold and smashed his face with the heel of his boot. Rory hit the ground hard and stayed there.

Nico was already behind the wheel and there was no sign of Alicia anywhere. Diego could try to catch him, but that would take time he didn't have. Not if he was going to reach Vanessa.

He pivoted and took off in a sprint toward the bank,

dodging curious pedestrians and bank employees flowing out of the doors. He was up two steps on the stairs in front of the bank when an explosion ripped through the building. He was too late.

Every molecule in his body screamed in protest. He must have misheard. She couldn't be dead. He never failed.

Dropping to his knees, he forced his gaze up the building to prove to himself that he'd been mistaken and the bomb hadn't detonated.

Smoke and flames streamed into the sky from the smashed-out windows of an upper floor. Numbly, he stared until the sight of the burning high-rise got scrambled up in his head with the tower Ossie died in. Ossie and now Vanessa.

He'd worked so hard to be a better man in Ossie's memory. He'd dedicated his life to taking care of the people he loved the only way he knew how. But Vanessa died the same way his brother did, in a building, alone. Diego should've saved her. He should've done more. What good were his skills if they couldn't save the people he loved most in the world?

He folded forward, hands on the hot concrete sidewalk.

Eventually numbness gave way to fury. After he lost Ossie, Diego's hands had been tied in a system of protocol and laws. No longer. Avenging Vanessa's death would be as easy as one, two, *boom.*

The beast inside him reared up, propelling him from the ground.

Ryan ran his way and seized both Diego's shoulders in his hands. "I heard it all and I couldn't get here. You sent me for the van, but it wouldn't start. Someone had messed with the engine. And then the fire department and the police were here and I couldn't get through."

His eyes rolled up to the burning building and he clasped Diego close to his chest. "I heard it all, bro."

But the fury working through Diego didn't need a hug. It needed vengeance. He shoved away from Ryan and strode toward Rory, who lay half in the gutter, obscured from passersby by two parked cars.

John intercepted Diego before he reached his target. "I heard everything, too, but I was caught up brawling with some of Chiara's men in the alley. Where's Alicia? Did Chiara take her? Is she alive?"

It was hard work to tear his eyes from Rory, but he managed. He grabbed John by the shirt and yanked his face close. "Why should I trust you?"

John had the wherewithal to look outraged. "You actually think I'd let something like that happen to Alicia—to all of us? Are you crazy? I don't know why Rory flipped on us, and I'm as pissed as you are about it."

It was an insult to Vanessa's memory that John would deign to compare his feelings to the lifelong grief Diego would have for the woman he lost. He shouldered past John, no longer interested in what he had to say.

But John wasn't done. "Rory and I went to war together—*war,* goddamn it—more than once. We were brothers. He betrayed me, too."

Not good enough. He sent John to the ground with a knife-hand strike to his neck. "We can't take any chances. Subdue him, Ryan."

He heard Ryan and John engaging in a fight behind him but didn't take the time to look. He needed something from Rory before he bled out in the gutter.

He dragged Rory up by the shirt. He came without resistance, licking at the blood in the corner of his mouth. He grabbed the hilt of the knife in Rory's back and gave it a slight twist. Rory gurgled and gasped.

"Where are the Chiara brothers? Tell me or you don't want to know how slowly I'm going to kill you. I have nothing left to live for anyway."

"I needed the money," Rory spluttered. "I… This job…it didn't come with decent pay, didn't come with respect. I figured if they were going to treat us like hired guns, I might as well make four times the money being my own boss, doing the same thing."

Diego blanched at his words. Greed. As long as he lived, Diego would never understand the price tag some people put on other people's lives. He twisted the knife again. "I don't care why. Tell me where I can find the Chiaras."

Rory let out a strangled moan. "Bahia Azul in Colón. The abandoned ship-building warehouse on the south side."

He patted Rory down until he'd recovered all the weapons Rory had taken off him. Rory's Kimber .45, he stuffed in his waistband.

Straightening, he looked first at John, who was lying on the sidewalk, his arms and legs bound. Then, bracing himself for how badly it would hurt, he took one last look at the broken building, the busted windows and fire where once Vanessa's office had stood.

She was gone. Because he hadn't protected her like he promised. Whatever man he thought he'd been, whatever goodness that had been in him, had died with her. Now that she'd been ripped from his future, all he felt was icy darkness.

He shucked his suit jacket and got rid of the tie. No need for a facade of civility any longer. As he rolled up his sleeves, he met Ryan's gaze. "Ready to find Alicia and kill the Chiaras?"

Ryan's jaw rippled. No shrug this time, but a decisive nod. "Been ready for a long time."

Diego nodded back. "Time to spill some blood."

Handcuffs dangled from Vanessa's hands like macabre jewelry, the connecting chain broken, shredded with one shot of her handgun.

Her heart ached, thinking of Diego and Alicia on the floor, unconscious and injured. She might not have been able to stop the submarine sale, but she would save their lives. She had to. The alternative was too horrendous to consider.

The peal of the smoke alarm stayed with her through the deserted hallway. To escape the building, she had to get five levels down to the fourth floor to initiate the first phase of her Leroy plan—the only part of the plan that still made sense. Sloshing over the water-soaked carpet, she kept her face on her feet as a buffer against the rain from the fire sprinklers, a technique she'd mastered while hiking through the jungle with Diego.

The only way to get to where she needed to go was via the stairs. She dreaded the exposure. What if Nico Chiara or Rory returned to make sure she was dead?

The safest move by far would be to hide out in a janitorial closet or office, her gun at the ready, and wait out the post-explosion chaos. But she had to save Diego, and Alicia, too, if she'd survived the gunshot wound.

She may not have the skill set to go after an international crime ring, but she had courage. And right now, with the life of the man she loved on the line, courage would have to be enough.

The smoke alarm was louder in the stairwell. It

pierced her skull and crawled into her bones, rattling her teeth. The noise meant there was no need to be quiet, but it also meant she wouldn't hear trouble if it came. She peered over the railing for any flash of movement on the stairs below, but it seemed she was alone.

With a steadying breath, she decided to make a break for it in one long sprint. She scurried down the stairs on the balls of her feet, making U-turn after U-turn in the descent until she stood at the doorway to the fourth level.

She pushed through, praying danger wasn't waiting on the other side. It wasn't. Just another waterlogged, empty hallway. Her ex-fiancé, Dave's, former office was the fifth door on the right.

She went through his office. She had history here, evenings working late to be near him though he ignored her, and one night of mediocre sex on his desk. The computer in the center of the desk had been doused with water from the fire sprinklers along with everything else in the building, rendering it unusable. But she needed an address to go with the scraps of information Mr. Tavares had given her before he died, moments before she escaped the blast.

She tugged the top desk drawer open. Bingo. A cell phone that looked like the type equipped with internet access. She stuffed it in her bra and kept moving.

Time for the reason she'd chosen this particular office as an escape point. The window, which looked onto a decorative planter, was one of the few in the building that opened.

On her first attempt, the window stuck, like it hadn't been opened in years, but finally it relented and pushed out. She put her foot through the screen and climbed into the vines and shrubs. Dave used to sneak out here to smoke, and she often joined him, so she knew about the ladder on the far side that dropped to the planter on the third floor.

The problem came when she got to the second floor planter and there was no ladder, or even a planter on the first floor she could drop onto. This part of the plan had been a bit fuzzy in her mind. She'd hoped that once she got here, inspiration would strike.

She walked to the far end, tripping over a garden hose, and looked over the edge into the plaza among the buildings where people usually ate lunch and took their smoke breaks. The fountain was running, and an abandoned coffee cart sat inert to her left. Sirens echoed through the plaza. The flashing red lights of emergency crews reflected off the neighboring buildings. But the plaza itself was empty.

The garden hose would have to do.

She knotted it the best she could around the pipe it was attached to. Then she shimmied on her belly over the edge of the planter, her hands on the hose, and slid down it like a rope. It got her a good two meters from the ground. She dropped the rest of the way and welcomed the feel of concrete beneath her shoes.

She scooted along the perimeter of the plaza in the shadows of the other high-rises and came out on the far side. The sidewalk was crowded with pedestrians walking fast in both directions—those who were curious about the explosion and moving in for a closer look as well as those hustling to leave the area. Joining the latter group, she tucked into the flow of foot traffic and withdrew the phone, navigating to the internet.

After a couple minutes of searching, she found what she was looking for and picked up her pace. Five blocks to the people who were her only hope for saving Diego.

Please let him be alive.

To keep her rising fear at bay as she jogged, she pushed the sleeve back on her left arm and dialed Diego's voice mail.

"I know you're not going to get this message right now, but I want you to know I'm getting help and then I'm going to find you and tell you face-to-face that I'm in love with you." She swallowed over the lump in her throat. "You better be alive, damn it. Hang in there a little bit longer. I'm coming to get you."

She ended the call and swiped at the tears clouding her eyes.

The sign on the building's door confirmed she was in the right place. She opened the glass front door and marched to the receptionist desk. Behind the counter, three men stood in a whispered conversation that looked intense. One lifted a radio to his mouth and said, "Stand by outside the bank. Backup's on its way." Guess they were aware of the explosion.

She pressed her palms on the counter and cleared her throat to get their attention. All heads turned her way. "I need to speak to an agent immediately about a matter that's life-or-death."

A handsome, well-dressed man who looked to be in his mid-thirties stepped forward, astonishment playing on his features. "Miss Crosby? I'm Agent Aaron Montgomery. How did you get here and why are you alone?"

Chapter 21

Colón stretched toward the Atlantic Ocean like Panama City's peasant cousin. A nothing town that marked the eastern opening of the canal, plagued by the same lawlessness and poverty as it was founded on a century earlier during its days as a mercenary trading port.

The grungy, dark-alley ambiance fit Diego's mood precisely. Nothing separated him from the muck of the earth, not anymore. He was done with following rules. Done with humanity. Rory and John's betrayal had strung his body tight, like a wire rod threaded through his torso. He'd trusted them with Vanessa's life, and they'd killed her. He'd killed her, when it came down to it.

Ryan stayed silent. No surprise there. Whatever grudge Ryan held against the Chiara brothers, he'd never confessed to Diego. But his willingness to accompany Diego on this mission spoke volumes.

The abandoned shipyard came into view in the distance, surrounded by a chain-link fence with strips of fiberglass threaded through the holes. Along a busy street, they'd abandoned the car they'd stolen, then stalked the rest of the way on foot to a small hill overlooking the yard—as close as they could without giving away their presence.

Armed guards paced over the blacktop inside the fence. The car Nico had driven sat in a cluster of other vehicles, its trunk cracked open. They'd taken Alicia's body out. If she was still alive, Diego would save her. And if she'd died, he vowed not to leave before finding her so he could return her body to her family in Arizona.

The building that most likely housed the submarine sat to the left and extended over the waterline like an enclosed dock.

"What's the plan?" Ryan asked.

Diego scrubbed a hand over his neck. "Lots of bodies around. The sale's going down soon. I'd blow the whole place up if human cargo wasn't a factor and Alicia wasn't somewhere in there."

"Can't risk it." The words died in Ryan's throat as Leo Chiara strode across the parking lot to the enclosed dock.

Diego brought his Sig up to aim. "Oh, it's on now."

"Hooyah," Ryan said, withdrawing his Ruger. "You can take Leo or Nico, but Enzo's mine."

Diego lined up Leo Chiara's head in his sights and positioned his finger on the trigger.

In the distance, a helicopter sounded in approach. Leo turned to look, giving Diego a perfect shot. Before he could squeeze off a round, three naval vessels swerved to a stop in the water outside the yard. Two armored vehicles crashed through the chain-link gates.

The helicopter he'd heard hovered overhead, almost blocking the sound of guns being drawn behind them. Ryan and Diego spun around.

"There's nowhere to run," said a man dressed in ICE agent gear. "Drop your weapons."

In the heat of the moment, Vanessa never guessed the ICE agents she turned to for help wouldn't allow her to accompany them on Diego's rescue. Not only had Agent Montgomery and the others been impervious to her rants and demands, but they actually told her that what happened next didn't pertain to her.

Like hell it didn't.

She told them as much, and that was when two agents bullied her into a windowless room on the second floor and left Agent Montgomery to interview her.

He battered her with question after question about her time with Diego from the minute the safe house delivery was aborted to the minute she walked through the ICE attaché office door.

She answered the best she could, leaving out the shift in her feelings, their connection and the love she'd found with him. Their time together was too precious to share with a stranger during an interview in a sterile room, and anyway, probably wasn't allowed between an agent and the person he was protecting.

In turn, she pestered Agent Montgomery to check in with the team sent to retrieve Diego and Alicia. He refused. Pestering soon turned into begging, as fear for their lives became an oppressive weight over her heart.

An hour into the interview, a call chimed on Agent Montgomery's phone. Her breath caught in her throat.

Was this the call that was going to tell her if Diego had been rescued unharmed, or the call that would tell her they'd arrived too late?

She clamped a hand over her mouth, waiting.

After a few clipped words, he ended the call and looked her way with a thin-lipped smile.

"It's time to go."

"What?"

He stood and smoothed a hand over his tie. "ICE's private plane is ready. We're getting you out of the country and into protective custody in the U.S. before the Chiaras get a lead on you again."

She dug her fingers into the arms of the chair. "I won't leave without knowing if Diego and his crew are safe."

"Miss Crosby—"

"Don't tell me it's none of my business. Those people saved my life. Agent Santero, he's..." What could she say? That he was the most honorable, capable and loving man she'd ever met? That he taught her how to be brave or that he was the love of her life and if anything bad happened to him a huge part of her would die, too? "I owe him everything."

His expression turned patient. "I haven't gotten word on his status yet. As soon as I do, I'll pass that information to you, but I have an explicit command from way over my pay grade to get you on a plane right now. If you won't come with me willingly, I'm going to have to subdue you—and I really, really don't want to do that."

He opened the door and swept his arm across the threshold in invitation.

"It's safe here. Why can't I wait here for Agent Santero?"

"Because if you're right and Agent Alderman is

working for the Chiaras, this building isn't secure. He has all the access codes, knows every entrance and exit. For all I know, he's bugged this room. The codes and locks will be changed and the office swept for bugs, but that requires time. Your life is worth more than taking such a risk."

It was odd, hearing him echo Diego's argument against her returning to the bank. Numb at her lack of options, she stood, swaying in place. "Will I ever see Agent Santero or his crew again if they're rescued alive?"

"I don't expect so, ma'am."

She had his personal voice mail number and his real name, so she could theoretically find him once she was in the States, but that wasn't good enough. She'd finally found a man worth chasing after, and she wasn't about to let him slip through her fingers without a fight.

Which meant only one thing. She was about to do something that was either really courageous or really stupid.

She waited until they were in the alley behind the building, then reached into her concealed holster.

She'd never held a gun on another person, and now that she was, she didn't like it. At all. But she wasn't getting on the plane without knowing whether Diego was alive or dead, and if he was alive, she wasn't going anywhere until she told him she loved him face-to-face, as she'd vowed in the voice mail message to do.

Agent Montgomery held his hands in front of him, palms out, and cast worried eyes at her trigger finger. "You don't want to do this, Miss Crosby."

The gun bobbed in her hand. She steadied her grip with the other hand and tried to recall the body positioning techniques Diego had taught her. "You're right.

I don't. But you don't understand. I'm not getting on that plane. I'm not leaving Panama without seeing Agent Santero, and I'm not going to let you stop me."

She walked backward toward the main street, praying for a taxi to drive past at the exact right time. Agent Montgomery followed at a distance, his eyes never leaving her trigger finger.

"Do you think he'd want you to put yourself in danger like that after all he did to keep you safe?" he said, stepping closer.

No. He'd be furious with her, but she couldn't think about that now. She raised her hand to hail a cab.

Agent Montgomery took another step closer. "The U.S. and Panama military have launched an offensive at the location you told us the Chiaras' submarine sale was taking place. The only intel I've gotten is that artillery fire has been exchanged. If you got in the middle of that, you'd distract the soldiers from their mission and might jeopardize a lot of men's lives. Including Agent Santero's."

She closed her eyes. Damn it. He was right, and she hated him for it.

"I promise you, when I learn more, I'll tell you immediately." His hand touched her arm. "But right now, you have to trust me to keep you safe."

His words were so similar to Diego's, her heart contracted. *Diego, you'd better be okay. If you're alive, I'll find you and I won't stop looking until I do.*

She let him take the gun from her hand. With an arm around her shoulders, he guided her back to the alley and into the waiting car.

It hadn't been tough for Diego and Ryan to convince the ICE agents of their identities. Their badges and reputations took care of that. The worst part was standing in the sun as the agents who'd found them co-ordinated with their bosses and got approval for Diego and Ryan to participate. Freakin' Feds and their chain of command. By the time the details were ironed out, the boathouse raid was pretty much over.

They jogged into the heart of the action anyway, though it was too late to do any good. Although, when Diego thought about it, he had to acknowledge that a lot of good had already been done.

In the center of the crumbling wood boathouse sat a submarine like a giant bullet in the water. American navy soldiers stood on top of it, preparing to breach. The narco-traffickers would've used it to pump millions of dollars' worth of drugs into the U.S. Seizing the watercraft made it that much harder for the bad guys to do their jobs and kept up the good fight in the drug war.

On the wooden dock surrounding the submersible, the Panama army had lined up more than a dozen men against the wall at gunpoint. Men who would no longer threaten the innocent. He returned his focus to the submersible as a frail woman in tattered clothes and snarled hair was being helped out—and she looked to be the first of many.

You did it, Vanessa. You helped save lives and made the world a safer place today. I hope you can see that right now.

He lowered his gun and closed his eyes as impotent rage pulsed through him. Vanessa might've helped make the world safer, but it would be a far bleaker place without her.

"Agent down! Agent down!" It was Ryan's voice.

Diego whipped his head to where Ryan knelt on the ground above a woman's body. He ran as fast as he could and dropped next to Alicia. Her eyes fluttered open when Ryan pressed his fingers to her throat.

Diego reached for her hand as relief swept through him. The bullet wound in her chest looked bad, but at least she still had a chance to make it out of this hell-hole alive. A slim chance, given her blood loss, but he had to have hope. "Medics are on their way, Alicia. Hang in there."

A noise bubbled up from her throat like she was trying to speak.

A pair of medics pushed Ryan and Diego out of the way. They staggered back to give the men room to work.

The boathouse was crowded and getting more jam-packed by the moment.

"Let's get out of here and figure out where they're holding the Chiaras," Ryan said. "I want to see the looks on their faces when they get cuffed and hauled to the slammer."

Agent Dreyer and a handful of armed agents and officers were positioned near the chain-link fence, standing guard over two prisoners—Leo and Nico Chiara.

"You're missing one," Diego said to Dreyer. "Where's Enzo?"

Nico laughed. "Sorry about your girl. She was a pretty one. Would've looked good under me, no?"

His tenuous control snapping, Diego rushed Nico and crushed his fist into the scum's face. He raised his arm to strike again, but a hand clamped around his wrist.

"That's enough, Agent Santero," Dreyer said. "Vincenzo Chiara isn't here. Never was, by the looks of it. We've got the place surrounded—land, sea and air. He wouldn't have gotten past us. Mark my words, we will catch up to him and bring him into custody."

Ryan sniffed. His face was stone-hard, but Diego

had known him all their adult lives and he read the rage behind the calm. Ryan scanned the horizon, like the scumbag might've levitated as a means of escape.

Diego looked out over the ocean, too, struck by the finality of the moment. He'd failed in every way. Under his care, Vanessa died. He'd held her safe in his arms that morning, the first woman he'd ever loved. He'd told her to trust him…and he'd ushered her straight to her death. Then he'd failed at vengeance. He'd even failed Ossie. The realization leeched the rest of the fight out of him like a bad adrenaline crash, filling his limbs and heart with lead.

All he had left to do was quit ICE. He wasn't worthy of the title or the badge.

Ryan's hand settled on his shoulder and squeezed, offering his support. But would Ryan understand what he was about to do?

"How did you find us?" Ryan asked Dreyer.

Diego was only half listening as he felt in his back pocket for his badge.

"Vanessa Crosby."

Diego's hand froze. He shook his head. "The Rio-Bank explosion… Vanessa was…" His stomach lurched. How could he say it when he couldn't even think it without wanting to puke?

"She's not dead, if that's what you were going to say. She walked through the ICE office doors an hour ago and told us you needed saving and that she knew where to find you."

Ryan maintained a hand on Diego's shoulder. And it was a good thing because Diego swayed on weak legs. Like a wuss. Like a man who hadn't spent the past seventeen years looking the Devil in the eye.

"Is she okay?" Ryan asked.

Dreyer grinned. "Not a scratch on her."

Diego didn't remember how it got started, but the next thing he knew, he was nodding like crazy. She was alive. She'd thought he was in danger and had tried to save him. Holy crap.

It took a few tries to find his voice. He swallowed, still nodding like an idiot. "Where is she?" he croaked.

"On a plane with Agent Montgomery. Headed for the States to enter protective custody."

The wheels were spinning in his head, but they weren't going anywhere. ICE was moving her out of Panama that fast? For what purpose?

Then it hit him. It didn't matter why. All that mattered was stopping that plane from taking off. Because if he didn't see her, didn't touch her with his own hands right the hell now to prove to himself that she was alive and well, he was going to explode—and it wasn't going to be pretty.

"Call the pilot. Hold the plane."

"Too late for that, Agent Santero. The plane's probably on the runway already. Besides, your part in this operation is done. Agent Montgomery will take over Miss Crosby's protection from here."

He met Ryan's gaze. Ryan tipped his head toward the ICE helicopter sitting in the shipyard parking lot. He felt the life come back into him, the clarity of purpose that came with a new objective.

"Hey, Dreyer, who's piloting that chopper?"

"Agent Vance. Why?"

But Diego was already at a dead run. "Because he's going to need a ride," he called over his shoulder. "I've got a plane to catch."

In the air, he got on the radio. "This is Agent Diego

Santero. Patch me through to Aaron Montgomery, stat."
Good thing Montgomery still owed him for saving his
girlfriend last year in Mexico because it was time to
collect.

Chapter 22

Diego touched down on the edge of a private government runway, as close as he could get to the jet in position for takeoff. The passenger door was still open, the stairs out. Montgomery had come through for him.

Sighing and laughing with relief, he sprinted the distance to the plane. Montgomery appeared in the doorway and sauntered down the stairs, his arms crossed and a look of annoyance on his face.

"Let me get this straight," Montgomery said. "You went after the Chiara brothers—hijacking my mission, mind you—without calling it in and without backup, like you're some Wild West vigilante. And then you stole a million-dollar military helicopter."

Diego stopped moving. He scanned the windows, searching for a glimpse of Vanessa but seeing nothing but the reflection of the sun. "Yeah, so?"

"So…I have explicit instructions not to let you on this plane."

He couldn't keep his eyes on Montgomery. They kept shifting to the doorway, waiting for Vanessa to appear.

"She's in the cockpit, talking to the pilots. I didn't tell her you were coming." Montgomery set his hands on his hips. "Give me one good reason why I should go against direct orders to help you."

He wasn't in the mood for a chess game. All he wanted was to hold Vanessa in his arms. But if Montgomery wanted to get snitty about things, Diego could too. "That girlfriend of yours I rescued last year, what's-her-name, are you two still together?"

Montgomery's eyes narrowed. Yeah, he got the message. He held up his left hand and wiggled his gold wedding band. "And a baby, too."

"Congratulations."

His eyebrows did a quick up and down. "What is it you want with Vanessa Crosby?"

Diego drilled him with a long, silent look.

Aaron flinched first, snorting. "It's like that, is it? I would've never guessed that for you."

They were getting way too close to touchy-feely territory for Diego's taste. When the hell was Vanessa going to emerge from the cockpit? Tamping his impatience, he answered, "I don't have to tell you what that's like. You know the script."

Aaron whistled. "Do I ever. You think you've got it all figured out, then someone comes along and you realize all those things you thought mattered don't mean jack anymore."

Diego huffed. That pretty much covered it. "You going to give me trouble, or are you going to let me see her now?"

Aaron made like he was giving it some serious thought. Jackass.

The cockpit door opened. And then Vanessa was there, alive. A strangled sound erupted from her throat when she saw him. She clamped a hand over her mouth and stood trembling in the doorway.

The world fell away. There was nothing except her and his need to hold her close and never let go again.

Aaron blocked his passage up the stairs with his body. He pressed a hand on Diego's chest. "We're even now."

Diego flicked a look in the other man's direction. "Yeah, we're square."

Aaron moved out of the way and finally, *finally,* Diego was up the stairs and pulling her against him. It was the best feeling in the universe to bring his arms around her body and smell her and feel her warmth.

He moved them farther into the plane while she cried into his shirt, hard but quiet.

Montgomery kept his distance but set a box of tissues on top of the stewardess station. The gesture evoked within Diego a memory of the day he and Vanessa met, how they'd joked about him keeping tissues in his utility belt. Her spark of toughness and humor in the face of danger had touched something inside him, some part of himself he'd let languish for too many years. Even then, he was starting to figure out how special she was—how perfect she was for him. He pushed away the tissues and hugged her tighter.

What he needed to do was articulate everything she'd come to mean to him, so she'd know without a doubt. He never could seem to say the right thing to her, but today that wasn't going to be a problem. This, he could handle.

He tightened his arms around her and put his cheek against hers, his lips next to her ear. "I love you."

And, damn, it felt good to say.

She turned her face in and nuzzled his cheek. "I love you, too."

At her words, a shiver ripped through him. He, who prided himself on always being the toughest bastard in the room, trembled at the words of a woman. Because she loved him and it was the most humbling, mind-blowing discovery of his life.

He'd deny the shiver happened until he was blue in the face if any other person had noticed, except that he hoped Ossie saw it, looking down from on high. He hoped his brother realized how important Vanessa was to him and approved of his choice.

He kissed her, slow and gentle. Perfect. And he thought, for the rest of my life, this is the woman I'm going to kiss. The realization nearly made him laugh, he felt so lucky.

The cabin darkened. The door clicked closed. At Montgomery's hushed directive to find some seats, Diego tugged her to the nearest ones. The plane began its taxi down the runway.

"I've got a lead on a job for you that I think you'll like, but there are strings attached," he told her.

"I'm intrigued. Go on."

"This morning while you were in the shower, I reached out to my buddy at ICE's Bulk Cash Smuggling Center in Vermont. He'd already heard of you and the algorithm you created, and when I told him you were looking for a new place to run your numbers and save the world using your computer, I could practically hear him salivating over the phone."

Her smile stretched all the way across her face and

up to her eyes. "That sounds like exactly the kind of job I'm looking for. What are the strings attached?"

He toyed with her bare ring finger. Yeah, he was going to solve that problem as soon as humanly possible. "Me. I'm the strings attached. I'd come with you. Of course, we'd have to stop by New Jersey. My family's going to want to meet the woman who's so important that I'm quitting black ops and moving to Vermont, of all the God-forsaken places."

Her hand stiffened. "What about your job and your gift? I don't want you to change who you are because of me."

The plane angled into the air. He released her hand and draped his arm across her shoulders, gathering her near. He'd figured she'd protest him quitting black ops—hell, he'd made a big point over and over about how important his job was to him—so he'd come up with an answer that even her super brain couldn't counter.

"Here's what you're not getting. I already changed, thanks to you. And I don't ever want to go back to the man I was. Not now that I know what I'd be missing without you. I'm no brainiac, but I'm smart enough to know I'd better hold on to the best thing that's ever happened to me."

Her eyes glowed with love, and it made him feel damn proud to know he put that look on her face.

"Besides," he added, "I've got a new job idea for myself, too."

She smoothed a hand over his chest. "Let me hear it."

"Instead of leaving ICE altogether, I'm thinking of transferring to personal security. You see, I have it on good authority that ICE is hiring a woman who's going to revolutionize their counterterrorism approach on a global scale. A woman like that would need to be protected 24/7, don't you think? She'd need her own personal chauffeur, someone to make sure one of the nation's VIPs is safe and happy at all times."

She planted a big kiss on his lips. "I like the way you think, but what about the third Chiara brother? Agent Montgomery told me ICE only arrested two. Will you be able to sleep at night, knowing one brother is still on the loose?"

Diego swatted the air with his hand. "Ryan's on the job. He's been obsessed with the Chiaras for a long time. He won't stop until he puts Vincenzo Chiara behind bars or in the ground. He's like what's-his-name, the pirate who's obsessed with Moby Dick."

She tapped her chin. "I thought Moby Dick was the name of the pirate."

"That's what I thought, too, but it turns out Moby Dick's the name of the whale, not the dude."

She pulled her face back, scoffing. "That's ridiculous. Who names a whale?"

"I know, right? That's my girl." Grinning like a crazy man, he pulled her onto his lap, feeling absolutely sure he'd never been this happy his whole life. "Okay, so I thought of a great math question for you. If I live another sixty years and my average heart rate is forty-five beats per minute, how many times for the rest of my life will my ticker be beating just for you? Don't forget to factor in my heart rate speeding up with age."

She worked her fingers into his hair. "Do I get to factor in all the times I make your heart skip a beat?"

He tried to fake a scowl but couldn't get the corners of his lips to turn down. "That's a terrible joke. You kill me with that stuff. Now get busy. You have a lot of calculations to make. Make sure you do them out loud, so I can hear your brain working."

The plane leveled at cruising altitude with Vanessa rattling off numbers and Diego loving every second of it.

* * * * *

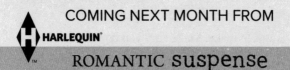
Available July 1, 2013

#1759 OPERATION BLIND DATE
Cutter's Code • by Justine Davis
A stubborn, clever dog and a fiercely loyal woman plunge Foxworth Foundation operative and ex-marine Teague Johnson into a case that rings too close to home, changing his life forever.

#1760 THE COLTON RANSOM
The Coltons of Wyoming • by Marie Ferrarella
Burned-out ex-cop Trevor Garth finds help from a ranching heiress when his daughter is kidnapped. He learns the value of love and family, but will it be too late?

#1761 FRONT PAGE AFFAIR
Ivy Avengers • by Jennifer Morey
Arizona Ivy wants her story on the front page. Investigating weapons smuggling, she gets mixed up with a sexy military weapons engineer. She's found her story, but might have lost her heart.

#1762 THE PARIS ASSIGNMENT
House of Steele • by Addison Fox
Security genius Campbell Steele goes undercover to out the internal threat sabotaging Abby McBane's company. But when Abby becomes the target, Campbell sees a greater threat to his heart.

HRSCNM0613

REQUEST YOUR FREE BOOKS!

2 FREE NOVELS PLUS 2 FREE GIFTS!

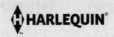

HARLEQUIN®

ROMANTIC suspense

Sparked by danger, fueled by passion

YES! Please send me 2 FREE Harlequin® Romantic Suspense novels and my 2 FREE gifts (gifts are worth about $10). After receiving them, if I don't wish to receive any more books, I can return the shipping statement marked "cancel." If I don't cancel, I will receive 4 brand-new novels every month and be billed just $4.74 per book in the U.S. or $5.24 per book in Canada. That's a savings of at least 14% off the cover price! It's quite a bargain! Shipping and handling is just 50¢ per book in the U.S. and 75¢ per book in Canada.* I understand that accepting the 2 free books and gifts places me under no obligation to buy anything. I can always return a shipment and cancel at any time. Even if I never buy another book, the two free books and gifts are mine to keep forever.

240/340 HDN F45N

Name _____ (PLEASE PRINT) _____

Address _____ Apt. # _____

City _____ State/Prov. _____ Zip/Postal Code _____

Signature (if under 18, a parent or guardian must sign) _____

Mail to the **Harlequin® Reader Service:**

IN U.S.A.: P.O. Box 1867, Buffalo, NY 14240-1867
IN CANADA: P.O. Box 609, Fort Erie, Ontario L2A 5X3

Want to try two free books from another line?
Call 1-800-873-8635 or visit www.ReaderService.com.

* Terms and prices subject to change without notice. Prices do not include applicable taxes. Sales tax applicable in N.Y. Canadian residents will be charged applicable taxes. Offer not valid in Quebec. This offer is limited to one order per household. Not valid for current subscribers to Harlequin Romantic Suspense books. All orders subject to credit approval. Credit or debit balances in a customer's account(s) may be offset by any other outstanding balance owed by or to the customer. Please allow 4 to 6 weeks for delivery. Offer available while quantities last.

Your Privacy—The Harlequin® Reader Service is committed to protecting your privacy. Our Privacy Policy is available online at www.ReaderService.com or upon request from the Harlequin Reader Service.

We make a portion of our mailing list available to reputable third parties that offer products we believe may interest you. If you prefer that we not exchange your name with third parties, or if you wish to clarify or modify your communication preferences, please visit us at www.ReaderService.com/consumerschoice or write to us at Harlequin Reader Service Preference Service, P.O. Box 9062, Buffalo, NY 14269. Include your complete name and address.

HRS13R

When the infant daughter of Trevor Garth, ex-cop and head of security at billionaire Jethro Colton's ranch, is mistaken for the Colton heir and kidnapped, Trevor's desperate to get her back before the kidnapper realizes his mistake. And he finds help in the unlikeliest of allies—Jethro's youngest daughter, Gabrielle.

Read on for a sneak peek of

THE COLTON RANSOM

by *USA TODAY* bestselling author
Marie Ferrarella, coming July 2013 from
Harlequin Romantic Suspense.

Turning his back on Gabby, Trevor strode out of the living room.

The moment he did, Gabby immediately followed him. Since the area was still crowded with people, she only managed to catch up to him just at the front door.

Trevor spared her a look that would have frosted most people's toes. "Where do you think you're going?" he asked.

He sounded so angry, she thought. Not that she blamed him, but she still wished he wouldn't glare at her like that. She hadn't put Avery in harm's way on purpose. It was a horrible accident.

"With you," she answered.

"Oh no, you're not," he cried. "You're staying here," he ordered, waving his hand around the foyer, as if a little bit of magic was all that was needed to transform the situation.

Stubbornly, Gabby held her ground, surprising Trevor even

though he gave no indication. "You're going to need help," she insisted.

Not if it meant taking help from her, he thought.

"No, I am not," he replied tersely, being just as stubborn as she was. "I've got to find my daughter. I don't have time to babysit you."

"Nobody's asking you to. I can be a help. I *can,*" she insisted when he looked at her unconvinced. "Where are you going?" she wanted to know.

"To the rodeo."

That didn't make any sense. Unless— "You have a lead?" she asked, lowering her voice.

"I'm going to see Dylan and tell him his mother's dead," he informed her. "That's not a lead, that's a death sentence for his soul. You still want to come along?" he asked mockingly. Trevor was rather certain that his self-appointed task would make her back off.

Trevor was too direct and someone needed to soften the blow a little. Gabby figured she was elected. "Yes, I do," she replied firmly, managing to take the man completely by surprise.

Don't miss
THE COLTON RANSOM
by Marie Ferrarella

**Available July 2013 from
Harlequin Romantic Suspense
wherever books are sold.**

HRSEXP0613R

HARLEQUIN®

ROMANTIC suspense

All Arizona Ivy needs is one good story to get her career kick-started. Investigating weapons smuggling, she gets mixed up with sexy military weapons engineer Braden McCrae. While one lead after another brings them closer to exposing the arms dealer who appears to have kidnapped his sister, Braden begins to realize he and Arizona have more in common than a thirst for adventure. She's found her story—but she might have lost her heart.

Look for **FRONT PAGE AFFAIR**
next month by Jennifer Morey.

Available wherever books and ebooks are sold.

Heart-racing romance, high-stakes suspense!

HRS27831

⬧ HARLEQUIN®

ROMANTIC suspense

Security genius Campbell Steele goes
undercover to out the internal threat sabotaging
Abby McBane's company. But when Abby
becomes the target, Campbell sees a greater
threat to his heart.

Look for *THE PARIS ASSIGNMENT*
next month by new
Harlequin® Romantic Suspense®
author Addison Fox.

Available wherever books and ebooks are sold.

Heart-racing romance, high-stakes suspense!

Love the Harlequin book you just read?

Your opinion matters.

Review this book on your favorite book site, review site, blog or your own social media properties and share your opinion with other readers!

Be sure to connect with us at:
Harlequin.com/Newsletters
Facebook.com/HarlequinBooks
Twitter.com/HarlequinBooks